The Bays are Sere
&
Interior Monologue

Édouard Dujardin

The Bays are Sere

and

Interior Monologue

Translated and introduced by

Anthony Suter

Libris

Libris
10 Burghley Road
London NW5 1UE

Les Lauriers sont coupés first published in
La Revue Indépendante, 1887
Le Monologue intérieur first published
by Albert Messein, Paris, 1931
This translation first published, 1991
Translation copyright © Libris and Anthony Suter, 1991
Introduction and notes copyright © Anthony Suter, 1991

British Library Cataloguing in Publication Data

The bays are sere: and, Interior monologue.
I. Title   II. Dujardin, Édouard
III. Monologue intérieur. *English*
IV. Dujardin, Édouard. Lauriers sont coupés
843.8 [F]
ISBN 1-870352-70-X

Designed and produced by Cinamon and Kitzinger, London
Typeset by Wyvern Typesetting Ltd, Bristol
Printed in Great Britain by Billing and Sons Ltd, Worcester

Contents

Acknowledgements

The thanks due after the preparation of this book are of a direct and an indirect nature. Indirectly, I am indebted to some of my first teachers of French literature, in particular, Mr Neville Walton, Dr E. J. Kearns and Professor D. J. Mossop.

Next – direct thanks these – I am grateful to Libris for giving me the opportunity to prepare this work. It was not only a great honour to replace the late Richard Ellmann, who had to withdraw because of his last illness, but also a chance to combine my interest in the literary influence of Wagner, literary translation, and the French late nineteenth century, out of which came Dujardin's masterpiece, which I had read with great enthusiasm many years before. Posthumous thanks are also due to Rayner Heppenstall whose article in *London Magazine* in August 1960 provided the title of this translation of *Les Lauriers sont coupés*.

I must also thank my wife, Odile, librarian at the University Library, Toulouse, for her invaluable help in preparing the bibliography and in procuring on inter-library loan the works without which this study and translation would not have been possible.

Anthony Suter
Toulouse, 1990

Translator's Note

A new translation of *Les Lauriers sont coupés* requires an explanatory note, but by no means an apologetic justification. Partly prompted by James Joyce, Stuart Gilbert produced a first translation which he entitled *We'll to the Woods No More* (New Directions, 1938). Joyce had some hand in the actual translation, thus prompting Vivian Mercier to say that what resulted was often too Joycean in tone.* The problem with *Les Lauriers sont coupés*, and indeed with Édouard Dujardin, is the paradoxical one of influence on Joyce, as well as Dujardin's return to some form of critical recognition through Joyce and Valery Larbaud. If the reflected glory is merited, it also *deflects* attention from the novel's real merits. In his introduction to the second edition of the Gilbert translation, Leon Edel concludes patronizingly with the assessment: 'the minor work which inaugurated a major movement'.†

Dujardin's fame comes from the influence he had on major *non-French* writers. This has meant that the majority of critics writing about his work have been Anglo-American specialists considering Dujardin in the light of later developments rather than focusing their attention on the author himself. Some attempt to redress the balance has been made in my introduction, but the weight of critical opinion has come down against Dujardin as an original writer. Even specialists in French literature, such as Kathleen M. McKilligan, while attempting to trace the techniques deployed by Dujardin, have failed to see the brilliant transposition of

* Vivian Mercier, 'Justice for Édouard Dujardin', *James Joyce Quarterly*, no. 4 (1966–7), pp. 209–13.
† New Directions, 1957, p. xxvii.

Wagnerian material and effects in *Les Lauriers sont coupés*, and emphasize its charm over its more durable features. In the latter case, the critic cannot have over- looked the *French* text, but many English-language critics working on stream-of-consciousness technique seem to have had no more than a working knowledge of French, or to rely on the first published translation. Such a procedure is of course somewhat inadequate, even for the study of the influence of the book on an English- language writer, because Joyce was an excellent linguist who lived for many years in France.

Failure to read the original French in all its pro- fundity has led to the general view of *Les Lauriers sont coupés* as a 'trivial' work, the adjective Leon Edel uses near the beginning of his introduction, which goes on specifically to deny the novel's right to be a 'great book' or a 'best book' (p. vii). It is this sort of denial that led Vivian Mercier to demand 'Justice for Édouard Dujardin', a demand that extends to Stuart Gilbert's translation as well. Sometimes, Mercier says, the over- Joycean Gilbert fails to be Joycean enough, and he com- pares his own rough translation of part of Chapter VI, the evocation of Daniel Prince reacting to the barrel-organ tune in the streets of Paris, where Gilbert fails to observe the repetition of the word 'calm', for example (pp. 47–8 below). Gilbert's version is smoothly elegant, but misses the musical function of repetition of such words. This is no doubt one of the reasons why Melvin Friedman, one of Dujardin's most perceptive critics, quotes extracts both from the French text and in his own translation.* I suspect that the Wagnerian, and perhaps even the Sym-

---

* Melvin Friedman, *Stream of Consciousness: A Study in Literary Method*, New Haven, Yale University Press, 1955, Chapter 6, pp. 139–77: 'Édouard Dujardin and Valery Larbaud: the Use of Interior Monologue'. Significantly, Friedman is one of the few critics to take into account the musical aspects of stream of consciousness.

bolist aspects of Dujardin's work escape Stuart Gilbert to some extent.

This is not to deny the great merits of Gilbert's work, especially in bringing *Les Lauriers* to a public of English-language readers for well over a generation, thus serving the cause of the literary-historical importance of Dujardin, however double-edged this service has been for the author's reputation. Stuart Gilbert's translation, though, pulls Dujardin's work towards an Edwardian idiom, when *Les Lauriers* is both late nineteenth-century and has a timeless quality about it. The familiar expressions, especially those of endearment and enthusiasm – 'awfully fetching girl', 'high stepper, by gad', 'deuced good', 'capital' – sound 'old hat' (!), and probably bring an (inappropriate) smile to the lips of the late twentieth-century reader. At the same time, the narrator's visit to the lavatory, introduced by Dujardin not only for realism but also for comic relief before the tense moment when Daniel Prince will ask Léa whether he can stay the night, is treated much more obliquely than in the original. Gilbert also introduces Gallicisms: 'adventure', for example, when the French means '(love) affair'. He does not always respect Dujardin's type of punctuation, and does not always follow his use of marks of suspension consistently, whereas I have insisted on the musical importance of such features (see p. xlv below). Gilbert's translation also notably omits the musical notation on page 47.

It would be pointless and impossible to make a detailed comparison which would require the equivalent of a chapter or article. The fact remains that important works of literature periodically require new translations.

In his introduction to *The Translations of Ezra Pound* Hugh Kenner says, 'the best of his translations exist in three ways, as windows into new worlds, as acts of homage and as personae of Pound's'.*

* Faber and Faber, 1970, p. 10.

Stuart Gilbert's translation of Dujardin was partly an act of homage. I hope mine will provide a new window into Dujardin's world. Each age translates according to its own view of the period and the language it is translating from. I have set out in my introduction what I see as the basically Wagnerian features of Dujardin's work. Dujardin's next translator – and I hope another generation will be sufficiently interested in his work to produce one – will translate from his or her own viewpoint. Over one hundred years after the first publication of *Les Lauriers sont coupés*, it is time for a new translation, in which I trust I have allowed Édouard Dujardin to speak more for himself than before, and to our own times.

The second work in this volume requires no explanation, except to belie Leon Edel's description of it as a 'rambling discourse' under a 'portentous' title,* and to place before the reader its first ever English translation.

* In the New Directions edition of *Les Lauriers sont coupés*, p. xii.

Introduction

I A traditional introduction to Édouard Dujardin would begin with the young James Joyce picking up a copy of *Les Lauriers sont coupés* from a station book-stall in 1903;'* that is to say it would not begin with the man at all, and even his book would not be studied in its own right, but only in the light of its (indirect but immense) influence. A precursor like Dujardin becomes so framed by successive areas and layers of influence that his central place in the picture is lost through infinite regress. However, he merits not only a prominently central place in the practice and development of a Wagner-inspired literary technique (interior monologue), but was also a very important figure in European cultural history.

Who then was the author of *Les Lauriers sont coupés*? Édouard Dujardin was, or was to become, law student and lover, musician and musicologist, France's 'Perfect Wagnerite', literary magazine editor, press baron, Symbolist, poet, novelist, dramatist, essayist and critic. Literary historian and memorialist, student of Hebrew and historian of religions. European and Germanophile. Gambler, duellist, business speculator, 'collaborator'. A man essentially of his times (which spanned ninety years), chameleon-like if not Protean, but also Nietzschean, seeing individual life as a brief space of light (to be recorded in literature) between the infinite passages of dark, in the cyclic process of recurrence.

Even when we have traced the main outlines of the life, and filled them out by evoking the times, the literature and other works, the impression will remain of

* See Notes on pp. lix–lxvii.

a man constantly pulled to one field of interest, then to another, then away to another, with the only common element being the passionate force of his attachment to everything he undertook. Taking this passion as a lead, we can wonder whether the very diversification of his interests was not the sign of a search: a search for his essential self, for a form of truth beyond this self, for communication and for love. Seen thus, Dujardin's life could seem less inconsistent, more of a unity enclosing diversity, the life of a traveller with his eye on the horizon, rather than the dabbling dilettante.

He wrote without recognition, but *Les Lauriers*, his chief claim to fame, a slim volume that instigated a revolutionary literary technique, has already proved that recognition can eventually come to the truly revolutionary artist. His work is re-created by his literary public. In this little volume by Dujardin we find the key to a literary process and to an epoch in European cultural history; technique reveals the leading motifs of a life: the ordinary individual struggling with sacred and profane love, and the heightening of these through a (partly Wagnerian, musical) art form. Dujardin was the match of his mentor Mallarmé for purity, an archetypal Symbolist to the end.

Édouard Dujardin's beginnings were typical of the assiduous schoolboy, later student, who dreams from under the shell of his studious outer self of some great artistic project. He was born on 10 November 1861 at Saint-Gervais-la-Forêt, near Blois in the Loir-et-Cher department. However, the family soon returned, in 1866, to its native Normandy, nearer to the sea which was to inspire the settings and archetypal metaphors for some of Édouard Dujardin's extravagant dramas. Dujardin's father, Alphonse, was a sea captain, so it was natural for him to set up in Rouen, which was at the time an important commercial and maritime centre, as well as being the overgrown provincial capital that inspired Flaubert's greatest anti-bourgeois scorn.

From 1870, Dujardin attended the Lycée Corneille before being sent on ahead of his parents to Paris as a boarder at the Lycée Louis-le-Grand (1878) where he studied in the 'classes préparatoires' which provided the super-sophisticated cramming classes for entry into the prestigious École Normale Supérieure. Édouard Dujardin's family settled for a while in Paris, but soon returned to their native Normandy, leaving their son their Paris flat – and to his own devices. After a passing phase when he thought (not insignificantly in view of his later study of religions) he wanted to become a priest, Édouard channelled his idealism into literature and music. He had failed his entrance exams for the École Normale Supérieure, and made a desultory attempt at studying history at the Sorbonne. Again, this experience was a thread to be picked up later, for he was subsequently to make a historical study of religion. For the moment, literature (especially poetry) and music were to be his main interests.

The year 1879 also saw him enrolled at the Conservatoire, where he met Debussy and Paul Dukas. His only poetico-musical composition (if one discounts the use of musical parameters in *Les Lauriers sont coupés*) is *Litanies, six mélopées pour chant et piano*, a poetic melodrama of interlinked songs, but again, the art form adopted is significant for its deliberate conjunction of text and music. This was perhaps the early result of his first encounters with the music of Richard Wagner, excerpts from whose works were to be heard at the concerts of the great conductors – Jules-Étienne Pasdeloup, Charles Lamoureux and Édouard Colonne. Acquaintance with the genius of Wagner may also have persuaded the young Dujardin to concentrate rather on a literature into which he could transpose musical elements. His lifelong passion for the works of Wagner dates from this period; his interest could not be assuaged by mere extracts, and he was one of a group of French enthusiasts to travel to London

to hear his first complete *Ring* cycle on 5, 6, 8 and 9 May
1882 at Her Majesty's Theatre. This was the touring
version of the *Ring* organized by the impresario Angelo
Neumann, with members of the original Bayreuth cast
conducted by Anton Seidl, which Dujardin reviewed for
La Renaissance musicale (14 May 1882). The very fact of
Dujardin's writing a review is a lead to one of the other
main threads of his life: journalism – especially musical
and literary. In concluding his review, Dujardin deplores
the fact that there has so far been no complete *and*
French-language *Ring* in Paris: he was already preoccupied with the necessity of making Wagner known as a
literary and musical figure to a non-German audience.

One essentially important literary personality to
whom Dujardin helped introduce Wagner's music was
the poet Stéphane Mallarmé, whose Tuesday 'At Homes'
at the Rue de Rome he regularly attended.[2] The result of
these meetings was reciprocally beneficial. To Mallarmé,
Dujardin presented the vision of an ideal total theatre, a
kind of realizable dramatic parallel to the aesthetically
sacred 'Livre' the Symbolist poet was striving to achieve.
To Dujardin, Mallarmé was the mentor of poetic purity.
That ideal and that master Dujardin never denied, as was
shown by his *Mallarmé par un des siens*, his commemora-
tive appreciation of the Symbolist achievement,
published a generation later.

Édouard Dujardin's enthusiasm for Wagner
naturally led him to Bayreuth in 1882, the year of the
Parsifal 'première', and he was back there for the same
work in July of the following year, when he made another
encounter that was to prove decisive for his life and
work: his meeting with Houston Stewart Chamberlain. A
proof that Dujardin kept faith beyond death is to be
found in his memorial volume *Rencontres avec Houston
Stewart Chamberlain* (1943), which mixes memoirs and
the correspondence of an intellectual friendship.
Dujardin met Chamberlain again in Paris in 1882 – after

a further Wagnerian tour to the Munich *Ring* – and once again in Munich and Bayreuth in July 1884. It was out of these meetings that the idea of a journal to propagate Wagner's works and ideas (even ideology) grew.[3]

Over a hundred years after this period, with Wagner tainted for some by misuse, or salvaged for the political left by others, it is difficult to imagine the quality of enthusiasm generated by him: perhaps – to use an image much favoured by the Symbolists – his works offered a mirror for nascent musico-philosophical aspirations, a possible justification of the belief that the world *could* be 'saved' by an artist and his works of art. Whatever the truth of the matter, such a Wagnerian movement was certainly the product of a Europe very different from the one which succeeded it in the twentieth century. Important figures such as Bertrand Russell in his autobiography and Sir Thomas Beecham in *A Mingled Chime* anticipated the view, suggested in A. J. P. Taylor's prelude to his *England, 1914–1945*, that pre-Great War Europe offered possibilities of international exchange to a number of privileged intellectuals and those rich enough to travel (then passport-free). There was, to a certain extent, a cosmopolitan intellectual European community, which partly explains the hostility of some (Bertrand Russell, for example) to European war in 1914, and the later blindness of others (like Dujardin) when it came to war again in 1939.

The *Revue Wagnérienne* first began as a monthly on 8 February 1885. Édouard Dujardin was joined on the review by Teodor de Wyzewa. De Wyzewa's daughter, Isabelle, sees him as the prime mover intellectually.[4] For her, Édouard Dujardin was more of an organizer. He certainly found the necessary financial sponsors, the banker Lascoux being his main backer, but a glance through the pages of the complete review shows that Houston Stewart Chamberlain was also responsible for some of the explanatory material published. It was here that Chamberlain began to work out ideas that later formed the basis of his Wagner books. Neither was Édouard Dujardin a mere organizer. Apart from reviews and short no:ices, he published 'translation-paraphrases' of parts of the *Ring* (*Rheingold*, Scene 1, and the Wanderer's invocation of Erda in Siegfried, Act III, plus Amfortas' lament from *Parsifal*, Act I). The significance of these goes far beyond their apparent importance. Wagner became – to use the stereotypical Symbolist image again – the musico-dramatic mirror for their literary gestures. Writing *about* another creative artist can become an aesthetic catalyser. Édouard Dujardin commissioned Fantin-Latour engravings based on scenes from the *Ring* and he instigated the famous series of Wagner sonnets: one by Mallarmé, and another by Verlaine, whence came T. S. Eliot's literary collage – 'Et, O ces voix d'enfants, chantant dans la coupole!' George Moore describes with wry humour how he accompanied Dujardin to fetch the sonnet from an alcoholic Verlaine who had gone over his deadline.[5]

According to Isabelle de Wyzewska, the literary merits of the *Revue Wagnérienne* partly accounted for its eventual demise: it was too literary and especially Symbolist-orientated, for musicians and music-lovers who did not necessarily want their music reinterpreted. It would probably be closer to the truth to say that, like all inter-disciplinary journals (and it was a genuine prototype for these), the *Revue Wagnérienne* was certainly too Symbolist for musicians, but also too musical for mainstream 'literati' who did not necessarily feel writing should be reassessed in musical terms.

Another factor in its demise was the supra-national nature of its views; while promotion of a German musician might please the European-minded members of the privileged intelligentsia described above, it went against the grain with musical 'patriots' who felt offended by Richard Wagner's Francophobe farce, *Une Capitulation*, which derisively delighted in France's defeat in the 1870 war against Prussia, and whose effects Édouard Dujardin tried to smooth over. Things went badly wrong for the review after what was known as the '*Lohengrin* affair' in 1887, in which Dujardin and his associates quite naturally championed the cause of those who wanted a complete performance of *Lohengrin* in Paris. Lamoureux backed down in the face of 'little French' musical patriotism. Again, this sort of incident must have influenced Dujardin in his persistent Germanophilism later on. In the summer of 1887, the *Revue Wagnérienne*, now financially very shaky, went bi-monthly; then on 15 July 1888, it brought out, after a six month's gap, a farewell issue. It had confirmed Édouard Dujardin as a Wagnerian, but it had also coincided with other literary ventures and adventures on the part of its founder, who was to prove himself to be the perfect *literary* French Wagnerite.

By taking over the *Revue Indépendante* in November 1886, which he ran concurrently with the *Revue Wagnérienne* until the latter ceased publication in 1888, Dujardin gave himself both a platform to promote the kind of literature he favoured without undue interference from others (i.e. anti-Symbolist musicians, for instance), and the chance to publish some of his own writings against a backcloth of works of his own choice. Here we reach an important stage in his literary development, because the *Revue Indépendante* published the first version of *Les Lauriers sont coupés* in serial form in 1887.

Dujardin needed all the managerial and organizational skills he had begun to develop on the *Revue Wagnérienne* (where he even arranged bookings and travel for the Bayreuth Festival and published information pages) to keep his balance on a financial tightrope.[6] He even procured a little advertising revenue from railway companies, but according to Jean Ajalbert: 'His only credit was illusions, will power, and imperturbable con-

xviii

Introduction

fidence which was his greatest strength.'[7] Editorial policy
was to pay contributors only upon their *second* appearance in the magazine, and although this led to problems
with the impecunious Villiers de l'Isle-Adam and with
Verlaine, for example, Édouard Dujardin was able to
assemble a distinguished 'stable' of writers, some of
them already famous, others – especially Mallarmé – to
be counted among the greatest innovators of pre-
Modernist literature. Since Dujardin was taking on an
ailing periodical (which had first appeared in 1884 and
was to continue publication until 1892 after Dujardin's
resignation from the editorial board in December 1888),
he sought to reassure present subscribers and attract new
readers in a brief statement of editorial policy:

> The *Revue Indépendante* will adhere to its policy as a
> publication devoted to all forms of Art. A constant
> preoccupation with this aim will allow it to accept –
> provided they are genuine – both the most traditional
> and the boldest projects, and to remain truly
> independent, no less independent of outworn tradi-
> tions than of futile decadent agitation.[8]

It was to this implicit appeal that the following
writers responded: Mallarmé, Jules Laforgue, Barbey
d'Aurevilly, J.-K. Huysmans, Paul Bourget, Octave
Mirbeau, Edmond and Jules de Goncourt, José Maria de
Hérédia, Villiers de l'Isle-Adam, Verlaine, Anatole France,
Maurice Barrès ... a wide-ranging group indeed, but
not without a tinge of the 'decadence' Dujardin said
he was avoiding. Mallarmé, apart from appearing as
a poet, was responsible for theatre criticism, and Dujardin's old friend, Teodor de Wyzewa, took on the review
pages. The *Revue Indépendante* was also international in
approach, as attested by the publication of translations of
Tolstoy, de Quincey, E. T. A. Hoffmann, Ibsen ... and
George Moore, a member of Dujardin's circle in Paris
at the time, and a lifelong friend and correspondent.[9]

The magazine also had a music section which frequently chronicled Wagner performances.

Apart from serializing the first version of *Les Lauriers sont coupés*, which does not appear to have elicited any printed reviews or response (for direct, personal responses to the author see pp. 88–90 below), Dujardin published several shorter pieces in *La Revue Indépendante* which throw some light on his preoccupations at this period of his life. First of all – and very naturally – he was unremittingly Wagnerian. While the *Revue Wagnérienne* had obliged him to follow certain proprieties and prescriptions (his Wagner 'paraphrase-translations' are at least a fair reflection of the original text), here he could allow his imagination to play freely at Wagnerian transpositions. 'Pour la vierge du roc ardent' (*Revue Indépendante*, September 1888) makes an obvious reference in its title to Brünnhilde, and the text also refers to *Siegfried* and to *Tristan und Isolde*. But the originality of the work comes from its (mainly) contemporary setting, and its deliberate juxtaposition of prose and verse forms. The prose corresponds to the evocation of a modern love affair at some unidentified seaside resort, while the poetry evokes a dream world of reference partly based on Wagner. By gradual osmosis, the poetical and Wagnerian effects filter through to the prose sections, till we have a prose-poem transposition of the Tristan and Isolde idea to the late nineteenth century: 'Every woman is Isolde to a Tristan . . .'.[10] Dujardin was thus, in the same period as *Les Lauriers sont coupés*, attempting to give an archetypally Wagnerian dimension to a love theme, an indication that Wagner was often present in the conception of his literary works. His obsession with the idea of lost and hopeless love is further indicated in two 'Suites' of poems (of great stylistic banality) that appeared in the January and September issues of 1889.[11] And a link with the only half-veiled reference to Daniel Prince's first sexual experience with a prostitute is suggested by the

'Ballade des authentiques courtisanes' (January 1888), a poem which plays on imagery of light and darkness so often to be found in the near contemporaneous *Les Lauriers*.

The banality of expression of parts of the verse pieces suggests Dujardin's true field was rather to be the prose-poem, and *Les Lauriers sont coupés* could indeed be viewed as a kind of extended example of that genre. The subject matter suggests that he could by this time keep his distance when handling romantic themes, as the very act of writing indicates. Certainly he could no longer have been a provincial greenhorn of the Daniel Prince variety, even if he might once have been. He had a wide circle of literary, and other friends, like Toulouse-Lautrec, who included him – yellow-haired and bearded – in voyeur-istic satyr's posture, in his poster, 'Le Divan japonais'. This conjunction of art and experience was one of the conditions and necessary paradoxes of Édouard Dujar-din's life. The man who felt familiar enough with the formally-minded Mallarmé to ask for his daughter Geneviève's hand in marriage in May 1885, even if it was refused, and then have the same somewhat aloof figure, Mallarmé, witness his marriage (his first, in 1896), also frequented a mixed crowd of literati and Bohemian art-ists at the Café d'Orient, rue de Clichy (transposed as the Café Oriental in *Les Lauriers sont coupés*).

The period atmosphere of this Paris can be sensed in Maupassant's novel *Bel-Ami* (1885). There is a veneer of frenetic pleasure over an apprehension of anguish through financial instability and, even more seriously, the gnawing threat of sexual disease. The *apparently* facile colouring of Toulouse-Lautrec pictures from his Moulin Rouge period fill structures that are scaringly skeletal despite the seemingly ample forms of the women displayed. Death was beneath the flesh in a period con-scious of its own ephemeral nature. Love was a disease or despair under the superficial mask of pleasure-seeking.

'They don't seem to believe in their own happiness ...'[12] said Verlaine, a poet Dujardin knew and even (?unconsciously) parodied in *Les Lauriers sont coupés* (see p. xlv below). Verlaine's ability to mirror the social veneer of polite expression that covered a desperate search for pure, idealized passion, is reflected in his love poems, such as the 'Bonne Chanson' cycle Fauré was later to set to music. Perfect poetic form mirrored the perfect (and impossible) love. Music too was to echo the shifting, transitional consciousness of the end of this nineteenth century, with the work of Debussy, based on fragmentation and shifting harmony.[13]

Dujardin, as we have seen in his earliest works and as shown in *Les Lauriers*, was preoccupied with this pursuit of an ever-receding love. He also looked like a dandy of the period. Dujardin summed up some of the conflicting aspects of the period, but it was mostly his dandified appearance which struck William Rothenstein:

> Édouard Dujardin, a Wagner propagandist, and associated with the Symbolist movement in literature, was a close friend of Anquetin and Toulouse-Lautrec, and a frequenter of Montmartre. How much better off he was than most of us, I cannot say but he had the appearance and manners of a French dandy. With full brown beard and eye-glass, well-cut clothes and spotless linen, he looked a figure apart ...'[14]

Rothenstein also noted Dujardin's involvement in 'affairs of honour'. Indeed, Dujardin became the chronicler of the main duels fought in the Paris area over the years 1880–1889, in *L'Annuaire du duel*, which he published under the pseudonym Ferréus in 1891.[15] Most of these duels involved, aristocrats, military men, members of the National Assembly and representatives of the press. Being a newspaper editor appears to have been a dangerous business! One entry is of particular interest:

9 November 1889

M. Édouard DUJARDIN, ex-managing editor of the *Revue Indépendante*

M. Victor JOZE

(Altercation following upon which M. Dujardin esteems he has been insulted.)

Witnesses for M. Dujardin: MM. Jules Courtier and Aristide Marie;

For M. Joze: MM. Myrton and Jules Livet.

Encounter with pistols in the Bois de Boulogne.

Two shots exchanged without result.[16]

Ajalbert implies in his memoirs that people who saw Dujardin casually were far from grasping the range and depth of his activities – especially his literary ones, although these are the ones most insisted upon by his artistic collaborator, Teodor de Wyzewa, in a profile contributed to the 'Hommes d'aujourd'hui' series of pen-portraits. The truth of the matter must have been that Dujardin was leading a double, even triple life: man about town, musico-literary promoter and creative artist. Literature could never have been far from his thoughts, as this was the time when he produced the work which is his greatest claim to fame, inventing interior monologue in the process.

It is perhaps significant that the writer who seems to have most profoundly understood the conjunction of literary illusionist and pragmatic realist was George Moore, whose records of random thoughts are in flashes reminiscent of interior monologue;[17] and in common with Dujardin George Moore was a Wagner enthusiast and Wagner-influenced.[18] His correspondence with Dujardin contains frequent references to Wagner, and to the respective literary projects of the two friends.[19] Respect was mutual, the influence coming probably more from Dujardin, especially with regard to Wagner and his own subsequent biblical and theological studies. In the rather rambling manner of his autobiographical trilogy, *Hail and Farewell*, Moore acknowledges the stimulating effect of Édouard Dujardin's conversation when it came to Wagner and religious studies.[20]

It is Moore who reveals how Dujardin had devised a special system of betting that kept him afloat financially for some large part of the eighteen nineties.[21] Unfortunately, George Moore is not very precise over his dates, nor especially about the dating of his account of Édouard Dujardin's accident detailed below. In case this betting should appear to indicate a superficially mercenary streak in Dujardin, let it be said that in his 1924 preface to the *Les Argonautes* trilogy, which deals with a Wagnerian *Ring* type conflict between love and money, Dujardin states that he believes a creative artist ought to earn his living from activities having no connection with his art, so as to leave that art untainted by the commercial influence of having to earn money by it. Unfortunately, Dujardin's winning streak was brought to a sudden end by a carriage accident that obliged him to pay exorbitant damages.[22]

We can surmise, however, that his speculations on the turf and elsewhere had allowed him sufficient financial independence to pursue his literary ideals without undue contamination of their purity. The utter seriousness with which Dujardin was working towards his literary goals has already been suggested by our mention of certain short pieces that appeared in the *Revue Indépendante*. He had also – as a prelude to and a preparation for *Les Lauriers sont coupés* – published a volume of short stories, *Les Hantises* (1886).[23] *Les Lauriers sont coupés* itself was no haphazard flash of 'inspiration', but the product of *conscious* literary artistry, as a study of the draft manuscripts has shown.[24]

Édouard Dujardin was already behaving like the proto-Modernist writer which his later influence on James Joyce proved him to be. And he was later to lay claim to another literary 'invention' in addition to interior monologue, i.e. free verse.[25] Although Dujardin continued to employ recognized traditional verse patterns as well (*La Comédie des amours*, 1891), his experimentation with mixed forms (*Trois poèmes en prose mêlés de vers*) and poetic prose inclined him towards a kind of free verse that cannot have been without Wagnerian influence, especially as he was preparing and producing a major Wagnerian project in the early 1890s.[26] This was *Antonia*, a Wagnerian trilogy whose very title suggests that Dujardin was reprocessing ideas he had sketched out previously. *Antonia* is also the title of the first (1886) of the *Trois poèmes en prose mêlés de vers*, and Dujardin makes an inter-textual reference to it in *Les Lauriers sont coupés* when Daniel Prince is dropping off to sleep at Léa's (p. 56 below). 'Antonia' symbolizes unfulfilled desire and hopeless love. While these themes were well integrated into *Les Lauriers sont coupés*, which at least enjoyed a critical success,[27] they were part of a near fiasco when deployed with an over-obtrusive Wagnerian reference system in *Antonia*, the trilogy.

The vast scale of Dujardin's dramatic work is obviously Wagnerian; the three parts of the trilogy are *La Légende d'Antonia* (1891), *Le Chevalier du passé* (1892) and *La Fin d'Antonia* (1893); and it would not be too fanciful to consider Dujardin's previous Wagner-orientated works as forming a 'prelude' thematically to what then becomes a '*Ring*'-type dramatic poem based on a cosmic-scale version of the eternal feminine within a cyclic time-structure. A. G. Lehmann has rightly identified the central figure Antonia with Kundry,[28] just as Kathleen M. McKilligan easily recognizes some of the *Parsifal* references in the plays – the 'Flower Maidens', for example – but *Antonia* has generally impressed more for the disastrous reception it received[29] than for its intrinsic qualities.[30] Dujardin put the different parts of his dramatic work on at his own expense in front of an invited audience which he did not choose carefully enough for Parts II and, especially, III, which was nearly laughed off the stage of the (unfortunately named) Vaudeville Theatre. Typical of press reaction was the following (*Le Gil Blas*, 16 June 1893):

> If you now tell me Mr Dujardin is not a fraud, I won't believe you; Mr Dujardin is a fraud, the father of frauds, the convinced poetic fraud.[31]

This sort of blow to his 'vanity' was mollified by the reaction of Stéphane Mallarmé who recognized, for his part, Dujardin's masterly use of verse and his creation, beyond his Wagnerian models, of a perfect theatre of suggestion and illusion.[32]

Dujardin's *Antonia* trilogy continues his Wagner-based dialectic of woman as part whore, part pure virgin, with the reference to Kundry (Wagner's own amalgam of the two sides in one figure) giving a mythical dimension to his character: the epigraph to *La Légende d'Antonia* is 'Ich sah ihn und lachte' ('I saw him and laughed') from *Parsifal*, Act II, where Kundry is deliberately made a female equivalent of the Wandering Jew. At the same time, Dujardin acknowledges a technical debt by dedicating the third part, *La Fin d'Antonia*:

en hommage au maître du drame moderne,
à Richard Wagner.

There are indeed reminiscences of Wagner, situations borrowed from Wagner, imagery transcribed from Wagner (the light/darkness symbolism from *Tristan und Isolde*, for example). We follow (a) Man's (i.e. the poet's) search for (the ideal) Woman, through the stages of his life, and through the ages. Although *Antonia* is supposedly set in modern times, it has a timeless quality about it, emphasized by the fact that the main character seems to move through multiple metempsychoses (like Kundry's), from life to life, from age to age. Dujardin's eternal woman (in best Wagnerian fashion with Kundry encapsulating Venus, Elisabeth, Brünnhilde, Isolde, etc.) incorporates in everlasting reminiscence aspects of her earlier selves. *La Légende d'Antonia* moves from a Siegmund–Sieglinde type evocation of love towards a form of 'Liebestod'. Subsequently, *Le Chevalier du passé* enacts a form of reincarnation whereby Antonia (like Kundry in Act II of *Parsifal*) has become a super-whore figure who is visited by a (reincarnated) version of her former lover. This means that Part III of Dujardin's triptych can be devoted to a theme dear to Wagner from *Tannhäuser*: the conflict between sacred and profane love. Antonia returns here as an itinerant beggarwoman, her lowly status a preparation for a form of psycho-spiritual redemption enacted in an atmosphere redolent (through imagery of a reawakening nature) of Wagner's 'Good Friday music'. Thus Dujardin gives voice and verse to the redeemed Kundry, who is seen but barely heard in Act III of *Parsifal*.

The above is a mere outline that cannot do full justice to all of Dujardin's Wagner borrowings, some of which can seem *too* obvious to the initiated Wagnerian. Even this, however, cannot detract from Dujardin's technical expertise in using a collapsible time-scale which derives from Wagner, but which is a sophisticated transposition and assumption of Wagner's use of narrative monologue: narrative is employed to evoke the past and to unfold the future in a kind of ever-moving present reminiscent of both musical development and Daniel Prince's stream of consciousness in *Les Lauriers sont coupés*.

Antonia never enjoyed public performance again. No doubt discouraged – and doubly so because of the legal battle connected with his accident – Dujardin operated a twofold retreat, which was eventually to involve an advance on another front. During what remains a rather obscure period of his life, he indulged in speculation in the press and was involved at various times during the very last years of the nineteenth century with newspapers such as *Jean qui rit*, *L'Éclair*, *La Journée* and *Fin de Siècle*, the latter entailing several brushes with the obscenity laws, indicating that the psychological battle over notions of sacred and profane love was still being fought out in him. This was the time when he first married (in 1896) a certain Germaine, whom we can surmise from an oblique reference in the correspondence with H. S. Chamberlain, that he divorced. This was also the time when he was working on his second novel (published in 1899), significantly entitled *L'Initiation au péché et à l'amour*, in part as a further reference to a *Parsifal* theme that is one of the leading threads in his biography.

Unlike *Les Lauriers sont coupés*, *L'Initiation au péché et à l'amour* is in traditional novel form, and reads not unlike a less sophisticated, more diluted version of Flaubert's *L'Éducation sentimentale*. And perhaps not surprisingly, it also reads, stylistically, not unlike the sequel Dujardin's second wife, Marie, was to write to *Les Lauriers sont coupés*: *La Belle que voici* (pp. xxxvff. below). *L'Initiation* . . . – this is the thematic link – reads like a possible background scenario to the encounter which provides the 'story' to *Les Lauriers* . . .; indeed Marcellin Deyruyssats, the naïve hero, a law student from the provinces, is cheated in the course of his 'sentimental education' by an unscrupulous adventuress. The novel also allows Édouard Dujardin to work out the early versions of some of his religious notions in the form of conversations between Marcellin and his friend, Henri. Thus Marcellin says: 'I am dubious about your divine origin, Jesus, and maybe you are only a beautiful legend.'[33] *L'Initiation au péché et à l'amour* is the story of a 'poor wretch living life';[34] and life, Dujardin insists in his preface, is as much made up of physical as spiritual love. It is difficult not to think of this book as other than the ironically yet affectionately self-parodistic portrait of the youth its author had long left behind, torn between the sacred and the profane, but now in maturity reaching a lovingly ironical acceptance of the inevitably weak nature of man defeated by life's complexities.

Another transition in Dujardin's life was his move in 1901 from Paris to 'Val Changis', near Fontainebleau, a manorial residence he had had built to designs prepared with the help of the painter Anquetin. The 'Val Changis' became a retreat in which Édouard Dujardin could play host to his numerous friends from the Symbolist period, for whom he remained, according to Aristide Marie,[35] the prime mover, instigator and inspiration of inalienable ideals. This partial retreat from the 'world' corresponded to a further new intellectual undertaking on Dujardin's part. At the turn of the century he took up the study of Hebrew and of religions at the Sorbonne. The history of religions was to occupy him, on and off, for the rest of his life.

The year 1904 saw a new collection of poetry, *Le Délassement du guerrier* and also the launching of a periodical (in a better class than the pornography of one of his previous journalistic ventures!), *La Revue des Idées*, on which he collaborated with another friend from the Symbolist period, the novelist and essayist, Rémy de Gourmont.

La Revue des Idées, which lasted until 1907, indicates the widening of Édouard Dujardin's field of interests at this time. It was as if the study of religions from what he considered to be a scientific point of view had awakened him to the necessity of study in as many directions as possible. The new review, according to its prospectus, aimed to be inter-disciplinary and was based on critical inquiry by specialists but still remained intelligible to the intellectual layman; and true to its aim, it published articles in the fields of philosophy, psychology, mathematics, physics, music, biology, medicine, botany, paleography, ethnography, anthropology, geology, archaeology, military history, sociology, philology, literary history, theology and law.

When it ceased publication in 1907, Dujardin became for a time 'chargé de cours' (part-time lecturer) in religious history at the Sorbonne, so far had his researches advanced. He had in 1906 presented a thesis on 'Les Prédecesseurs de Daniel' and recycled much of his research material in *La Source du fleuve chrétien*, published by Le Mercure de France in the same year.

Dujardin worked from what he termed a 'sociological' angle on religion, inspired by such figures as Émile Durkheim, and also by the Comtist tradition (as indicated by the subsequent publication – the only other work by Dujardin, apart from *Les Lauriers*, to see the light of day in English before this present book – of his late work, *The Ancient History of the God Jesus*, by the Comtist publisher Watts and Co. in 1938). His aim was desacralization of the Scriptures or, at any rate, an attempt to deprive them of hierarchical superiority of insight over other sources, in order to see them as merely part of Man's attempt to come to terms with the meaning of existence. In *La Source du fleuve chrétien*, he disputes the historical veracity of the prophets' utterances, suggesting they were added *after* the historical events they were supposed to foretell as part of an attempt to rouse the Jewish people. As the subtitle of the book, 'Le Judaïsme', implies, his study tries to trace the early history of the Jews. Thus he sees the religion of 'one God' primarily in political terms as a brilliant device to reinforce nationalism. It is interesting that the author, who was later to be labelled a Nazi sympathizer and 'collaborator', points apparently disapprovingly in his book to the religious and national laws of Judaism which insisted on the exclusion of aliens to preserve the purity of the Jewish race.

After his relative disappointment with his literary projects (especially drama), Dujardin can be considered, albeit in a minor way, as reacting like Wagner in his years of exclusion and exile before he could complete his projected *Ring*: in the time gap before his mature masterpieces, Wagner wrote his main theoretical works in which he imagined his ideal theatre, and consequently and conjointly his ideal society. Dujardin, like Wagner, needed to discover – and to invent – a theoretical, socio-historic and religious origin to his thought and literary work.

The dramatic works which Dujardin continued to produce were also Wagner-inspired. In 1910–13, he wrote the first (and major) part of the trilogy that was to have the general title *Les Argonautes*. *Marthe et Marie* was produced at the Théâtre Antoine on 31 May 1913, as part of the inauguration of Lugné-Poë's 'Théâtre de l'Oeuvre', which was thereafter to play such an important role in the promotion of French poetic drama. If *Antonia* is Dujardin's *Parsifal*, then *Les Argonautes* – and especially *Marthe et Marie* – is, while containing reminiscences of other Wagner works, his *Ring*. This stems from its basis in a dramatic conflict between 'Gold' (commerce) and 'Love' (pure idealism):

> *Les Argonautes, Marthe et Marie, Les Epoux d'Heur-le-port, Le Retour des enfants prodigues* contain the conflict between the two principles that Wagner symbolized by Gold and Love ... and more profoundly, Schopenhauer – the Will to Live and Renunciation.[36]

In the same preface Dujardin indicates his Wagner-inspired notion of an ideal theatre for an ideal public. He also insists on the necessity of transforming personal experience in aesthetic terms. It is here that he recommends the pursuit of an aesthetic ideal unshackled by commercial considerations (see p. xxiii above). The form and content of his work is highly reminiscent of Wagner. One of the main vehicles of dramatic expression is the extended monologue, a continuing preoccupation with which Dujardin vigorously defends:

> ... only superficial minds will deem that a monologue which lasts for nearly one act is automatically undramatic.[37]

Basically, *Marthe et Marie* is a 'rags to riches' story, ending in a Schopenhauerian renunciation whereby Félicien, the hero, returns with Marie to the village of their birth, where Marthe, her sister, plays the role of her double. In a part-*Tristan*, part-*Parsifal* inspired dénouement, Marie tears the bandages off the wound she has suffered in defending Félicien from her jealous former lover, and thus 'gives' Félicien to Marthe.

This was the idealism inspired by German philosophy which Dujardin's work reflected on the eve of the Great War. And *Marthe et Marie* was the work James Joyce saw advertised in his Swiss haven from a war-torn Europe in 1917, when he attempted to contact the author who had influenced the technique he was employing in *Ulysses*, in order to procure another copy of the novel he so much admired.[38]

In situating the essentials of his life and literature outside the European conflict, Joyce was to some extent leading a parallel idealized existence to Dujardin, who refused to follow the general anti-German movement in France at the time. Rather than cut himself off from what was happening politically, like Joyce, Dujardin, the former Symbolist and perennial Germanophile, attempted to study the possibilities of a negotiated peace. He went occasionally to Switzerland, less as a form of escapism than as a means of maintaining close contact with his old Wagnerite friend, H. S. Chamberlain, who had made clear his allegiance in 1914 by taking German nationality. Out of Dujardin's concern to maintain the kind of Europe he had known in his youth, with Germany

as a force for cultural regeneration, came his founding
of the *Cahiers idéalistes* in 1917.

This periodical, which appeared intermittently, even
erratically, until 1928, was anti-war (even pacifist
because it included articles by Romain Rolland), and
pro-German. In it Dujardin published his poetry about
the horror of war and, as far as the censor would allow,
expressions of his pro-German sentiment, culminating in
1919 in a denunciation of the 'revanchiste' Treaty of
Versailles. Together with his propagation of Wagner,
this publication was to become one of the elements in a
whole file of accusations that could be levelled against
Dujardin as 'collaborator'. The well-springs of his
thought, however, lay in philosophical idealism rather
than in a form of crypto-Nazism. This is one of the most
difficult aspects of Dujardin's life to analyse, as it eventually concerns one of the murkiest periods in French
history. That is why it is best to mention the sources of
the problem from its earliest signs. Otherwise, however,
only the most zealous political activist could denounce
Dujardin as being proto-Nazi at this period. First of all
he (vainly as far as gaining wide public success was concerned) continued his theatrical work: the two remaining
sections of *Les Argonautes* were presented, *Les Époux
d'Heur-le-port* on 3 June 1919, and *Le Retour des enfants
prodigues* on 9 February 1924. Then, genuine literary
esteem came with the 'rediscovery' of *Les Lauriers sont
coupés* by James Joyce and Valery Larbaud, the main
stages of which Édouard Dujardin himself accurately
describes in *Le Monologue intérieur*. The term 'accurately'
is important, because any attempt to see Dujardin as a
pathetic literary has-been trying to jump on the *Ulysses*
bandwagon would be totally out of character with the
exemplary idealist we have depicted so far. Joyce's debt
to Dujardin has been acknowledged by Richard Ellmann
in his definitive biography,[39] and it is also interesting to
refer to the first-hand account by Frank Budgen, especi-

ally as it begins in terms which recall Édouard Dujardin's own definition of interior monologue, the technique Joyce took over from him (see *Interior Monologue*, p. 113 below).[40]

Joyce himself appeared whimsically dismissive of Dujardin's full profundity, as in a letter to Harriet Shaw Weaver of 22 November 1929:

> I cannot get any satisfactory reply from anyone in London about Dujardin's book and the poor man thinks it is all settled, G.M.'s [George Moore's] preface and everything. You remember his dedication in *Les Lauriers*. Well he brought me his *Ulysses* and to give him cake for bread I wrote in it 'To E.D. Annonciateur de la parole intérieure, le larron impénitent. J.J.'[41]

He was no doubt very conscious of the effect his reflected fame had had on Dujardin. A letter of 6 June 1924, had found James Joyce recommending Svevo to Valery Larbaud, the other player in the *Lauriers* triangle in the twenties:

> If you manage a short notice on it [Italo Svevo's *Zeno*] somewhere or, as you suggested, give some pages of it in the second number of *Commerce* you would do much more for him than my mention of *Les Lauriers sont coupés* did for Dujardin.[42]

To be entirely fair to Joyce, he did everything in his power to promote the translation of *Les Lauriers*.[43] He eventually arranged for Stuart Gilbert, one of the translators of *Ulysses* (whose final version was looked over by Valery Larbaud, promoter of both Joyce and Dujardin) to translate the work, and tried – without success – to obtain a preface for the translation from Dujardin's old friend George Moore, who in the event sounded more dismissive of interior monologue than Dujardin would have liked to think. After pleading that he wished to devote the few remaining years that he might live to his own literary work, Moore claimed to 'know nothing of the question which apparently agitates France, the discovery of the *monologue intérieur*. In England we don't believe that any discovery has been made. We think, rightly or wrongly, that the *monologue intérieur* existed from time immemorial'.[44]

Joyce, however, was disinterested enough to help Gilbert translate *Les Lauriers*,[45] which no doubt enhanced Dujardin's role as a precursor, but helped to play down the Wagnerian origins of interior monologue,[46] when one considers Joyce's rather ironically hostile attitude to *Götterdämmerung* – 'I was going to squander a lira on *The Dusk of the Gods* tonight but am afraid that, in my present pendulous mood, I couldn't stand in the gallery for three hours',[47] and the spoofing references to Wagner in *Ulysses* and *Finnegans Wake*.[48]

Respect between the two men was mutual. Dujardin added his name to the petition against the unauthorized serialization of parts of *Ulysses* in the United States (February 1927), and he was present at the famous *Ulysses* luncheon in honour of the French translation of the book on 27 June 1929 at the Hotel Léopold in Les Vaux-de-Cernay near Versailles. In a letter to Joyce subsequent to this he acclaimed his reading of *Ulysses* in (for him!) suitably Wagnerian terms:

> The sentiment of swimming in an ocean of spirituality, the very one I experienced at twenty when I first heard (without knowing German) the four days of *The Ring of the Nibelungs*, something, in fact, which makes understandable what the mystics call the vision in God.[49]

Apart from proclaiming him as a literary innovator, the new attention brought to Dujardin confirmed him in a further, new role he had adopted: that of literary memorialist. This new aspect of his career had already partly taken off with an essay published in 1919, 'De Stéphane Mallarmé au poète Ezéchiel'. In 1924 he was prime mover in the foundation of the Mallarmé Society, and he further produced 'Mallarmé par un des siens', which became the cover title of a 1936 volume of essays also containing previously published articles – 'Les premiers poètes du vers libre' and reminiscences of the *Revue Wagnérienne*. This activity as literary historian was crowned by his lectures on interior monologue, in which he acknowledges his debt to Valery Larbaud, another writer with whom a deep degree of mutual admiration existed. After dedicating his first attempt at interior monologue, *Amants, heureux amants* to Joyce, Larbaud acknowledged his indirect debt to Édouard Dujardin by dedicating *Mon plus secret conseil* to him.[50]

Édouard Dujardin's life was becoming balanced between revaluations and new ventures. While his work as precursor of interior monologue was coming to light (a new, definitive edition of *Les Lauriers sont coupés* with a preface by Valery Larbaud came out in 1924 in the wake of this discovery), he had staged *Le Mystère du dieu mort et ressuscité*. Following that evening of 26 May 1923, he met a young writer over thirty years his junior, Marie Marguerite Chenou, who was to become his second wife on 26 June 1924. It is to Marie Dujardin that we owe a fragmentary pen portrait of Édouard Dujardin at this period as a piercingly blue-eyed, silver-haired sage in *La Belle que voici*, the sequel to *Les Lauriers* published in 1949, in which Daniel Prince, forty years after his brief liaison with Léa d'Arsay, has turned into a petty-minded, conservative, retired functionary, whose only pleasure is spending the occasional 'dirty weekend' in Paris. During one of these he encounters and pursues – intent on petty revenge – the daughter of the now deceased Léa, who has idealistically taken pity on the naïve hero she has read about in *Les Lauriers sont coupés*, but by whom she is going to be deceived and disillusioned. The evocation of

Édouard Dujardin comes from a preliminary chapter in which Daniel Prince coincidentally meets his 'creator' at the bookstore of the publishers responsible for Dujardin's work. During a discussion in a café, Édouard Dujardin has the opportunity to size up Daniel Prince as a narrow-minded philistine, while revealing himself in the process to be a perspicacious observer of human souls, and a perennial Wagnerian, a follower of Nietzsche, and pro-German into the bargain.

2 The way in which Dujardin's aesthetic, philosophical and political (or politically interpretable) views cohere in an ambiguous jigsaw pattern is the subject of this second section of the introduction.

This complex pattern is reflected in the continuingly variegated strands of Dujardin's activities during an old age that surpassed in energy and enterprise what many men achieve in their youth. The recognition accorded to Dujardin because of his invention of interior monologue must have been a spur to continued effort on his part. When discovering interior monologue was at the height of fashion, in 1923, he published the first volume of his *Histoire ancienne du Dieu Jésus*, planned as a six-part work, of which only three were published. The same year, as already noted, saw the performance of *Le Mystère du dieu mort et ressuscité*, a drama which is in part a reflection of his religious writings, and the tangible beginnings of the influence on his works of Nietzsche, whose cyclic view of existence and civilization formed one of the basic concepts behind Dujardin's final drama, *Le Retour éternel* (1932).

During the nineteen twenties and thirties Édouard Dujardin continued incessantly to work as a journalist and propagandist of ideas. In 1934–35, for example, he was involved in yet another journalistic venture, *Les Superbes*, a periodical devoted to social problems. He was

also throughout this time a frequent lecturer. *Le Monologue intérieur* first took shape as a series of lectures given
on tour in the Weimar Republic. Dujardin's various
activities were rewarded by the attribution of the Prix
Lasserre in 1934. In addition, he became a frequent radio
broadcaster, presenting adaptations of the classics in
1938–40.

The multifarious nature of his activities, stemming
from a whole lifetime of effort, is the key to his paradoxical position and attitudes during the Second World War.
As previously stated, his approach to the history of religions was non-doctrinal, and this earned him the
anathema of the Roman Catholic Church. The second
subtitle of *Grandeur et Décadence de la Critique. Sa
Rénovation* (Messein, 1931) is *Le Cas de l'abbé Turmel.*
The 'Abbé Turmel' referred to had been excommuni-
cated for questioning the interpretations of Saint Paul
and especially for questioning the Resurrection, saying
that it was absurd to say 'salvation' depended on parti-
cipating in someone else's death, that the death and
Resurrection of Jesus were only a pseudo-death and
resurrection.[51] Dujardin goes even further by stating that
the interpretations of Paul, based on this first fake, had
simply been foisted on the Church and had persisted,
generation after generation: not an attitude designed to
please conventional believers! And furthermore, Dujardin casts doubt on the historical veracity of the character
of Jesus.[52] Édouard Dujardin does this – and here we
can see the fiction writer and literary critic coming out
in him – by a clever abolition of hierarchy in the respective functions of reality and fiction: he sees basically no
difference between fictional and historical 'reality',
placing Jesus among fictional characters:

From the aesthetic and literary point of view, the
characters of Jesus, of Hamlet, of Père Goriot, of Mr
Bloom, as they emerge from the works in which they

are described, are as real, as true to life as those of Saint Paul, of Jean-Jacques (Rousseau), of Louis XIV, which emerge from the *Epistles*, the *Confessions* (whatever lies Jean-Jacques put in them), the memoirs of Saint-Simon.[53]

This non- or anti-hierarchical point of view also stems from Édouard Dujardin's reading of Nietzsche from whom he absorbed the idea that civilization was in a state of constant flux. The notion is echoed in the very title of his final play *Le Retour éternel* (1932). Dujardin's last two plays function – notwithstanding references to Antonia as a Kundry figure, and *Les Argonautes* as a simile-*Ring* cycle – as a *Parsifal*, Wagner's drama of decadence and regeneration. Dujardin firmly believed, from after the World War onward, that civilization (especially European civilization) was going into a period of decline which, in the eternal cycle of recurrence, was the necessary prelude to regeneration. *Le Retour éternel* shows this process in operation through four separate phases, corresponding to the 'tableaux' in the play, and ranging through the Stone Age, the Roman era, the nineteen twenties, and a vague future in a devastated Paris out of which new life will grow. As such it reads like a staid and Claudelian version of Thornton Wilder's *The Skin of Our Teeth*! However, other important elements feature in the play, not least a preoccupation with revolutionary socialism in Period Three (Modern Times), which reflects Dujardin's 1928 political work, *Demain, ici, ainsi, la révolution* where his distrust of capitalism (based on the old Wagnerian conflict between love and gold) tempted him into a temporary flirtation with pro-Bolshevism. Thus we can see him, like Ezra Pound with Social Credit, momentarily at least, absorbing undigested into his work, socio-political ideas that might seem to bolster up his essentially aesthetic outlook on life. In this way too, the former Symbolist convinced of the decline of cultural values, became a crypto-decadent ... years after the nineties and the 'fin de siècle'.

Fundamentally Dujardin was looking for some system that could temporarily halt – for his generation at least – the inevitable process of decline. This – again in order artificially to shield the aesthetic centre of his life – eventually led him to sympathize with Nazism, although there is no evidence to suggest that he was ever in direct contact with the Nazi Party, even if proto-Nazis had figured amongst his friends.[14] As with Wagner, it was the theoretical prose writings of Dujardin that got him into trouble, and then reflected back onto his art works, earning him a bad reputation politically. It is really very appropriate to make the Wagner comparison again here, because Dujardin's prose works increasingly became a rag-bag of confused reflections.

It is tempting to think that the projected *Histoire ancienne du Dieu Jésus* was left uncompleted because uncompleteable, as it became constantly side-tracked by issues like the 'Cas de l'abbé Turmel' cited above, and, even more significant, by a discussion of 'Le Christianisme hitlérien' which is Appendix IX to *La Première Génération chrétienne. Son Destin révolutionnaire* (1935). The, to say the least, very curious juxtaposition of terms in the title of the appendix is a reflection of Dujardin's curious and sometimes confused position. Claiming to have based his analysis of Christianity all along on an opposition between primitive, heroic Christianity and its interpretative debasement in the Gospels (and – see above – in Saint Paul) into the 'slave mentality' condemned by Nietzsche, he sees a parallel to early Christianity in Hitler's Germany which subsumes the individual in courageous service to the social collective. According to Dujardin, Hitler's Germany, however, while rejecting what Dujardin sees as the orthodox Christian confabulations of centuries, has also thrown out the essential feature of primitive Christianity, the myth of the sacrificed god-hero and his resurrection. This *revolutionary* (both in the accepted sense of the term and with the meaning of *cyclic* renewal) aspect of Christianity meant it could not be adopted by a counter-revolutionary albeit 'reformist' society like Hitler's. Dujardin sees in the modern world, on the one hand Bolshevism and Italian fascism as independent of religion, and on the other 'Hitlerism' (he never uses the word 'Nazism') conserving certain aspects of primitive Christianity. And he sees contemporary society as faced by a choice between these two extremes. His own belief seems to be in the original *myth* of sacrifice and renewal which he appears to believe is best represented in aesthetic form in Wagner's *Parsifal*. Thus, he appears to situate his arguments on a purely theoretical level. In choice of sympathies he was probably swayed towards 'Hitlerism' because it preserved at least some elements of essential, eternal myths and because his over-theoretical argumentation sees political choice in very extreme terms. Moderation he would probably have seen as the despised domain of petty-minded bourgeois of the despicable, retired Daniel Prince type!

He dismisses any attribution of 'racism' to what he terms 'national religions' (here is a further reference to the use of religion as a factor for national cohesion, as with the Jews), and he assimilates such atrocities as anti-semitism with the atrocities perpetrated regularly and everywhere in the cyclic course of history. Here again, an absolutely *theoretical* line of argument wipes out the *living* horror of such atrocities. But, whatever Dujardin's even later leanings were towards support of a strong head of state to maintain social cohesion against the decline of civilization,[55] there never is any trace of anti-semitism in his work. Indeed his play, *Le Mystère du dieu mort et ressuscité* (Messein, 1924) is positively pro-Jewish. Here, there is no specious theorizing, and the play contains a very moving evocation of the expulsion of Jews (p. 59) and their treatment as scapegoats (p. 73). In fact, in its celebration of three great religions and of religious tolerance, the play reads like a new version of Lessing's *Nathan der Weise*.

One has the impression that the man who had once mirrored perceptions through the consciousness of a fairly ordinary young man, lost contact with the realities of everyday life when he had been taken over by a cosmic vision of eternal recurrence ... The year 1943 saw another compromising publication, that of his *Rencontres avec Houston Stewart Chamberlain*, in which Dujardin unblinkingly quotes his late friend's acclamation of Hitler in 1923. Dujardin on the very first page accords Chamberlain the title of 'prophet of the Third Reich', but the very fact that he was writing this memoir (in fact of great documentary value) shows that he was beginning to live in the past. IIis previous works as *literary* memorialist had revealed the well-springs of the future. Now he was enclosed in the circle of his own mind, which allowed him to see H. S. Chamberlain behind the racial theories of the Third Reich, but meant that he blinded himself to their essential race hatred. Perhaps his mind, though still capable of theoretically logical thought, had developed a remarkable degree of self-deception. (Anyway, his 1943 publications were as insensitive to possible reactions as Wagner's republication of *Jewry in Music* under his own name.) Possibly and plausibly, Dujardin saw Chamberlain's racist thought as a logical extension of his own theory of *Jewish* national religion. This is the part of Dujardin's life which has earned embarrassed excuses or lame moralizing from critics,[56] and put Édouard Dujardin on the Resistance black list. This meant Dujardin spent his extreme old age in disgrace and necessary obscurity, entombed in his Paris flat, Rue Singer, where he died on 31 October 1949, still working on an author who had become one of the

principal preoccupations of his later years: Friedrich
Nietzsche. Dujardin never managed to finish his projected *Le Cas Friedrich Nietzsche*.

Edouard Dujardin had become a writer out of contact
with the political realities of his time. His overview was
millennial rather than twentieth-century. His view of
Jewish monotheism was unorthodox – unfortunately so
at a time of institutionalized anti-semitism in Germany,
but then Freud's own view of Moses and the Jews was
seen as the work of an apostate.[57] What, finally, we must
remember – in order to understand, although definitely
not excuse – is that Dujardin lived over a quarter of a
century of his intellectual life at a time when Europe's
frontiers were open. There had existed on a cultural level
a sort of intellectual brotherhood which was forcibly split
up by the 1914–18 War, as Romain Rolland who
published in Dujardin's *Cahiers idéalistes* deplored, and
which partly came together again in a grotesquely parodistic form of impotent nostalgia in 1940. A lifelong
Germanophile like Édouard Dujardin was unable to
reject this even then, and his 'collaboration' thus sym-
bolically represents an important feature of French socio-
cultural history of the period.

A few hours before dying he had heard a radio broadcast of the 'Liebestod' from *Tristan und Isolde*, as Marie
Dujardin attests:

> I had often imagined that when the moment when
> this world would no longer appear to him came, I
> would like him to be rocked to sleep by the music of
> Wagner which had been the great love of his life. My
> wish was miraculously granted by chance. I had not-
> iced that day that an extract from *Tristan* formed part
> of a concert broadcast on the radio. I had worked out
> by pure guesswork the time when this work would be
> on, and at the precise time I switched on the radio,
> the performance began. As from the first chord he

recognized it, saying it was 'the death of Isolde'! I anxiously watched the time coming up to the scheduled end of the broadcast. Chance that day continued to work miracles. The broadcast went on longer than the time announced, and the man who was listening with his last reserves of emotion to the fragment from the Wagnerian drama, was able to hear it played to its conclusion.[58]

3 Édouard Dujardin died, as he had lived, a Wagnerian. And this is the essential thread of his life and literary work, which was on the scale of a Modernist epic, attempting to reassemble the century's fragmentation of culture into a jagged kaleidoscope. Dujardin's Wagner fixation meant that he was willing to harness immense and sophisticated means to an apparently simple subject and story in *Les Lauriers sont coupés*, just as in music, Richard Strauss, for example, could employ a huge orchestra to portray his family life in his *Sinfonia Domestica*, or Debussy could deploy a vast orchestral apparatus to suggest a hidden psycho-symbolism in *Pelléas et Mélisande*. What then did the lifelong Wagnerian Édouard Dujardin learn from his mentor that is important for a reading of *Les Lauriers sont coupés*? The answer to the question touches on a whole range of subjects and techniques that make *Les Lauriers* the accomplished post-Wagnerian work of art that it is.

Les Lauriers sont coupés is in part written in a poetic prose that certainly owes much to Wagner and to contemporary experiments in free verse. Much of its imagery is based on Wagnerian references filtered through a Symbolist aesthetic – in particular the obsessive patterning of allusions to light and darkness. These ultimately serve to characterize the different aspects of Woman in the work: Léa is 'blonde' and 'nocturnal'; and these aspects also come to symbolize a view of Woman (part virgin, part

mother, part whore) who is created as much through the
symbolization process as through ordinary 'characteriza-
tion'. Woman becomes an idealized motif. Dujardin
builds his metaphorical patterns into a time structure
which owes much to Wagnerian techniques of transition,
but follows a strict, classical scheme of Unities inspired
by Racine. Within a plan of 'Prelude' (the opening of
Chapter I) plus three 'Acts' (three chapters per 'Act'), the
consciousness of the first-person narrator functions in an
ever-evolving process of rehearsal and re-enactment like
that of a Wagnerian monologue. Narrative thus becomes
a function of premonition and memory within a human
mind. This very special narrative development is signposted by a series of leitmotifs which are both references
to a concrete reality and the recycling of this 'objective'
reality through a subjective consciousness.

Wagner opened up not only a new, purely musical
world, but to the literary-minded like Dujardin showed
new poetic possibilities. Producing paraphrase-translations of selected passages for the *Revue Wagnérienne*
forced Dujardin into trying to write an equivalent of
Wagner's alliterative verse ('Stabreim'). Antoine Goléa
has attested to the difficulties of translating Wagner into
French, and that only when he had achieved what could
pass as a good *singing* version of the original was he
satisfied with the results.[59] Dujardin in his *Rheingold*
translation reflected Wagnerian alliteration to the point
of exaggeration. This sort of experiment had an obvious
influence on his poems, and on the strongly accented,
short rhyming lines of his early dramas, sometimes to the
point of ridiculous banality (see above, p. xix). It is vital
to note, however, that Dujardin was intent upon producing a sound world of words to reflect his characters'
consciousness. Furthermore, his early pieces that alter-
nate prose and verse forms indicate that he was working
at an osmosis of the two that was to result, on the one
hand in free verse, on the other, in poetic prose. For that

most difficult of styles, poetic prose, Wagner helped Dujardin to be superbly equipped, so that he had at his disposal a medium for exploring the very limits of conscious thought, as when Daniel Prince is in a state of fervent ecstasy (Chapter IV), or drifting into somnolence (Chapter VII).

Being an early master of free verse also helped Dujardin to regulate the rhythmical patterns of his prose. His own definition of free verse is of a poetry based on the 'rhythmical unit'.[60] A friend of Mallarmé, Dujardin absorbed the master Symbolist's use of punctuation as a guide to tempo from the 'score' provided by the printed page. This accounts for his persistent use of semi-colons to mark off thought units in *Les Lauriers*, plus the use of suspension marks to denote the 'reverberation' of a word or phrase like a note or chord prolonged by the pedal.[61] A translator would be unwise, therefore, to smooth over units as prescribed by Dujardin's markings (see Translator's Note above).

Another musically orientated French poet who may have influenced Dujardin for *Les Lauriers* is Paul Verlaine, author of the famous *Parsifal* sonnet. Some of the love language of *Les Lauriers*, when Daniel is dreaming of a future life with Léa (Chapter IV) sounds as if it is drawn from 'La Bonne Chanson' (1869–72). Verlaine's imagery – the moon in the night-time scene, the greenery of foliage – is part of a poetic stock-in-trade of the period which he rescued from any hint of conventionality, through his deliberate pointing at conventions to give a distancing effect, and through his musicality.

Much of this imagery is shared by Wagner, who in his turn had taken a preoccupation with the opposition of light and darkness from Novalis. Dujardin's *Les Lauriers* reflects the Wagnerian imagery that was part and parcel of the Symbolist epoch. Imagery of the spring comes from *Die Walküre*, Act I, where the rebirth of the forest greenery, made to shimmer verdant silver in the

moonlight as Siegmund and Sieglinde offer themselves
up to each other, is the discovery of (re)nascent love.
This corresponds to Daniel Prince's sense of young love
on a Paris night in April. Another vision of the forest is
from *Tristan und Isolde*, Act II, where the foliage
encloses the lovers deliberately cutting themselves off
from the daylight world of reality, as they sink into a
protective simile-death of night orgasm. Dujardin
transposes the meeting of Tristan and Isolde on to his
Chapter IV where Daniel Prince surveys the night world
around him from his balcony. The foliage creates a deep-
dappled psycho-landscape fashioned by the narrator's
fusing idealized love and the concrete sights and sounds
around him. The sound of the barrel organ is a dia-
chronic reminiscence of Daniel Prince's walk through the
streets in the previous chapter. There is also an insistent
Tristan und Isolde-like play on the pronouns 'You' and 'I'.
Dujardin's aim, like that of many authors towards the
end of the nineteenth century – George Moore and
Gabriele d'Annunzio, for example – is an impressionistic
evocation of a remembered sound world.[62]

Dujardin's preoccupation with light and shade was
probably also influenced by the lithograph reproduction
techniques of his time. Subtle gradations through grey
form the basis of much of the work of Félicien Rops
whose work was displayed in the gallery attached to the
Revue Indépendante offices. So, both musical and graphic
works were connected with Dujardin's imagery. Light
and shade are the two basic, contrasting but interlinked
poles of the Symbolist world.[63]

The Symbolists' emblematic use of references to light
and to the colour white build into a coherent pattern of
imagery, the most interesting feature of which is its total
(and deliberate) ambiguity. 'Blanc' in French signifies
both 'white' and 'blank'; therefore, on the one hand it is
associated with purity, the sun of the Absolute set in the
azure Ideal of the sky, and on the other hand with

sterility and fragility. 'Glace', means both 'mirror', a window of perception onto the self, and 'ice', frosted fixity. Light against darkness is the warning torch of *Tristan*, Act II, extinguished in order to plunge the lovers into the psycho-sexual underworld of mutual discovery.

Taking a wider view, light/dark patterning becomes part of the very cyclic nature of existence. Orphism, which Kearns (see note 63) terms 'an anthropomorphic dramatization of the cosmic cycle' organizes different levels of existence into four part cycles. Thus, an individual's life consists of birth, maturity, death and (tenebrous) not-being or absence, which in a yearly cycle corresponds to the four seasons, beginning with spring and ending with winter. Similarly, the span of one day consists of sunrise, noon, sunset and night. The cosmic cycle, with its microcosmic variants in an individual character's life, is continually evoked in Wagner's *Ring*. And the daytime span that mirrors an individual's existence is at the basis of *Les Lauriers sont coupés* where, even if only approximately, six hours of 'real' time are followed directly: a whole day's cycle is presented with the aid of re-enactment in the memory. Thus, Dujardin's evocation of the individual can be related to what he later formulated as his view of history and civilization: Daniel Prince, the stereotypical ordinary individual, 'appears' from the crowd to become the archetypal human being for an evening. Human history – a perpetual flux with cycles of decadence and resurgence for Dujardin – could even be related to the way in which his book, *Les Lauriers*, returned to life out of the mass of possible books written and forgotten.

Patterns of white purity and dark sexual evil are, furthermore, essential to the Symbolists', Wagner's and Dujardin's view of Woman. Here the ambiguity of the emblem white comes into play: it is not merely a guarantee of virginity, for virginity, while an absolute, bears the

concomitant but opposite connotation of lack of fulfil-
ment, frigidity and sterility. Daniel Prince insistently
refers to the alabaster purity of Léa d'Arsay's skin, to the
ideally light blonde of her hair, but these he is hardly
ever allowed to touch: he remains constantly, gnawingly
unfulfilled sexually. At the same time, there is a sexual
purity he wishes desperately to preserve. He frequently
tries to repress his jealous awareness of the fact that Léa
has had and has other ('fulfilled') lovers, but when despair breaks through, he considers Léa as little more than
a worthless whore. Daniel's 'decision' disinterestedly to
break with Léa (which he never carries through) is a
symbolic gesture of 'pure' renunciation that mirrors his
naïve search for a pure ideal. In counterpoint to this
stands not only his fearful fascination with Léa's body,
but also an obsessive aversion to prostitutes. He is wary of
being accosted by them (Chapter III) but relates to them
through a sense of attraction–repulsion. From a flashback
in Chapter VI – 'in a room, bare, indistinct, high-
ceilinged, bare and grey, in the smoky candle light, in the
somnolence of the tumult of the swarming street; yes, a
narrow, high-ceilinged room, and the mean bed, and the
lascivious lips, swelling and swelling again while the beast
groans and pants for breath . . .' – it is obvious that he has
been initiated by a prostitute, and remains shamefully
self-conscious about the fact, because he does not want to
be seen in an area where friends might think he is 'on the
prowl'. An undercurrent of interlaced fear of and fascination with sex, means he tries to keep Léa on a higher
plane in an uncontaminated corner of his mind, even if at
the end of the book his sexual desire gets the better of
him, only for him to receive a humiliating refusal.

Léa is blonde and nocturnal: the two adjectives of the
final sentence of *Les Lauriers* express her dual nature as
perceived by the narrator. This duality comes from a
distillation of Symbolist imagery and iconography.
Creamy white blonde purity is straight from Puvis de

Chavannes, while the night world of the whore is reflected in the works of Félicien Rops, who pictured Man as Woman's carnal slave.[64] Nocturnal carnality is also mirrored in the garishly 'cheap' colourings of the Toulouse-Lautrec paintings of prostitutes: colour is rendered garish and ghoulish by the artificial lights of cabarets and brothels.

Woman's duality comes insistently in Wagner, whose heroines often embody one of two opposite poles: innocent maid willing to sacrifice herself to achieve the salvation of the hero, and temptress wanting to ensnare the male. Senta in *The Flying Dutchman* is of the former type, but, more interestingly, Wagner's two other early period works present women in pairs: virgin Elisabeth is opposed to Venus in *Tannhäuser*; Elsa to the sorceress Ortrud in *Lohengrin*. But even more pertinent here is the way in which Wagner encapsulates the two tendencies in Kundry in *Parsifal*. Kundry is never seen as a pure virgin but *becomes* pure through her redemption at the end of the work where producers such as Jean-Pierre Ponnelle sometimes dressed her in white to contrast with her mourning black prescribed by Wagner for her servant role at the beginning of Act III, and with the adornments of the sexual temptress of Act II.[65] We thus have the colour symbolism of Dujardin's period, an external reminder of the fact that he took Kundry as his model for Antonia.

Dujardin projects his narrator's consciousness, not through any intrinsic interest in him as a subject, nor merely through inherited patterns of images and motifs. It is the very process of thought forming that interests him. In organizing his material, however, Dujardin wishes to avoid the incoherence into which the presence of random thoughts might have tempted him. *Les Lauriers sont coupés* is thus very strongly structured. The structure, as much as the insight into human souls – as acknowledged in his dedication to Racine – he owes to the French classical tragedian. Basically, *Les Lauriers* adheres to a deviant form of the Unities. Duration is limited to six hours (which we have already seen as a mental telescoping of one day). The action is limited to what can conceivably be experienced, remembered and recounted by a single human mind during that time. The place (or space) of the dramatic action is less Paris (even though the way in which the city glimmeringly impinges itself on the narrator's consciousness is very evocative) than the narrator's mind, through which all information is presented, even if this entails the dramatic trick of having the narrator reread Léa's letters to himself. The book consists, therefore, of a kind of artificial 'staging' introduced by restriction to an interior point of view. The technique owes its artificiality, in a way, to French classical tragedy where, by convention, characters could only do what was in conformity with *les bien séances*, being obliged to recount the rest. In Dujardin, this accounts for Daniel Prince's apparently self-conscious manner, when he is describing, for example, his clothing, getting dressed, etc. At the same time, however, this results in such a heightened perception of the 'real' world, that as readers, we begin to look at every concrete object as potentially metaphorical.

The character on the stage of his own mind is placed in a three-part structure that comes not from classical tragedy but from Wagner, who could adopt a very strict, almost 'bare' pattern when he wished, as in *Tristan und Isolde*, for example.[66] *Les Lauriers sont coupés* consists of three 'Acts': Act I = Chapters 1–3; II = Chapters 4–6; III = Chapters 7–9. As such, the chapter groupings could be labelled: I – exposition; II – development, and idealized climax within the narrator's mind; III – dénouement. Each 'Act' is prefaced by a short 'prelude', the first of which functions as a general prelude to the whole novel. In general, the chapter openings function like the very short preludes in the *Ring*, which serve briefly to situate the action in time and space, with an orchestral indication of the main elements in play in the ensuing action. Further coherence is lent to this structuring by the use of a literary leitmotif system (on which see pp. lii–lv below).

Partly because of the interplay of these leitmotifs, these theoretical 'Acts' do not appear as rigid divisions. Wagner's work operates through perpetual transition from one section to another; rigid convention of set-pieces is abolished. Constant modulation, furthermore, produces a constant effect of nervous tension in the listener.[67] Similarly with Daniel Prince in *Les Lauriers*, we are within a constantly shifting consciousness.

The narrative act itself is a form of transition, and very Wagnerian. In Wagnerian narrative the characters are constantly going over material from the(ir) past, recycling it, then moving forward. The mind of the narrator is constantly within a process of rehearsal and re-enactment. Wagner can make the process involved even more complex through use of his orchestra, as when the orchestra at the end of *Parsifal*, Act I, can 'repeat' what is going on in Gurnemanz's mind when he thinks about the 'wise fool' after the Grail ceremony. Dujardin attempts an equivalent of this by showing us from within Daniel Prince's ever-moving mind, the sights and sounds that surround him, interpreting them into his memories of past experiences with Léa, then projecting them onto his future imaginings about her. This is a central feature of Wagnerian narrative in that the narrator controls the time span of the actions recounted. Thus, the character who is no doubt Wagner's *super*-narrator figure, Gurnemanz, *controls* time and space in *Parsifal*: 'Der Raum wird hier zur Zeit' ('Here space becomes time'), he announces to Parsifal before the Act I 'Transformation music'.

Memory and the future exist within a present which is the time – and the *tense* (the French use the same word for both) – of narration. This is not an ordinary narrative present,[68] more a prefiguration of the New Novelists' use of the present tense. Therefore, there could be no question in translation of transposing the French present tense into an English past narrative. Everything narrated exists *only* through the ever-moving present of the narrator's consciousness. This is musical and, in particular, Wagnerian.[69]

The constant preoccupation of the musically obsessed literary artist is simultaneity: how to suggest the contrapuntal complexity of the different layers of a score with literature, where the eye can only take in one layer of meaning at a time. The answer is the *suggestion* of simultaneity in the present through the foreshortening of time through memory, and projecting the future.

Simultaneity can be suggested too, through a sophisticated literary leitmotif technique. Again, Dujardin's debt to Wagner is obvious. Somewhat surprisingly, however, Dujardin's own definition of the leitmotif (see *Interior Monologue*, pp. 111–12 below) is lacking in sophistication in that he sees it mainly as a kind of labelling technique. Here, he shows himself to be the victim of the definitions of leitmotif of his own time, but after Wagner's ... Wagner himself used the term 'Grundthemen' (basic themes), which indicates their structural possibilities and the fact that they could be developed. This seems to concord with the nomenclature 'motiforgane' employed in Dujardin's own *Revue Wagnérienne* – the 'organic motif' which can evolve according to its own nature and, above all, according to its placing in a large-scale structure in a context. In discussing the leitmotif in *Interior Monologue*, Dujardin talks of it too much in isolation.

Dujardin is here very much of his time, in that the term 'leitmotiv' was invented by Hans von Wolzogen (1848–1938), a well-known Bayreuth acolyte in the early Cosima years and a frequent contributor to the

Bayreuther Blätter. The term – and the simplified use it
implies – was necessary at the time because of the unpre-
cedented vast scale and complexity of Wagner's works,
which needed to be 'signposted' for a neophyte audience.
The 'signposting' system was taken up by the great
French Bayreuth pilgrim, A. Lavignac, whose famous
guide book, *Le Voyage artistique à Bayreuth* (first
published in 1897) labelled, after Wolzogen, not only
characters, but also objects and emotions. To some
extent this represents a certain truth. The Giants in *Das
Rheingold* (the work in which, as prelude to the whole
Ring, motifs are first set out) have their own recognizable
theme, as does the gold, and love. But a problem arises
once the motifs are used over and over again. Musically,
they can be employed again in the same way, but *dramatically* this is not true. Even an exact repetition at a different point in the drama brings an accretion of the
motifs' associations in previous contexts. This is where
the term 'Erinnerungsmotiv' (literally, 'memory motif')
is particularly useful. First used of recognizable motifs in
operas by Weber, it was taken up again by Alban Berg
who was conscious of how the memory could work in
recalling the past associations of a musical theme. In this
way the 'Erinnerungsmotiv' is dramatically more
sophisticated than Berlioz's 'idée fixe' which, as the name
suggests, called up a fixed and obsessive idea. Wagner
himself was conscious of the fact that motifs had to
develop musically according to the dramatic context
while remaining recognizable. For example, the 'Walküre' motif (one of the most easily recognized) can be
heard to go into fragmentation as Brunnhilde is losing
her divine status; and fragments of the same motif return
as her former state is recalled to her (for example, with
her reference to her steed, Grane, in *Siegfried*, Act III,
and the reunion with Waltraute in *Götterdämmerung*, Act
I). A *developing* leitmotif is the one related to the notion
of 'Heim' ('home') employed (for dramatic irony) in the

quite different contexts of monologues by Hunding and Fricka in *Die Walküre.*

In actual fact, Dujardin employs the leitmotif in a far more sophisticatedly Wagnerian manner than his own definition would imply. Paradoxically, he himself is conscious of the use of 'memory motifs' to organize dramatic narrative, quoting the way in which elements from early chapters in *Les Lauriers*, especially Chapter I – the woman near the Louvre stores – are recalled in *deliberately* modified form: the woman is later in the evening remembered as blonde, not redhaired, thus underlining the fickle way the narrator treats a woman's reality (see *Interior Monologue*, p. 112 below). Chapter IX contains a reworking of many motifs from Chapter I. And again, this is a function of narrative. Just as the Wagner character redefines his past life in relation to his interlocutors, the novelistic 'I' narrator is redefining himself and his recent past in relation to a 'non-hearing interlocutor', his ideal audience or fictive psychological 'alter ego'. The narrative leitmotif works not only in relation to the past, but with regard to the future. Some of the fragmentary thoughts that go through Daniel Prince's mind very early on in the narrative are not made fully explicit until later on. This is the equivalent of what I shall term a 'premonitory motif' in music drama, i.e. the statement of a motif without any precise means of identification the first time round: for example, what becomes the 'Sword' motif in *Die Walküre* is heard as the gods are going into Valhalla in *Das Rheingold*. Only later will this become apparent as an intuition in Wotan's mind. Thus the future – like the past – is encapsulated in the present.[70]

Memory in first-person narrative works in two ways: as an obvious signposting for the reader, and as a (devious) series of recollections by the narrator. This contributes to our sense of a narrator uneasily poised between memory and anticipation. It is further complicated by that fact that Dujardin's narrator lives partly in an unrealizable dream world. This is evoked, for example, in the crypto-musical parody of *Tristan und Isolde* (Act II love duet) in Chapter IV, with the voices rising above each other in an evocative approximation to orgasm. Wagner himself uses a passage based on 'falsely' premonitory motifs when in *Tristan und Isolde*, Act III, Tristan deliriously imagines he can see Isolde coming to him.

The repeated references to Wagner in my critical exposition should by now have made obvious not only the extent of Dujardin's debt, but the fact that he was inventing nothing 'after the event' in claiming to have put a Wagnerian scheme into place for *Les Lauriers*. Historically, because of his almost contemporaneous association with the *Revue Wagnérienne*, and technically, the Wagnerian project seems so obvious that he would not have had to set it out in any correspondence, as K. M. McKilligan suggests he ought to have.[71] Despite the serious background research this critic has done on Dujardin, she seems to skirt warily round the Wagnerian aspects of his work. One of the few critics to have taken this aspect of Dujardin's work seriously, recognizing the *Tristan und Isolde*, Act II reference, for example, is Erika Höhnisch in *Das gefangene Ich*, where she analyses time and space structures of *Les Lauriers*, free verse patterns, movement between the inner and outer worlds in the narrator's mind and, above all – in doing so in a study devoted to similar technical aspects of Valery Larbaud and Michel Butor – accords him the status of a serious artist in his own right.[72] Carmen Licari also does this by indicating the conscious effort involved in Dujardin's adaptation of his novelistic material to the interior monologue form. As conscious artist, as well as in his lifelong attempt to master a compendium of literary and human knowledge, Dujardin was a prototypal Modernist author. This is to contradict Dujardin's many detractors who see him as a technical innovator in a work of little intrinsic importance.[73]

Yet Dujardin's life did have an 'after-life'.[74] The very fact that so many critics mention him testifies to his permanence.[75] However a summary of these would be more of a descriptive bibliographical catalogue than a vital element in an introduction. Furthermore, a detailed treatment of influences could turn an introduction into more of a critical study than it already is, while attracting attention away from its central subject. A few important figures have to be mentioned, however, if only to insist through their stature on the importance of Dujardin himself and the validity of his claim to have invented interior monologue.

The most important and obvious is James Joyce. An interesting minor feature of the process of influence is the fact that in spite of his aversion to Wagner (p. xxxiv above), he still inherited the method from Dujardin. There is clearly sufficient evidence in the text of *Ulysses* itself, even if the *whole* of the novel does not consist of interior monologue from the point of view of a single character. Detailed analysis would require a volume, but what points to Joyce's similar preoccupations are the framing devices for interior monologue that resemble Dujardin's in *Les Lauriers*. First, like Dujardin, Joyce creates a mental itinerary through a city which provides some of the 'raw material' impinging upon the human consciousness, and in the space of a few hours 'Princesday' becomes 'Bloomsday'. Second, he provides a mythical framework: the story of Ulysses functions as a hierarchical, universalizing parallel in the same way as Dujardin's Wagnerian parameters and references. Both Joyce and Dujardin are therefore employing a kind of 'mythical method', like T. S. Eliot's, where fragmented classical and literary references mirror the loves and ordinary preoccupations of the present on an apparently 'higher' plane.

It is this level of reference which is lacking in Valery Larbaud's attempts at interior monologue, which remain rather slight in comparison with *Les Lauriers sont coupés* which, as we have seen, is a coherently structured work with a symbolic reference system far beyond its surface level. It is tempting to think of Valery Larbaud as trying his hand at a technique that he saw was in vogue. His relation to Dujardin is more important for its contribution to literary history than to the potentialization of a formal procedure.

In any case, the influence of the technique was put into practice years before Valery Larbaud: in Arthur Schnitzler's story *Leutnant Gustl*. Even though Dujardin remains 'only begetter', this fact of literary history does contradict what Dujardin reports in *Le Monologue intérieur* (see p. 97 below), where he states that Schnitzler himself in 1926 denied knowing anything about *Les Lauriers*, which was supposedly pointed out to him by Georg Brandes. In an article by Barbara Surowska, Schnitzler is revealed as having been influenced by Dujardin.[76] Surowska quotes from Schnitzler's letter to Georg Brandes of 11 June 1901: 'The first incitation to the form, however, came to me from a story by Dujardin entitled *Les Lauriers sont coupés*.'[77] *Leutnant Gustl* is remarkable for the fact that it is written in interior monologue throughout its whole span and without making the slightest concession to the reader.[78] This narrative technique makes for dramatic tension: we are not told till near the end why the title character has decided to commit suicide. He has allowed himself to be dragged into a quarrel with a baker, his social inferior, with whom he realizes he cannot stoop to fight. The full information is only revealed – like a dramatic trick at the very end of the story – almost simultaneously with the news of the baker's death. Schnitzler's technical expertise makes Barbara Surowska place *Leutnant Gustl* above *Les Lauriers*, but although there is a striking indirect evocation of Vienna through the eyes of a right-wing, anti-semitic army officer, it lacks the framing devices Dujardin provides from Wagner to universalize his story.

Wagner again comes to the fore in such a way that his mature works could perhaps be indirectly credited with the invention of interior monologue. The chain of influence can be read backwards in time like this: without Joyce and Larbaud, there would have been no 'resurrection' of Édouard Dujardin; without Dujardin there would have been no interior monologue in the form we know it in Joyce; but without Wagner there would have been no Dujardin, as we know him after this necessarily Wagner-orientated exposition of biography and ideas.

It is furthermore significant that two of the other major twentieth-century novelists to employ forms of stream of consciousness technique – Virginia Woolf and Malcolm Lowry – were also both influenced by Wagner, as part of a reference system as regards characters and in an attempt to suggest an impression of musical simultaneity.[79]

To prolong, broaden and deepen the cataloguing of the authors influenced by *Les Lauriers sont coupés* would require at least a chapter of a book or, in brief, would make the final section of this introduction read like a parody of Dujardin's own final section to his *Interior Monologue* (see pp. 141–4 below), where he lists authors who, however intermittently, employ the technique. This is but another proof of the 'after-life' of *Les Lauriers sont coupés*.

However, even more essential is its potential after-life among present-day writers and readers, who can now turn to 'a beautiful little work that I loved when it first appeared and that sent me searching for someone to admire it with me ...'.[80] The words are George Moore's, and what follows is for all those ready to accompany him in this monodrama of the mental loneliness of modern man.

Notes to the Introduction

1. See Richard Ellmann, *James Joyce*, new and revised edition, Oxford University Press, 1983, p. 126.
2. See 'Richard Wagner, rêverie d'un poête français', in Mallarmé, *Oeuvres complètes*, Gallimard, Paris, 1945, pp. 1592–3.
3. See *Rencontres avec Houston Stewart Chamberlain*, Grasset, Paris, 1943, especially p. 12.
4. Isabelle de Wyzewska, *La Revue Wagnérienne, essai sur l'interprétation esthétique de Wagner en France*, Librairie académique Perrin, Paris, 1934.
5. *Conversations in Ebury Street*, Boni and Liveright, New York, 1924, pp. 198–99.
6. See Kathleen M. McKilligan, 'The Trials and Tribulations of a Symbolist Editor', *Nottingham French Studies*, Vol. XX, No. 2, 1981, pp. 37–50.
7. 'Il n'avait provision que d'illusions, de volonté et confiance imperturbable qui composait le plus fort de sa force' (Jean Ajalbert, *Mémoires en vrac. Au temps du Symbolisme, 1880–1890*, Albin Michel, Paris, 1938, p. 199).
8. '*La Revue Indépendante* demeurera fidèle à son programme: une publication consacrée à l'Art sous toutes ses formes. La constante préoccupation de cet objet lui donnera le moyen d'admettre également, pourvu qu'elles soient sincères, les formules les plus réservées et les plus hardies, et de rester vraiment indépendante, indépendante non moins des traditions académiques que des vaines agitations décadentes (unnumbered page in *La Revue Indépendante*, 2 series, vol. 1, Slatkine reprint, 1968).
9. See Bibliography: George Moore.
10. Lack of space precludes quoting longer sections of this work.
11. Note that persistent, insistently obvious rhymes here point to over-indulgence in Wagnerian verse patterns taken to a parodistic absurd, for instance, in 'Courtisanes':

Les reines de caresses
les princesses de morbidesses
Les triomphatrices déesses
Emmêlent leurs kermesses
Et les pêcheresses
Epandent leurs tresses

Les enchanteresses
Aux voix d'allégresses
Mènent des liesses.'

12. 'Ils n'ont pas l'air de croire à leur bonheur' from 'Clair de lune' in *Fêtes Galantes* (1869).

13. For this, see Pierre Boulez (sleeve-note to his 1966 recording of *La Mer, Jeux,* and *L'Après midi d'un faune,* CBS 72533).

14. *Men and Memories, vol. I: 1872–1900,* Faber and Faber, 1931, p. 69.

15. Perrin et Cie, Paris.

16. op. cit., p. 266:

ANNÉE 1889 / *9 novembre*
9 novembre
M. EDOUARD DUJARDIN, ex-dir. de *la Revue Indépendante,*
M. VICTOR JOZE.
(Altercation, à la suite de laquelle M. Dujardin se juge offensé.)
Témoins, pour M. Dujardin: MM. Jules Courtier et Aristide Marie;
Pour M. Joze: MM. Myrton et Jules Livet.
Rencontre au pistolet, au Bois de Boulogne.
Deux balles sont échangées sans résultat.

17. *Conversations in Ebury Street,* pp. 215–16.

18. See William F. Blissett, 'Literary Wagnerism' in *George Moore's Mind and Art,* edited by Graham Owens, Oliver and Boyd, Edinburgh, 1968, especially pp. 61–3.

19. *Letters from George Moore to Édouard Dujardin, 1886–1922,* Crosby Gaige, New York, 1929.

20. See *Ave* (volume 1), Tauschnitz edition, vol. 4314, Leipzig, 1912, especially pp. 63–5 and 186–9; and *Vale* (volume 3), Tauschnitz edition, vol. 4490, Leipzig, 1914, pp. 244–8. These pocket editions are in themselves an indication of the European intellectual community of the time.

21. *Conversations in Ebury Street,* pp. 213–14:

A strange system it was, one never practised, I believe, by anybody but Dujardin, strange and yet reasonable if one considers it; for the backer of horses is turned hither and thither by what he reads in the newspapers, by omens, by the advice of tipsters, by the weights, by the show of a certain horse in the preliminary: one and all allies of the bookmaker;

but relieved from all knowledge of the horses, in other words,
relieved from all prejudices, the backer rises triumphant and
ruins his foe, the Ring. Go to the race-course ignorant, said
Dujardin, and never bet unless at the very last moment a horse
advances suddenly from shall we say ten to one to five to one; if
this happens, put all the money you can on the horse, for if a
horse comes from ten to one to five to one in the last half-hour,
we may reasonably suppose that the stable is backing him; a
system without doubt, which whilst followed won for Dujardin large sums of money and made him feared at Longchamps.

22. *Conversations in Ebury Street*, p. 214:
But the soul is perfidious and life beset with accidents, and
one day returning from Longchamps the horse that Dujardin
was driving took fright and descended the Champs Elysées at
a gallop, Dujardin unable to stop it but just able to keep to his
side of the road, crying to the vehicles in front of him to make
way, which they did. At the Rondpoint it seemed that the
horse would weary and stop before he reached la Place de la
Concorde; but as he entered the last reach of the avenue a
carriage driven by a sleepy or deaf coachman failed to take
heed of the advancing danger till it was too late. Crash went
the tilbury into the carriage; two old ladies were carried out
fainting; the sergent de ville arrived; an action for damages
was begun, and Dujardin, whose taste for litigation did not
allow him to compromise, was mulcted – a mulct of ten
thousand francs was the adjudication of the court, a sum so
out of all proportion to the damage he had done, that discouraged by this experience in jurisprudence, and perhaps
weary of the slow accumulation of Sundays needed to acquire
a fortune at Longchamps, he deserted the Parisian race-
courses for Monte Carlo, and it was not long before the
croupiers raked in all the money he had won at Longchamps
and Auteuil; whereupon Dujardin ceased to be a punter and
became a journalist, and a successful journalist, as the house
in the Val Changis testifies.

23. This is one of the main arguments of Kathleen M. McKilligan's *Dujardin's 'Les Lauriers sont coupés' and the Interior Monologue*, Occasional Papers in Modern Languages, No. 13,
University of Hull Publications, 1977.

24. See the introduction (in French) to Carmen Licari's edition of
Les Lauriers sont coupés and *Le Monologue intérieur*, Bulzoni,

Rome, 1977, in which she indicates that Dujardin began in a conventional mode, only to rewrite his novel later from an interior point of view.

25. See 'Les premiers poètes du vers libre', pp. 105–83 in *Mallarmé par un des siens*, Messein, Paris, 1936. Such an 'invention' or 'discovery' is in fact impossible to date precisely, as Dujardin himself says of interior monologue (see below, p. 132), being the product of an age and an intellectual climate. However Jean Cassou, 'Édouard Dujardin et l'évolution du symbolisme', *La Revue Européenne*, 1 March 1924, pp. 16–24, supports Dujardin's individual contribution (see especially page 19).

26. I must insist (against Kathleen M. McKilligan, op. cit. [note 23]) on how *natural* Wagnerian interior monologue technique must have been in the context of Dujardin's predominantly Wagnerian literary preoccupations before and after *Les Lauriers sont coupés*.

27. See Dujardin's own account below, *Interior Monologue*, pp. 86ff.

28. *The Symbolist Aesthetic in France, 1885–1895*, second edn, Blackwell, Oxford, 1968, p. 197.

29. Convinced of the banality of the drama, Kathleen M. McKilligan bases her article 'Theory and Practice in French Wagnerian Drama: Dujardin and *La Légende d'Antonia*', *Comparative Drama*, vol. XIII (1979–80), pp. 283–99, more on the circumstances of the performances, etc., than on a detailed study of the Wagnerian aspects of the text.

30. Another sign of lack of interest is the fact that the reprint of 1944 is in an edition of three hundred copies, as much because of lack of potential buyers as because of wartime restrictions.

31. 'Si vous me dîtes à présent que M. Dujardin n'est pas un fumiste, je ne vous croirai pas; M. Dujardin est un fumiste, le père des fumistes, le fumiste poétique et convaincu' (reprinted in Joseph Rivière: *1893–1923. Notes à propos des représentations du 'Mystère du dieu mort et ressuscité' d'Édouard Dujardin'*, Éditions de Soi-Même, chez Picard, Paris, 1923, p. 10).

32. Stéphane Mallarmé, 'Crayonné au théâtre', pp. 322–28 in *Oeuvres complètes*, Bibliothèque de la Pléiade, Paris, 1945.

33. 'Jésus, je me méfie de ton origine divine, et peut-être n'es-tu même qu'une belle légende . . ., *L'Initiation au péché et à l'amour*, Mercure de France, Paris, 1899, p. 233, but the idea of 'redemption' (cf. *Antonia*) finds more favour in his eyes (p. 234).

34. 'Un pauvre bougre qui vit la vie . . .', op. cit., p. 244.

35. See *La Forêt symboliste*, Firmin-Didot, Paris, 1936; Chapter III is devoted to Dujardin.

36. '*Les Argonautes, Marthe et Marie, Les Epoux d'Heur-le-port, Le Retour des enfants prodigues*, c'est le conflit entre les deux principes que Wagner a symbolisé dans l'Or et dans l'Amour (l'Amour au sens chrétien du mot, ou, avant lui et plus profondément, Schopenhauer dans la Volonté de Vivre et le Renoncement' (Preface to Théâtre, vol. II, *Les Argonautes*, Mercure de France, Paris, 1924, p. 13).

37. '... seuls les esprits superficiels jugeront qu'un monologue qui dure quasiment un acte est, *a priori*, anti-dramatique ...', op. cit., p. 11.

38. See below, *Interior Monologue*, pp. 91–2 and Richard Ellmann, op. cit., p. 411n.

39. op. cit., pp. 95, 126 and n, 358, 411n, 520 and n, 529 and n, 615, 617, 634n, 637, 665, 668, 759, 791.

40. Frank Budgen, *James Joyce and the Making of 'Ulysses'*, Oxford University Press, 1972, p. 94:

> The function of the interior monologue is, of course, the same as that of any monologue spoken on the stage – to make us acquainted with the persons and aware of their inner conflicts.
>
> All writers of fiction do this in one way or another. The interior monologue is simply a convenient and intimate way. And although the device is largely associated with Joyce's *Ulysses* he never claimed any originality in the use of it. In the course of a conversation in his flat in the Universitätsstrasse Joyce said to me:
>
> 'I try to give the unspoken, unacted thoughts of people in the way they occur. But I'm not the first one to do it. I took it from Dujardin. You don't know Dujardin? You should.'
>
> It was not until 1923 or '24 that Joyce met Dujardin. By that time Joyce's acknowledgement of his debt to the French writer was everywhere known. M. Dujardin presented Joyce with a copy of his book, *Les Lauriers Sont Coupés*, reprinted after thirty-five years of oblivion, containing the inscription: '*A James Joyce, maître illustre, mais surtout à celui qui a dit à l'homme mort et enseveli: Lazare lève-toi*' ('To James Joyce, renowned master, but above all the one who said to a man dead and buried: Lazarus, come forth.')
>
> Some years later I called at Joyce's flat while he was writing

on the flyleaf of the French *Ulysse*. He showed me the flyleaf. On it stood: '*A Édouard Dujardin, annonciateur de la parole intérieure. Le larron impénitent, James Joyce*' ('To Édouard Dujardin, herald of interior speech. The unrepentant thief, James Joyce').

41. *The Letters of James Joyce*, vol. I, edited by Stuart Gilbert, Faber, London, 1957, p. 287.

42. *The Letters of James Joyce*, vol. III, edited by Richard Ellmann, New York, Viking Press, 1966, pp. 97–8.

43. See letter to Eric Pinker, dated by Ellmann 25 July 1929, *Letters*, vol. II, p. 192.

44. In a letter of 10 May 1930, *The Letters of James Joyce*, vol. III, p. 197.

45. See Ellmann, op. cit., p. 665.

46. See 'Édouard Dujardin's claim in *Interior Monologue*, pp. 110ff. below.

47. Letter of 11 February 1907 to Stanislaus Joyce, *Letters*, vol. II, p. 213.

48. Pointed out by Bryan Magee in *Aspects of Wagner*, Alan Ross, London, 1968, pp. 73–4.

49. *Letters*, vol. III, p. 191–2; Ellmann's translation of: 'Le sentiment de nager dans un océan de spiritualité, le même que j'ai éprouvé à vingt ans la première fois que j'ai entendu (sans savoir l'allemand) les quatre journées du 'Ring des Nibelung', c'est-à-dire quelque chose qui fait comprendre ce que les mystiques dénomment la vision en Dieu.'

50. Larbaud's relations with Dujardin are fully chronicled by Frida Weissmann and in the correspondence between the two writers that she published: 'Autour du monologue intérieur: La Correspondance Dujardin-Larbaud', *Cahiers Valery Larbaud*, no. 14, March 1976, reprinted as an appendix to *Du Monologue intérieur à la sous-conversation*, A. G. Nizet, Paris, 1978, pp. 111–37. See also 'Valery Larbaud et le monologue intérieur (d'après ses lettres inédites à Édouard Dujardin)', in Th. Alajouanine, *Valery Larbaud sous divers visages*, Gallimard, Paris, 1973, pp. 114–36.

51. *Grandeur et Décadence* . . ., p. 82.

52. Not an entirely outlandish view at the time; the historical reality of the person of Jesus has often been questioned by serious thinkers (see A. N. Wilson, *Jesus: the Evidence*, Weidenfeld and Nicolson, London, 1986).

53. 'Du point de vue esthétique et littéraire, les figures de Jésus,

de Hamlet, du Père Goriot, de M. Bloom, telles qu'elles se dégagent des oeuvres où elles sont décrites, sont aussi vraies, aussi vivantes que celles de Saint-Paul, de Jean-Jacques, de Louis XIV, telles que celles-ci se dégagent des épîtres, des *Confessions* (quelques mensonges que Jean-Jacques y ait semés), des mémoires de Saint-Simon' (*Grandeur et Décadence de la Critique*, p. 121).

54. A detailed study of Dujardin's unpublished correspondence might establish leads on this.

55. *De l'ancêtre mythique au chef moderne*, published 1943, makes the association with Hitler all the more obvious.

56. The latter from Kathleen M. McKilligan, op. cit. (note 23), the former from Jean Mabire, 'Un Héraut wagnérien: Édouard Dujardin, 1861–1949' in the journal of the French New Right, *Nouvelle École*, nos 31–32, Spring 1979 (Richard Wagner special issue no. 2), pp. 94–117.

57. See Estelle Roth, 'Freud, Moses and Rushdie', *Observer*, 5 March 1989, and *Sigmund Freud. His Life in Pictures and Words*, edited by Ernst Freud, Lucie Freud and Ilse Grubrish-Simitis, Penguin Books, London, 1985, p. 319.

58.   J'avais souvent songé que lorsque viendrait pour lui le moment où la figure de ce monde passerait, j'aimerais qu'il soit bercé par cette musique de Wagner qui avait été le grand amour de sa vie. Un hasard miraculeux exauça mon souhait. J'avais noté ce jour-là qu'au programme d'un concert donné par la radiodiffusion, figurait un fragment de *Tristan*. J'avais déterminé au jugé le moment où passerait cette œuvre, et à l'instant précis où j'allumais l'appareil, l'exécution en commença. Dès le premier accord, il la reconnut et la nomma: «La mort d'Yseult!» Je regardais, anxieuse, s'avancer l'heure exacte à laquelle devait cesser l'émission. Le hasard, ce jour-là, continua à se montrer miraculeux. L'émission se prolongea au-delà de la minute prévue, et celui qui écoutait avec une ultime émotion le fragment du drame wagnérien, put l'entendre se dérouler jusqu'à son terme.

Marie Dujardin, 'Souvenir d'Édouard Dujardin', *Synthèses* (*Revue internationale*, Brussels), vol. 14 (May 1959), no. 15, pp. 90–8; quotation, p. 97. I am grateful to Kathleen M. McKilligan for supplying me with a photocopy of this memoir of Dujardin.

59. 'Le Langage poétique de Richard Wagner', *Obliques* (Richard Wagner special issue), 1979, pp. 125–38.

60. 'l'unité rhythmique' (see op. cit., note 25).

61. For the influence of Mallarmé's punctuation system on an English poet, see my article 'Basil Bunting et Mallarmé', *Caliban*, XIII (1976) (Annales de l'Université de Toulouse-Le Mirail), pp. 137–40.

62. See George Moore's *Evelyn Innes* (1898) and *Sister Teresa* (1901); and D'Annunzio's *Il Fuoco* (1900) with its crypto-Wagnerian love-death.

63. I am grateful to Dr E. J. Kearns, formerly of the University of Durham, whose pioneering work on this subject forms part of his (unpublished) doctoral thesis, *L'Image dans la poésie symboliste française*, 2 volumes, University of Reading, 1958, which he kindly lent me during the preparation of this study and translation.

64. For Félicien Rops, see the catalogue published by Flammarion for the Rops retrospective, Paris, 1985; for Pierre Puvis de Chavannes and other similarly orientated painters, see *Le Symbolisme* (texte de Robert L. Delevoy) Skira, Paris, 1982.

65. See my review article, 'Pre-Raphaelite *Parsifal*', *Wagner News*, no. 57, October–November, 1987, pp. 3–7.

66. The German musicologist, Alfred Lorenz, author of *Das Geheimnis der Form bei Richard Wagner*, believed tripartite structures to be basic to all of Wagner's major works. Lorenz's major large-scale studies have not been translated into English, but see his short article 'The Musical Structure of *Tristan und Isolde*', *Wagner* (New Series), vol. 2, no. 3, 1981, pp. 74–7.

67. See David Huckvale, 'Wagner and the Mythology of Film Music', *Wagner* (New Series), vol. 9, no. 2, 1988, pp. 46–67.

68. As remarked by Rayner Heppenstall in a perceptive piece on Dujardin, 'The Bays are Sere', *London Magazine*, August 1960, pp. 47–51.

69. It is no accident that Alain Robbe-Grillet has employed Wagnerian techniques in his cinematographic works; see my 'Wagner and the Progressive Slide into Pleasure: Wagner in the films of Alain Robbe-Grillet', *Wagner*, vol. 7, no. 3, 1986, pp. 73–83.

70. Wagner's references to 'balsam' in *Parsifal*, Act I, are especially complex: a reminiscence for one character's mind is premonitory for another, and hence for the audience.

71. op. cit. (note 23).

72. Erika Höhnisch, *Das gefangene Ich*, Carl Winter Universitätsverlag, Heidelberg, 1967.

73. For example Francis Scarfe in *The Art of Paul Valéry*, Heinemann, London, 1954: 'Dujardin's novel develops an essentially trivial theme and in a light manner' (p. 110). Robert Humphrey, *Stream of Consciousness in the Modern Novel*, University of California Press, Berkeley, 1954, is similarly dismissive, limiting himself to a theoretical discussion of Dujardin's discussion, without applying it to Dujardin's own work. A. W. Raitt, *Villiers de l'Isle-Adam et le mouvement symboliste*, Librairie José Corti, Paris, 1965, p. 338, is most derogatory: '. . . de tout cela il n'est pas resté grand'chose' ('. . . not much of all that has survived').

74. I have borrowed this expressive term from Jonathan Miller, *Subsequent Performances*, Faber and Faber, London, 1986.

75. See Bibliography.

76. 'Schnitzlers innerer Monolog im Verhältnis zu Dujardin und Dostojewski', in *Theatrum Europaeum: Festschrift für Elida Maria Szarota*, Wilhelm Fink Verlag, Munich, 1982, pp. 549–58.

77. 'Mir aber wurde der erste Anlass zu der Form durch eine Geschichte von Dujardin gegeben, betitelt *Les Lauriers sont coupés*' (quoted by Surowska, op. cit., p. 552).

78. Very aptly, the French translation by Dominique Auclères, *Le Lieutenant Gustel*, Calmann-Lévy, Paris, 1983, reads very like Dujardin.

79. Malcolm Lowry was well aware of the Joyce/Dujardin connection, as he indicated in a punning inter-textual reference to his garden signboard in *Under the Volcano* (where Chapter 5 is a reinterpretation of the Garden of Eden story) (see Malcolm Lowry, *Selected Letters*, edited by Harvey Breit and Margerie Bonner Lowry, Penguin, 1985, p. 319: 'Le gusta este Dujardin?').

80. George Moore, *Conversations in Ebury Street*, op. cit., pp. 218–19.

Nous n'irons plus aux bois,
Les lauriers sont coupés.
La belle que voilà
Ira les ramasser

Voyez comme on danse,
Entrez dans la danse.
Sautez, dansez,
Embrassez qui vous voudrez!

Traditional French children's song

The Bays are Sere

In homage to Racine,
supreme novelist of souls.

i An evening of setting sun, remote air, deep skies; and of obscure crowds; sounds, shades, multitudes; infinite vastnesses of space; an ill-defined evening ...

For from the chaos of appearances, amid periods and sites, in the illusion of things being begotten and born, one among the others, distinct from the others, yet similar to the others, one the same and yet another, from the infinity of possible existences, I appear; and this is time and space being defined; it is the Now; it is the Here; the clock striking; and, around me, life; the time, the place, an April evening. Paris, on a bright evening of setting sun, the monotonous noises, the pale houses, the foliage of shadows; a milder evening; and the joy of being someone, of walking; the streets and multitudes, and, stretching far in the air, the sky; all around, Paris sings, and, in the haze of shapes perceived, softly it frames the idea.

... The clock has struck; six, the appointed time. Here's the house I have to go into, where I shall find someone; the house; the entrance hall; let's go in. Night is falling; the air is mild; there is a cheerfulness in the air. The staircase; the bottom steps. Supposing he's left early? he sometimes does; but I want to tell him about the day I've had. The first floor landing; the wide, well-lit staircase, the windows. I've confided in him, in this decent friend of mine, about my love affair. What an enjoyable evening in front of me again! Anyway he won't make fun of me any more. What a delightful evening it's going to be! Why's the stair carpet turned up in that corner? it makes a grey blot on the rising red, on the red that goes up and up, stair by stair. The second floor; the door to the left; 'Chambers'; let's hope he hasn't gone out; where would I track him down? Oh well, I'd go along the boulevard. Let's go straight in. The main office

– Where is Lucien Chavainne? The huge room and the circular arrangement of the chairs. There he is, bending over by the table; he's got his hat and coat on; he's hurriedly arranging papers, with another clerk. The bookcase with the blue ledgers, at the back, with the tape in bows. I stop at the door. The sheer delight of telling him what's happened! Lucien Chavainne looks up; he sees me; hello.

'Is it you? You've come at the right moment; you know we leave at six. Will you wait for me? We'll go down together.'

'Very well.'

The window is open; behind it, a grey courtyard, full of lights; the high, grey walls, pale in fine weather; my lucky day. Nice the way Léa said 'See you this evening' to me ... She had her teasing, pretty smile, like two months ago. Opposite, at a window, a maid; she's look-ing; there – she's blushing; why? She moves back out of sight.

'Here I am.'

It's Lucien Chavainne; he's taken his stick; he's opening the door; we go out; the two of us, we go down stairs. He:

'You're wearing your bowler.'

'Yes.'

Sounds reproachful. Why shouldn't I be wearing a bowler? This chap thinks that elegance is about such trifles. The concierge's lodge; always empty; strange sort of house. Is Chavainne at least going to walk along with me a little? He never wants to go out of his way; he's so tiresome. We reach the street; a carriage at the door; the sun is setting the house-fronts ablaze; the Tour Saint-Jacques in front of us; we're heading for the Place du Châtelet.

'So, what about your love affair?'

He asks me; I am going to tell him.

'Still about the same.'

We are walking side by side.

'You've come from her apartment?'

'Yes, I've been to see her. We chatted, sang, and played the piano for two whole hours. She's arranged to meet me this evening, after her show.'

'Ah!'

And with such charm!

'And you, what have you been up to?'

'Me. Nothing.'

A silence. Delightful girl! She got annoyed with herself for not being able to sing her song; I was the one who wasn't in time, and I didn't admit I'd made a mistake. I'll be more careful this evening, when we start again.

'You know she's only on stage at curtain-up now? I'm going to wait for her around nine at the Nouveautés; then we'll go for a ride in a carriage; probably to the Bois de Boulogne; the weather is so pleasant. Then I'll take her back home.'

'And you'll try and stay?'

'No.'

Lord preserve me! Will Chavainne never understand my feelings?

'You amaze me,' he says, 'with this platonic love.'

Amazing . . . platonic love . . .

'Yes, old boy, that's how I see things; I obtain more pleasure by behaving differently from other people.'

'But look, my dear fellow, you're not taking into account the kind of woman you're dealing with.'

'A bit-part actress; true; and that's why I like behaving as I do.'

'You're hoping to touch her?'

He's sneering; he's unbearable. Well, no; she isn't the girl you'd take her for.

And anyway . . . Rue de Rivoli; let's cross over; watch the traffic; what a crowd this evening! six o'clock's the rush hour, especially in this area; the tram sounding its horn; let's walk somewhere safe.

'There aren't quite so many people on the right-hand side.' I say.

We walk along the pavement, close to each other. Chavainne:

'A pleasure like that isn't worth the candle. For the three months you've known this young woman . . .'

'I've been seeing her at her home for three months; but you know very well that I've known her for more than four.'

'As you wish. For four months you've been ruining yourself for nothing.'

'You're making fun of me, Lucien.'

'Before ever having spoken a word to her you give her five hundred francs via the chambermaid.'

Five hundred? no, three hundred. But I did, in fact, say five hundred to Chavainne.

'If you think,' he continues, 'that this sort of munificence incites an actress to corresponding generosity . . . Change your approach, my friend, or you'll obtain nothing.'

Irritating deduction. Does he really believe that, if I obtain nothing, it isn't because I wish to obtain nothing? I oughtn't to talk to him about these things. Let's put a stop to it.

'And I prefer such extravagance to mindlessly going on one-night sprees with ridiculous girls.'

Let that be a lesson to you. That's silenced him. Certainly a very good friend, Lucien Chavainne, but so stubborn about affairs of the heart. To love, and honour one's love, respect one's love, love one's love. It's warm, walking; I undo my topcoat; I won't keep my morning coat on this evening to go out with Léa; my frock coat will be better; I could take my silk hat; Chavainne is right in a way; besides, I'm being a fool! I can't wear a bowler with a frock coat. Léa hardly mentions my clothes at all; yet she must notice them. Chavainne:

'I'm going to the Français this evening.'

'What's on?'

'*Ruy Blas*.'*

'You're really going to see that?'

'Why not?'

I'm not answering. Does one go and see *Ruy Blas* in 1887? He:

'I've never seen the play, and I'm curious about it.'

'What an old romantic you are!'

'You, calling me romantic?'

'What if I am?'

'You're more of a romantic than anyone. What with this business about your great love. All because you went to the Nouveautés to hear I don't know what . . .'

Lovely she was that night!

'You've spent all winter getting worked up; and now you're doing any number of silly things. Seriously . . . And don't forget that I was the one who read the poster as we left the theatre and told you the lady's name. From that moment on you were enraptured; and now its platonic love.'

An elegant gentleman goes by with a rose in his button-hole; so I'll have to have a buttonhole this evening; I could still easily take Léa something. Chavainne is silent; the man's an idiot. Oh yes, it's strange, my love affair; well, so much the better. A street; Rue de Marengo; the Magasin du Louvre; the carriages head to tail. Chavainne:

'You know I'm leaving you at the Palais-Royal?'

Good! What a bore he is, always slipping off! Here we are under the arcade; near the shops; in the crowd. What if we walked in the road? Too many carriages. They're pushing here; never mind. A woman in front of us; tall and slim; oh! the arch of her body, that heady perfume and that lustrous red hair; I'd like to see her face; she must be pretty.

* See notes on page 80.

'Come to the theatre with me this evening ...' It's Chavainne speaking to me ... 'Later we'll go for a stroll somewhere.'

'I've already told you I've a rendezvous.'

The red-haired woman stops in front of the shop window; a distinctive red-head's profile, yes; a very lively look; dark eye make-up, a big white bow at her throat; she's looking in our direction; she's looked at me; what provocative eyes! We're near her. Fine-looking girl.

'Not so fast.'

'Your rendezvous is no obstacle; since you've made up your mind not to stay at Mademoiselle d'Arsay's, you'll come for the last act, or for the end, or no matter where, and we'll go for a midnight stroll.'

Is he making fun of me?

'You'll tell me everything you've said to Mademoiselle d'Arsay.'

Why not, as a matter of fact, this evening, after leaving her?

'That doesn't suit you? What do you do when you leave your friend then?'

'My dear chap, you're really being stupid.'

We fall silent; I think he's smiling; what stupid nonsense! The Place du Palais-Royal. And the young redhead, where is she? gone; what a nuisance! I can't see her. Chavainne: 'What are you looking for?'

'Nothing.'

Gone. All because of this gentleman. He:

'I'm going as far as the Théâtre-Français; I want to see what time the performance starts.'

Still harping on his show! Let's go. Yet before he leaves me, I'd like to tell him about my day; the little sitting-room slightly dimmed by the yellow curtains; Léa so nice; she was wearing her pale satin peignoir; her wasp-waist under the ample silky pleats and the wide white collar from which a little of her rosy bosom peeped out; she smiled when she came toward me; and her hair

cascaded in golden locks from her palish blonde head
onto her shoulders; she's not any age, the dear, and so
pretty; nineteen, or twenty perhaps; she admits to
eighteen; exquisite girl. Along the immobile length of the
Palais-Royal, along by the Palais we go. She held out her
hand to me; I kissed her on the forehead; very chastely;
she leaned on my shoulder, and for one moment we
stayed still; through the satin, in my hands, I felt the soft
warmth. How I love her, the poor little thing! And all
those people going by, hither and thither, going by,
ignorant of these joys, all these indifferent and ordinary
people, walking close by me!

'Here's a poster ...' It's Chavainne speaking ... 'It
starts at eight. You really won't come?'

'Of course not.'

'Goodbye then. I've got to go back home.'

'Goodbye. Have a good time.' Excellent friend ...
Have a nice meal, gentlemen. To please this woman and
be her lover ... God, I was with the angel ... He:

'Have a good time yourself and – above all – be
careful.'

'Don't worry.'

'You'll tell me what you've been doing.'

'Yes. Goodbye.'

Handshake. He turns. Goodbye! I'm going to walk
up the Avenue de l'Opéra; I'll have dinner at the café on
the corner of the avenue and the Rue des Petits-Champs;
I'll have time to reach home before nine. The post office.
I really ought to write home; I'm late; I'll write tomorrow; tomorrow, I've the Law School class; out of the
three courses I go to I'd better not miss that one. Lucien
Chavainne is going to the Français this evening. Yes, a
nice chap; rather affected, but pleasant to get on with,
you can talk to him; he understands; he has good taste
and is elegant; and a real friend; it's a pleasure to be with
him; next time I'll tell him all the reasons for my conduct; it's a pity I didn't explain my afternoon to him

more; perhaps he would have guessed the spell my love holds; but he's not sensitive to these things! A love which is content with friendship; a woman so loved and honoured! Two months have already gone by since our first, our only kiss; no, it was at the end, no, in mid-February. They're lighting the gas-lamps in the avenue; night falling. What will she be like when she's back? no doubt with her long blue shawl and the long hanging tress of her hair; she looks artless, like a little girl; some evenings she's so happy and laughing; one day, she was dressed in black and really imposing; another day, innocent with smoothed-back hair, all rosy, she was just out of the bath. I ought to help her more; my mother will certainly give me a bit of money at Easter; everything will work itself out. The corner of the Rue des Petits-Champs; the restaurant's already lit up; but all the shops in the avenue are lit up; how quickly night comes! 'Cafe Oriental, restaurant.' On the other side of the street, Duval's; what if I went there to save money? saving would be advisable; really the restaurant is better; and there's not much difference in price; Duval's is good too, not so comfortable but just as good; never mind, I'm going to treat myself to the restaurant. Inside, the lights, reflections of reds and golds; the street darker; the mirrors misted over. 'Dinner at three francs ... beer ... thirty centimes.' Léa would never want to eat here. Let's go in. Have to tweak up the ends of my moustache, like this.

ii Blazing with light, red, golden, the restaurant; the glittering mirrors; a waiter in a white apron; the pillars heavy with hats and overcoats. Anyone here I know? Those people are looking at me as I come in; thin man with long whiskers, what solemnity! all the tables taken; where shall I sit? an empty one over there; my usual place too; nothing wrong in having one's usual place; nothing for Léa to laugh at in that.

'Yes, sir . . .'

The waiter. The table. My hat on the stand. Let's take our gloves off; drop them casually on the table; these little things show a man's style. My coat on the stand; I sit down; ouf! I was weary. I'll put my gloves in my coat pocket. Blazing with light, golden, red, with its mirrors, this glitter; what? the restaurant; the restaurant where I am. I was tired. The waiter:

'Shell-fish soup, pea soup, consommé . . .'

'Consommé!'

'What will you have to follow, sir?'

'Let me see the menu.'

'White wine, red wine . . .'

'Red . . .'

The menu. Fish, sole . . . yes, sole. Entrées, lamb chop . . . no. Chicken . . . fine.

'Sole; chicken; with watercress.'

'Sole; chicken and watercress.'

So, I'm going to dine; nothing unpleasant about that. Rather a pretty woman there, neither brunette nor blonde; refined looking, my word; she must be tall; she's the wife of the bald man with his back to me; more likely his mistress; doesn't quite look the lawful wife; definitely rather pretty. If only she would look over here; she's nearly opposite me; how do I go about it? What's the use? She's seen me. She is pretty; and the man looks a bore; unfortunately I can only see him from the back; I'd like to know what his face is like too; he's a solicitor, a country solicitor; how stupid I am! And the consommé? The mirror in front of me reflects the golden frame; the golden frame must be behind me; these lights are bright red, with crimson burners; it's the pale yellow gaslight which illuminates the walls; yellow under the gaslight as well, the white tablecloths, the mirrors, the wine-glasses.

One's at ease here; comfortable. Here comes the consommé, the steaming hot consommé; careful the waiter
doesn't splash any on me. No; let's eat. This soup's too
hot; try again. Not bad. I had lunch a bit late and I'm not
very hungry; all the same, I must have dinner. Soup
finished. That woman's looked over here again; she's got
lively eyes and the man seems a dull dog; it would be
marvellous to get to know her; why not? Strange things
do happen; by looking at her for a long time first, I can
start something; they're having their roast; never mind!
if I want to I can finish at the same time as them; where's
the waiter, wish he'd hurry; they always keep you waiting in these restaurants; wonder if I could arrange to have
dinner at my place; perhaps the concierge would have
some cooking done for me every day for a small fee. It
wouldn't be up to much. I'm being ridiculous; it would
be a nuisance; what would happen on the days when I
can't get back home? at least one isn't bored in a
restaurant. What's the waiter up to? He's on his way;
he's bringing the sole. What strange fish! this sole only
has about three or four mouthfuls on it; there are others
they serve up for ten people; it's true the sauce has something to do with it. Let's start on this one. A mussel and
prawn sauce would really be much better. That time we
went gathering prawns; didn't find many, and the back-
breaking effort, and with my legs soaked, despite the
thick yellow shoes I bought near the Bourse. You never
finish picking away at a fish; I'm not getting anywhere. I
owe my bootmaker at least a hundred francs. Have to try
and learn about the Bourse; would be useful; I've never
understood what it was to buy in a bear market; what can
you possibly get out of securities that are going down in
value? let's pretend I have one hundred thousand francs'
worth of Panamas, and that they go down in value; so I
sell; yes; so I'll buy again next time they go up; no, I'll
sell. That fat solicitor having his meal ought to advise
me. Maybe he's no such thing. Oh! these fish-bones;

there's nothing to eat on this sole; still, it's good; let's leave these bits. On the bench, against the backrest, I lean back; more people coming in; one seems to be embarrassed; incredible pale-coloured coat; people haven't been wearing them for years. I've left a tasty-looking morsel of sole; not going to make myself look silly by having it now. Would be excellent that little white piece with stripes made in it by the bones. Too bad; I'm not going to eat it; I wipe my fingers on my serviette; a bit rough, my serviette; new maybe. The solicitor's wife has just looked round; seems to have signalled to me; she's got lovely eyes; how shall I go about talking to her? She's not looking any more. Shall I write a note? that would risk disappointment; still ... I'll show her the note; if she wanted to take it she'd manage to; I can write it in any case. And then? I have to go home, dress, be at the theatre before nine o'clock; unbearable all these complications.

'Finished, sir ...'

'Yes. You can bring the chicken.'

'Sir ...'

A drop of wine. Empty, the seats opposite; between the seat and the mirror, leather upholstery. I must see what happens with a note – anyway. My card-case; my address card, that's more suitable; my pocket-pencil; very well. What shall I put? A rendezvous for tomorrow. I must indicate several. If that solid solicitor knew what I was up to! I write: :'Tomorrow, at two, in the reading-room of the Magasin du Louvre ...' The Magasin du Louvre, not very chic, but still the most convenient; and then, or somewhere else? The Louvre? go on with you! At two o'clock. Need to allow enough time; at least from two till three; that's it; I change 'at' to 'from' and I'm going to add 'until three'. Next 'I ... I will wait for you ...' No, 'I will wait'; that's it; let's see. 'Tomorrow from two in the reading-room of the Magasin du Louvre, until three will wa ...' That's not right at all; how do I put it?

I don't know. Yes; 'at two o'clock in the reading-room
...', etc ... 'till three. Will wait ...' Let's say until
four; yes; I'll take a book; what's-his-name's novel, the
journalist; I don't know why I bought it the other evening; but, since I did buy it, I'll see what it's like; I'll settle
down and wait quietly; it's draughty sometimes; rarely,
no, it isn't draughty. Now what about this note I'm
supposed to be writing? Let's carry on. 'Will wait until
...' but I'll have to put in 'at' instead of 'from'; right;
'tomorrow at two o'clock ...' My card's going to be
covered in crossings-out, hideous, illegible; this is ridiculous; I'm going to catch my death in that awful draughty
reading-room; and anyway that woman's not going to
accept my note. I tear it up; across the card; across again;
that makes four bits, again ... and that's eight; once
more; there – again; can't any more. Well, I can't throw
these bits on the floor; they'd be found; have to chew
them a bit. Ugh! Horrible. Onto the floor; that way it's
certain nobody will read what's written. That woman's
laughing; yet she didn't look at all just now; she's looking
now; she's laughing; she's talking to the man; pretty,
pretty, pretty girl! This chewed-up paper is vile; let's
have something to drink; this is taking the awful taste
away ... Let's see the menu; peas, asparagus; no, ice
cream, a coffee ice, that's it! I haven't much appetite.
Dessert, cheese, meringue, apple? The waiter serves the
chicken; looks good, the chicken.

'I will take a coffee ice; then, do you have any cheese,
Camembert?'

'Yes, sir.'

'Camembert then.'

Now for the chicken; wing; not too tough today;
bread; this chicken's going down well; one dines well
here; the next time I dine with Léa at her home, I'll order
the dinner from Rue Favart; it's less expensive than in
the big restaurants, and it's better. Only the wine here
isn't anything special; have to go to the best restaurants

for wine. Wine, gambling, women – there, there you are
– What connection is there between wine and gambling,
between gambling and women? Admittedly, people need
to work themselves up to make love; but gambling? That
chicken was extraordinarily good, excellent watercress.
The peace and quiet of a dinner nearly over. But gambling ... wine, gambling – wine, gambling, women ...
Women, dear to Scribe. It's not from *Le Chalet*, in *Robert
le Diable** rather. And that's by Scribe too. And always a
passion for the same three things ... Long live wine,
love and tobacco ... That leaves us the tobacco, admittedly. There, there you are ... The bivouac refrain. Do
you have to pronounce the 'c' in bivouac as in *tabac*?
Mendès, Boulevard des Capucines, used to say 'dom-p-
ter'; one must say 'dom-ter'.* Love and tobacco ... The
bivouac refrain. The solicitor and his wife are leaving.
It's senseless, ridiculous, ludicrous! letting them go! ...
    'Waiter!'
    The waiter's not there; it's sickening; I'm a fool, a
chance like that; I'll never have another, wonderful
woman. She didn't look over here when she got up; it's
not surprising, of course. They're going. It would have
been marvellous; I'd have followed her; I'd have known
where she was going; I'd have managed something some-
how. Which street can she have taken? they turned right;
she went up the Avenue de l'Opéra. Is there a performance today? Must be, Monday today. It will be a good
thing to take my little Léa soon; she'll like that.
    'Did you call, sir?'
    The waiter: what does he want? Did I call him? Must
have done.
    'I'm in rather a hurry ... you see ...'
    'Very well, sir ...'
    The waiter looks as if he's making fun of me. I am
being a real fool. And why bother about other women?
Haven't I got my fair share? what's the use of someone
else? wearing oneself out searching? More people leav-

ing. I'll spend all evening over my dinner. The ice cream; jolly good; let's have a taste; slowly; has to be savoured; the coolness; the flavour of coffee; on the tongue and the palate; flavoured coolness; can hardly get this sort of thing at home. Must be tired out, the little man who took his son to eat ices at Tortoni's;* I've never set foot in the place; I've never been in Tortoni's. What you're missing ... to the melody for *La Dame blanche*;* what you're missing; ice finished; too bad. The waiter's brought the cheese without my noticing. Have to drink a drop of water first. In about a fortnight's time I'll leave town; if the weather's good, the whole family will be staying at Quevilly; in April the weather's not good enough to go into the country. I'm leaving this cheese; I'm not hungry any more. What a bother always having dinner out in a restaurant! nobody to talk to here; nobody worth seeing; not one woman to look at; for a whole week not one woman; a bunch of gents not half as smart as they seem; they come in here out of poverty; on their uppers; then, country solicitors who think they're at Bignon's.* Three francs plus a ten sous tip; and good night. I get up; I put my coat back on; the waiter's pretending to help me; thank you; my hat; my gloves, here in my pocket; I'm going. There's a table where I'd have been more comfortable, on the right, near the pillar; people drinking glasses of beer; the big doors, massive, plate-glass; a waiter opens the door for me; good night; it's cold; let's button up my coat; it's the contrast with the warm inside; the waiter closes the door again; 'beer, thirty centimes ... dinners at three francs'.

iii It's dark in the street; it's only half past seven though; I'm going back home; I'll easily be at the Nouveautés for nine. The avenue isn't as dark as it first appeared to me; the sky is cloudless; the pavements light and clear, the light from the gas-lamps, from the triple gas-burners; not many people out; the Opéra over there, the foyer of the Opéra ablaze with light; I'm walking on the right-hand side of the avenue, towards the Opéra. I was forgetting my gloves; not long and I'll be home; and there's nobody about now. I'll be home soon; in ... from here to the Opéra, five minutes; Rue Auber, five minutes; as long for the Boulevard Haussmann; five minutes more make ten, fifteen, twenty minutes; I'll dress; I'll be able to leave at half-past eight, twenty-five to nine. It's dry out; it's pleasant walking after dinner; never many people in the avenue at this time of the evening. Léa leaves the theatre at nine o'clock, between nine and quarter past. What shall we do? a ride in a carriage; we'll follow the boulevard to the Champs-Elysées, up to the Rond-Point; to the Arc de Triomphe rather, in order to take her home by way of the outer boulevards; the weather's so mild; she'll surely let me hold her hand; she'll no doubt be wearing her black cashmere dress; I'll be careful we don't get back too late; she'll probably ask me to stay a while; I'll see her exquisite, unspoiled, impish smile; slowly she'll be washing and undressing for the night. 'Sit in the armchair and be good!' She'll speak to me with a lovely, ceremonious gesture; I'll probably reply: 'Yes, mademoiselle!' I'll sit in the armchair; the low, blue velvet one, with the wide band of embroidery round it; there she sat on my knee a fortnight ago; and I'll sit in the low chair, near her, opposite the wardrobe with the mirror; she'll be standing and will put her hat on the plush-topped table, arranging her hair with little movements of her hands to right and left, pausing, studying herself, from behind, with little delicate movements of her hands, looking at me, laughing, pulling faces, mischievously; sheer bliss! in her black dress and her black cashmere bodice; not tall; not small either; even if she looks small; no, it's not small she appears, but young, very young; and so plump; her ample hips, below her slim waist, softly curving downwards; her swelling bosom, which heaves so in moments of emotion; and her artful child's face; her hair all blonde and her wide eyes; lovely, darling Léa! The poor dear, I want to love her, and with a pious love, as one ought to love, not like others love. When we're back, it will be ten at least. Twenty-five to eight by the pneumatic clock. The Opéra. The terrace of the Café de la Paix is packed; nobody I know; the Opéra; Rue Auber; the house where Monsieur Vaudier lives; two months already since I last went to dinner there: maybe he's away; rich as Croesus, to possess a fortune like that; how much must it come to? a million from stocks and shares, I've been told. That comes at least to capital of about twenty million; nearly one hundred thousand francs a month; no, one million divided by twelve, that's twelve into a hundred ... nought, that leaves ... let's say ninety-six, nine hundred and sixty thousand francs; twelve into ninety-six is eight, eighty, eighty thousand francs a month. I'd like Léa to have a superb town house; sweet little girl; if I had that wealth this evening; let's pretend; I'd have suddenly come into money; it's such fun to make things up like that; so the solicitor would have handed over the deeds to me; I'd have money, gold-coin and notes, immediately, a hundred thousand francs; I'd go to Léa's as usual; as if nothing had happened; I'd suddenly say to her: Do you want us to go somewhere, Léa? Let's go, the two of us; I'm taking you with me; I'm taking you away, you're taking me away ... No, let's be serious; I'd say to her something like: Will you come? She'd certainly be

amazed; she'd say she couldn't. Why ... She'd explain
she couldn't leave everything; very simply and naturally
I'd reply to her: Oh! don't bother about anything any
more, I've had a bit of luck; I can help you; if you have
any debts, any liabilities, just let me arrange your
departure ... That's the right turn of phrase ... Let me
arrange your departure. I'd put ten thousand francs on
some item of furniture; and: – If you need more, you'll
let me know ... ten thousand francs; or only five; no,
better ten thousand to start with; and anyway it would be
so easy for me. Twenty thousand? That would be ridiculous; but ten thousand, fine. How astonished and pleased
she'd be! Do you want us to leave? I'd say to her. What
do you mean? leave? Yes, leave, leave everything here;
you'll find it all again a hundred times over; the two of
us, let's escape, leave, come on! And I'd take her in my
arms, I'd kiss her hair; I'd carry her off; and in a low
voice, in a low voice, she'd like to very much; it would be
like in Gautier's *Fortunio*;* only Fortunio sets fire to the
curtains, and carries his love off naked amid the flames;
with a private income of one million francs, I'd risk the
luxury of being a bit mad. The Eden Theatre; the gas of
the footlights; the electric lamps; the programme-sellers;
a little kid would open the door of a cab; what's the use of
a kid opening your carriage door? The Printemps stores
over there; not a soul on the pavement; there are usually
street girls here, insufferable stopping people; not a single one tonight; the street's dismal. Let's return to the
matter in hand; I want to play at dreaming how I'd
organize things if I became rich; yes, let's organize that,
while walking along. So, I'd have become rich; but how?
what's the use of looking for a reason? things would
simply be like that. As I was saying then, I'd have come
into money; this evening I'd have my fortune, and a lot of
money on me. I have no wish to live extravagantly at
home; I'd have a bachelor flat and set Léa up in a town
house; I'd willingly keep on my fourth-floor place in Rue

du Général Foy: something of the kind, but better; live at home in the style of a man with thirty odd thousand francs private income and spend one's million a year on one's mistress; I'd like to have a little ground-floor flat for myself in a house in the Parc Monceau area, it goes without saying; five or six rooms; a carriage-entrance; then two steps; the door; a hallway; in the front part a small drawing-room; a dining-room, a smoking-room; at the back, the kitchen, the privies, a big dressing-room and the bedroom; the bedroom opening onto a courtyard garden. The hallway wouldn't have to be too tiny; I'd make it into a kind of conservatory; the whole length of the apartment: that would be inconvenient; it would be better for it to finish on a level with the dining-room; so between the drawing-room and the bedroom a second hallway separated from the first by a door, by a curtain rather; and the young ladies who would slip away well hidden behind it ... How would all this be furnished? no useless luxury; in my own way; I've always dreamed of a white bedroom without any furniture; a square bed in the middle; brass rather than fabric, brass goes well with white; the walls covered in fabrics, satin, cashmere, white silk; the ceiling too; on the floor white animal skins; polar bear, naturally; and, above all, no furniture; the wardrobes in the dressing-room; only divans here ... There! I don't know where I am anymore or what I'm doing; ah! Boulevard Haussmann soon. To the left, the drawing-room door; to the right, the window; straight ahead, the dressing-room door; opposite, the bed; the chimney-piece? straight ahead instead of the dressing-room door; and this door? towards the corner; or no chimney-piece, or, chimney-piece in the corner; and there, in the corner, or in the middle of the ceiling, an alabaster night-light, a bit like in Léa's bedroom. The dressing-room marble of course. Would the hallway have to be marble? All along the wall, shrubs. How could this hallway be lit? a skylight isn't very neat looking. And then, I'd want the house in a quiet street. It would be perfect, in front of the house one or two square yards of garden, giving onto the street; a low wall with ordinary iron railings; the little garden; just a few lilacs; a little greenery, I don't know what; how wide? a metre or a metre and a half; I'm mad; two or three metres. That depends on whether a door in the apartment opens onto the garden; not really necessary; but no bother, as long as it's the dining-room; pleasant from time to time; so, garden – three or four square metres. Let's see; three square metres, therefore three paces easily, one, two, three; yes, that's it. When I'd want to have dinner at home, my servant would arrange things with Chevet or someone; it's important to live simply; besides, normally, I'd be living with Léa; from time to time I'd have her back in my little ground-floor apartment; an escapade; we'd make love to each other so beautifully in our white bedroom, on our white bearskins. This evening we'd have run off together; in two hours I'd arrive at her house; I'd have my twenty-five thousand francs with me; I'd arrive in the usual way. But I'm not going to her home, I'm going to the theatre; doesn't matter . . .

'Good evening, sir.'

What? A street girl. If it looks as if I'm looking at her, she's going to stop me.

'Sir . . .'

A shower of patchouli; heavens! hurry on. Ah! Léa, Léa, my lovely, good, lovely little Léa; how happy you'd be, and with the bad times over, how we'd love each other, when I'd tell you I'd become rich, for you, and when we'd run off together, this very evening. Where would we go? to my place first, and tomorrow we'd leave on our travels; tomorrow for buying everything we need; leave only the day after tomorrow; until then, together, at my place; and like that, therefore, this evening around nine o'clock, just as usual, I'd arrive at the theatre; I wait for her; she comes out; I greet her; she comes towards

me; I say to her: Good evening, mademoiselle ... To the
left, in the side street, that tall, thin young man, in a short
coat and top hat? It's Paul Hénart. He's coming this way,
Paul Hénart; always polite; and always with his elegant
rattan cane; he's noticed me, acknowledges me ...
    'Hello.'
    'Hello. On your way home?'
    'Yes. How are you? You're going this way?'
    'Yes; I'll walk as far as Saint Augustin's with you.'
    'Fine. What news?'
    'Nothing, nothing yet.'
    I'm glad to see him again; a very old, very honest,
very warm-hearted friend; very proper, a gentleman; I'd
trust him; very honest, very warm-hearted. We walk
along the boulevard. He's good looking, without being
affected. Where was he going? I ask him.
    'You're not going home this way?'
    'No; I'm going to the Rue de Courcelles.'
    Of course, it's the old business of his marriage; is that
still on?
    'Rue de Courcelles? You're going to the home of that
lady, whose daughter ...'
    'Exactly.'
    'You talked to me about it vaguely; some time ago;
how are things going?'
    'I'm getting married soon.'
    'Really?'
    'Really. Does that surprise you?'
    'No.'
    To get married; marry a woman you love; to be able
to marry a woman you love: to possess her. So these
things are possible, to get married, be together, have a
wife.
    'No,' I say, 'that doesn't surprise me ... But how did
it come about so quickly? ...'
    He's going to get married. What a man, with his love,
his marriage, these things that only happen to him!

'What do you expect me to say?' he replies. 'I love a young girl who loves me and I'm going to marry her.'

'And you're happy?'

'Happy.'

'You're lucky.'

'I've found a woman worthy and capable of love.'

He seems to believe himself to be the only one on earth who is loved and in love. Yet I remember . . .

'My dear Hénart, if I remember well the two or three things you've told me about it, you made the acquaintance of the young girl quite by chance.'

'Quite by chance, indeed; I saw her for the first time, one day, in a public park, with two other young girls. I was passing, strolling along rather; she was there, so fresh, so unaffected; more than six months ago already; I found out where she lived, then her name, what she was . . . That was that.'

That was that; he's admitting it; in a public park, three young girls; I sat down opposite them; I took out my monocle; I followed her; that was that.

'And once a mathematician feels he's in love, all is lost. You spoke to her.'

'Not immediately. She had noticed me; she told me so later. I found out she was living with her mother. You can guess the rest.'

'You sent her notes.'

'No. A friend of a friend brought me into contact with these ladies.'

Procuring; very good.

'And then?'

'I came to know a girl of deep feelings; a serious girl, with a trusting soul, of few words, a steadfast look, a genuine woman. I went to her mother's; her mother, she was so good, she understood, and she trusted me, the dear, honest, admirable mamma. A story out of Madame de Ségur,* isn't it? The mamma spends her evenings knitting, as one does at that age; she plays the piano too; we chat, Elise and I.'

What candour.

'And that's lasted for six months. One evening, we agreed to marry; she was all in white, sitting in an armchair; me, next to her, on a low chair; it was in a corner of their sitting-room; the mamma often persists in sight-reading difficult pieces, Iansen, for example; Elise, quite still, says to me in a very low voice, appearing not to move her lips, and as if some other person who might have been herself had spoken, she says to me: "The first evening you came here, if I had dared, I'd have said yes . . ." And she said to me: "My friend, I will be your wife . . ." She spoke these words to me . . . Can you picture the scene? . . . Then the mother turned round, she looked at us; and she exclaimed: "Well, children, we'll marry you; don't worry . . . Ha! ha! ha!" and she began to laugh, such a gay, open laugh; and . . . and so on, and so on.'

That's the moral of the story.

'Very, very good, my dear Hénart. Very good of you to tell me these things. And you're going to get married?'

'This summer, I hope.'

'Has she a little money of her own?'

'The mother has enough to live on decently; and since I've been with the company, I earn a little money.'

'Very, very good. She's twenty, didn't you say, and you're twenty-seven?'

'My life's honour and purpose reside in her; I'm going to be her husband, and I feel infinite joy.'

Infinite joy, her husband, infinite joy. We are walking, Paul and I, in the streets. Opposite us, Boulevard Malesherbes, the trees, the lights, the empty streets, a pale breeze. I'd like to be there, in the country, at my father's, alone in the fields at night, alone! alone and walking; it feels so good, at night, in the countryside, going stick in hand, straight on, dreaming of all things possible, in silence, in the wide, empty countryside, on the high-banked roads, it feels so good, so good! ... We are walking, Paul and I, side by side.

'You're a happy man, my dear Hénart.'

'I wish you something comparable; I'm going to see my fiancée right now; she's waiting for me; without seeming to be; otherwise her mother would tease me. But here we are at Saint Augustin's. You're going up Avenue Portalis?'

'Yes; I must get back home.'

'You've no attachment. Quite the opposite, I bet ...'

'Oh! nonsense. Good night, Paul.'

'Good night.'

'You'll come and see me?'

'One morning I'll come and wake you up, if it's not indiscreet.'

'Fear nothing, my friend.'

'Good night.'

'Good night.'

We say goodbye to each other. He goes that way. Is he, isn't he a happy man? He knows undivided love, mutual love. He thinks I'm chasing after women. Mutual love! He believes what he's saying, so he's happy; perhaps happy as nobody ever was; would he be the only one to have known what love is? He definitely believes it. And yet! it's not unusual to believe such things; and on what grounds! Rue de Courcelles; Elise; the mamma; and goodness me who? a young lady he met by chance one fine day; who frequents a public park with two friends; whom he followed; who received notes; at whose home he gave himself naïve airs for six months; and who'd have said yes to him immediately if he'd dared. And the mamma; with modest private means; certainly a widow; an officer's widow; the mother who pretends to be sight-reading Iansen; the romance of eternal love; I will be your wife; why not straightaway in the bedroom? what would our engineer have said? Ha! ha! ha! they kept their cards .

well to their chests those two women. And he's going to imagine, imagines, can imagine that he's in love; doesn't know he's taking himself in; wouldn't guess that in two months this passing fancy would be over; and is getting married. Real love stories aren't like that, they aren't based on this sort of thing, don't come about like this, and when a heart is moved, it isn't in the Parc Monceau, on a day when one is out strolling and following little milliners and widows' daughters, in order to play at being Paris in front of three beauties. The door of my house; I've arrived. True love? Me, me, me, sacrebleu.

iv 'Sir.'
Someone calling me; the concierge; he's holding a letter.

'The chambermaid who has already been several times brought you this letter, sir, a quarter of an hour ago. She said it was urgent.'

A letter from Léa no doubt.

'Give it to me . . . Thank you.'

Yes, a letter from Léa.

'Dear friend, don't pick me up from the theatre tonight. Come straight to the house around ten. I'll be waiting for you. Léa.'

Insufferable; always changing; one never knows what one will be doing; first one plan, then another; always the same fuss; why doesn't she want me to go and fetch her at the theatre? so as not to be seen with me? no doubt somebody new? Perhaps she might have been late as well; perhaps she has a reason? The third floor or only the second? The gas-lamp; it's only the second floor. This girl drives you to despair; still, lucky I've been told; sending her chambermaid at seven o'clock; I could have

not been coming back; this is ridiculous; if I hadn't had
her note and if she'd seen me at the theatre, she'd have
made a terrible scene; no, she's going to be frightened I'll
be there and come out by another door; these theatres
have more than a couple of dozen doors; and what sort of
a figure would I have cut there? She certainly knew I was
bound to go home beforehand; anyway ... My door;
let's open it; the dark; the matches are there; I strike one
... careful ... the sitting-room door; in I go; the
mantelpiece; the candlestick's on it; I light the candle;
match in the ashtray; everything's where it ought to be;
the table; no letters; yes; a visiting-card, dog-eared;
who's been? ... Jules de Rivare ... Oh dear! What a
pity! an old friend; we used to sit next to each other in
philosophy prep; what a goody-goody! He's been today;
the concierge doesn't tell me anything; so dear old de
Rivare's in Paris; with his black moustache and cavalry
officer's looks; another one who knows what's what; he'll
be back; absent-minded of him not to say where he's
staying! ah! on the back of his card, I forgot to look,
there's a note: 'I'll be awaiting you for lunch tomorrow;
meet me at eleven, Hotel Byron, Rue Lafitte.' I'll be
there; I'll be there. And what about my law lecture at
two? if I haven't time to go, I won't go. He must be rich,
old de Rivare; this country nobility; who knows? Tomorrow, at eleven, Rue Lafitte. For the moment, I have to
dress for going to Léa's; I've more than an hour and a
half, all the time in the world to get ready. My hat and
coat, on a chair. I go into my bedroom; the two stork-
shaped candlesticks with double holders; let's light them;
there we are. The bedroom; the white of the bed against
the bamboo, to the left, there; and the old tapestry
drapes above the bed, the red designs, blurred, purplish-
blue, soft-toned, a blackish blending of red-back and
blue-black, worn shades; the dressing-room needs a new
mat; I'll choose one at the Bon Marché; would be better
in the Avenue de l'Opéra. I'll wash. What's the good? I

mustn't stay at Léa's, must be back here; yet who knows
what may happen? who knows how things may turn out?
what the occasion may offer? when will the day of our
love come? What's the point. I'll wash. I've more than
enough time, it's only twenty minutes to where she lives;
no use hurrying; lovely and warm this evening, mild,
balmy; prospect of joy; we'll chat in the carriage, the two
of us, we'll ride through the darkened streets, in the mild
and balmy air, the happy atmosphere; lovely evening.
What if I opened the window? yes; I open it wide. The
semi-darkness of the night; night milk-whitened by the
first stars; ill-defined half-shadows; bright night; behind
me the bedroom, the reflection made by the candles, the
air closer in bedrooms, the heavy, humid atmosphere
close indoors. I'm leaning on the balcony, over into mid-
air; I'm breathing the evening air, vaguely looking at the
beautiful view; the beautiful, umbrageous, melancholy,
distant charm of the air; the beauty of the night; the grey
and black sky confusedly blueish; and the points of the
stars, like trembling drops, watery stars; the pallor, all
around, of the open sky; there, the clumps of trees and,
further off, the houses, dark, with lighted windows;
roofs, blackened roofs; below, in a blur, the garden, and
a chaos of walls and things; and the dark houses with lit-
up windows and darkened windows, and the immensity
of the sky, blueish, white with the first stars; the mild air;
no wind; the warm air; breath of May beginning; a warm
well-being in the caressing nocturnal atmosphere; the
piled clumps of the trees, over there, and the sphere of
the grey-blue sky dotted with trembling lights; the dim
shade of the garden at night; the balmy air; lovely spring
breeze, lovely summer, night breeze! Léa, my sweet
dear, my little Léa, my loved one, my Léa! The darkness
of night mingles all things; my friend with the carefree
smile and laugh, with the laughing eyes, with the wide
eyes, little laughing mouth, yes, smiling lips! in the
shadows lie the dim gardens, under the cloudless sky,

and it's her pretty blonde head, mocking, childishly small, delicate nose, sweet face, fine blonde hair, white delicate skin, smiling child who laughs at me and makes fun of me and we cherish each other; tonight, on the shifting balcony, on the vague outlines of the walls, in the mild evening air, amid the disappearing surroundings; you are beautiful and you are graceful; divinely graceful you walk, with your hips swaying, and you walk softly, on the carpets, by the table with the flowers, in your delightful yellow sitting-room; by the flowers on the shimmering carpet you softly walk, inclining your head slowly to the right, slowly to the left, with pale smiles, ivory face with its unruly hair, smiling in slow waves, you come and go, you walk; your thin dress floats, creamy crêpe, the ripple of the crêpe where the silk ribbon falls, the pleated crêpe clasping your breasts and hips and childlike body, and you softly move your lips, my friend; I love you, the shadow of the great greenery rises high into the sky; my own one, you show through the clear shade, smiling, light, artless, sweet and good; I love you purely; I only want her love from her; and her kiss, and I I want it out of her love. I have received it, received it from one who did not love me! Night; the dark trees; the brilliance of the stars more intense; engulfing night; behind me is the bedroom; I cannot see it, I only know it is there; behind me the closer air of the bedroom; here, the cool mild of outdoors; leave the window, sorrowfully! go back in, busy myself with things, do things; it would be good to dream in an idle evening, at the window, dream of one's love, of one's loved one, and to reflect one calm evening, and dream, dream of a love one would like to be pure, of the loved one you would wish to be inviolate, one chaste evening; it would be good to dream in the calm ease of evening. Here, cool, dark night; cooler, darker night; behind me, the bedroom: warmer, closer, with the transparent candle flames; outside it's cool, inside warmer; outside it's cool, almost cold; this dark

becomes merely dull; it is distressing trying to pierce so
much stillness; this pallid sky, these clumps of trees,
these lights are of ice; almost sinister, this silence; I am
afraid of this vast, mute night; inside is soft, mild,
humid, warm, with the carpets, the fabrics, the enclosing
walls, the comfort of soft things; let's go back in ... I
straighten up, I turn round ... The candles on the
mantelpiece are lit; here's the white bed, soft, the carpets; I lean against the open window; outside, behind
me, I feel the night; black, cold, sad, sinister night; the
dark where appearances change; the silence where sands
murmur; the tall trees packed black together; the bare
walls; and the windows dim with the unknown, and the
windows lighted, unknown; in the pallor of the sky, this
vibration of the weeping eyes of the stars; the secret of
opaque, mysterious shadows, mixed into something fearsome; there, some unknown, fearsome thing ... I shud-
der; quickly, I turn round, grip the window, I push it to,
I close it, quickly ... Nothing ... The window's closed
... And the curtains? I draw them to, like this ... Night
is abolished. In the friendly light this is my room; how
comfortable one is at home! The bedroom soft and gentle
far from the terror of empty nights; comfort, light. I lean
against the wall. One feels absolutely confident, very
content, full of energy, the white light of the candles,
whitened gold; the softness of the carpets and hangings;
it is well-being, sweetness, happiness. I'm going happily
to prepare myself, here, in the peace of this narrow room.
Gleaming under the lights, shining white, colour of running water and of marble, the dressing-room; I must
dress, I have my grey trousers and my black jacket on; I
can go to Léa's like this; of course she's often seen me in
this get-up; but she's often seen me in everything I wear;
this is correct dress; a frock-coat? – not necessary; I'll
only be seeing Léa; I'm keeping these button-boots on
too; no buttons missing? no; they haven't got dirty; a
brush-up will do; but I must change my shirt; this one I

put on last night is still clean; the collar and cuffs are spotless; it's a bother changing; still, has to be done; if, by any chance, at Léa's tonight, who knows? ... lovely, dear girl, if tonight ... Sacrebleu, am I mad? Let's dress, and get out another shirt. My jacket, there, on the bed; my waistcoat on the bed too; now, in the dressing-room; my dressing-room is really very tidy; conscientious servant; the candles reflected in the big mirror over the wash-stand; the straw-coloured walls; the big, white bowl full of water; perfectly clear water, a few drops of musk, just a few; my shirt hanging up; I'm lucky not to have flannel shirts; they're ridiculous; the sponge; cold water on my hand; my head down into the water; the sudden chill! it's lovely having one's head in the clear water streaming down, plashing, trickling and slipping and running, flowing; my ears full of water and buzzing, my eyes closed then open in the sea-green water, my skin tingling and quivering, a caress, a voluptuous sensation; what happiness going to the seaside; we'll go to Yport no doubt; my mother likes that part of the country; the forest, the cliff; dive into the bowl; the sponge spurting onto my neck, the coldness against my chest, perfumed just a little, good old water; my towel; what a relief! I went for a shave at midday; that's enough for today; if only I could shave myself properly; one never gives oneself a good shave; my beard wouldn't have suited me. There, I'm presentable; one always has to be careful; I'm going to Léa's this evening; and what if I were allowed to stay there? would be fun ... Come on, come on ... Where's my hairbrush? It's strange how girls of easy virtue can put up with so many people; and what about us who accept all of them. I'm scrupulously clean; bravo! quick, must dress; I'd catch cold; a white shirt, let's hurry things along; cuff-links, collar-stud; clean linen; I'm being an idiot! hurry up; in my bedroom; my tie; my braces are a sight, I made a rotten choice; my waistcoat, watch in pocket; jacket; I was forgetting my button-boots; doesn't

matter! no, just a brush-up; with my clothes-brush; it's
only a bit of dust; one, two, now my jacket; tie's straight;
right; I'm ready; I can leave; my handkerchief; my card-
case; very good; what time is it? half-past eight; I'm not
leaving as early as this; so let's sit down, here, in the
armchair; I've an hour to wait; undisturbed here, quite
undisturbed and enviably so; nothing, my dear chap, like
a nice nap, in a nice armchair, after a quarter-of-an-hour's
wash and a good splash in cold water.

V Since I've nothing to do, let's examine, briefly but
seriously, how I'm going to behave at Léa's
tonight; obviously, stay with her until midnight or one
o'clock, then leave; she must understand the reasons for
my conduct; oh, how difficult it is to explain! I feel
uncomfortable here; let's go into the sitting-room; get
up; the candles on the desk; I can just walk up and down
in the sitting-room, in front of the mantelpiece and the
two windows; let's draw the curtains; casually up and
down in the sitting-room. What was I thinking about?
The trouble is, when I begin to think about something,
my mind wanders off at a tangent. I must know what I'll
do this evening, though; I can't leave everything to
chance; it's my duty to make Léa understand ... First of
all I must have the chance of leaving of my own accord;
several times already, because she didn't ask me to stay, I
looked when I left as if I had been politely shown the
door. This evening she'll perhaps agree to my staying;
supposing she agrees; then I'll tell her that I'd definitely
better leave her; why should I stay, if she doesn't love me
enough to keep me because she really wants me? That'll
be my reply. It's difficult; I don't know how I'll manage;
she'll be amazed; she'll look at me with her wide, exag-
geratedly wondering eyes, half mockingly; like the day I

wanted to scold her; with her lively way of coming and
going, her little movements, now rapid, now lazy; and
the day when she threw her hat into the window-box;
her pearl-grey hat; she started laughing, laughing; the
silly girl! ... What a scatterbrain I am! I'll never manage
to fix my mind on one single thing; it's enough to drive
one to despair. What if I wrote things down? That's a
good idea; I'm going to make a little plan in writing of
what I am going to tell her; at least that's useful for
working out ideas. I sit down; the blotter, paper, the
inkwell, the pen-holder; the nib seems to be all right;
very good. Opposite, the Chinese silk curtain; the vague,
white flowers of Chinese silks, where the slow stork floats
with its raised bill; the black silk very smooth against the
white embroidery; paper, on the blotter; that's it; let's
write ... What did she say in her latest letter? I ought
first to reread the letter; I've her letter here; let's see; in
the drawer, the packet of letters; here's all the correspondence, her letters and my rough copies. Here's her
first note four months ago.

Dear Sir,
It is quite impossible for me to accept your kind
invitation this evening. If you were willing to post-
pone it until tomorrow, I would be free then.
Yours truly ...

That's from the evening when I thought I was taking
her out to supper; I had been to see her for the first time
the day before; it was midnight when I went to ask for
her at the concierge's lodge at the theatre that I was given
this note. And next day? it was next day at the concierge's lodge that she sent me packing. This is her
second note, dating from a fortnight later.

Dear Monsieur Prince,
I am most grateful to you for the service you had
the amiability ...'

I had been back to Rue Stévens again. Once you have started something, you are reluctant to suddenly let everything drop; I'd given tips, written; I really couldn't let things rest there, leave everything, think no more about it. Louise was her chambermaid then; how many louis I must have given to the fat lass! During those two weeks while Léa was away, I only saw her, the worthy Louise, at Rue Stévens. And then that business of Mademoiselle d'Arsay having landed up in Champagne, exactly where I can't remember, without a penny; my six hundred francs had come through from my father; I acted on impulse, wanting to astonish, to dazzle, to show off; extravagant, though; giving three hundred francs like that, for a woman I had just caught a glimpse of twice and who had shown me the door; a fine gesture, certainly, but which tied my hands. That was when she wrote me her second note.

I am most grateful for the service that you had the amiability to render me. If I had known earlier that you were the author of this kind act I would have thanked you at once . . .

She had written 'earlier', and added 'at once' over it.

But I was only informed of your kindness a little while ago. I hasten to add that I shall be back in Paris on Wednesday evening and if you were so kind as to come and see me during the afternoon of Thursday towards four o'clock, you will be very welcome. In the expectation of the pleasure of seeing you, please accept my friendly greetings.
Léa d'Arsay

It had occurred to me to keep in a notebook a brief written account of my continuing relations with this woman; I was wrong not to keep this up; it would have become increasingly interesting; this summary of one three-week period is a curiosity in itself; the very weeks after Léa's return to Paris, the first three weeks of our liaison; this actually begins on the day after her return.

Thursday, 27 January: Four o'clock; I go to Rue Stévens; Léa invites me in; white dress; she tells me her troubles, the quarter's rent not paid; I offer to bring her two hundred francs, at midnight; agreed.

Midnight; she comes back from the theatre with her mother; sees me in her room; not very friendly, at first; I hand over the two hundred francs; she doesn't want me to stay; not feeling well; becomes more friendly . . .

Actually, as I'd begun, I had to continue; besides, I had grounds for believing that this recent, latest gift would overcome all difficulties; I could hardly act otherwise, and lose by a refusal the benefit of my earlier gifts.

Friday, 28 January: I send white lilacs.

Saturday, 29 January: I think I see her in a carriage Rue des Martyrs; arrive at Rue Stévens; Louise tells me she has gone out for dinner in town; I promise to come next day at one.

Sunday, 30 January: One o'clock, Rue Stévens; Louise tells me she has gone to the country for a few days; her mother has obliged her to; she is kept on a tight rein; I show my displeasure; I state that I will be out of Paris for a week; I find out about the allowance the consul used to pay her; five hundred francs a month, in addition to dresses and presents.

31 January to 12 February: My trip to Belgium.

5 February: My letter.

9 February: A reply.

10 February: My second letter.

I've the rough draft of my two letters and her reply. This is the first of my two letters:

I had hoped not to leave on Monday without having said goodbye to you . . .

Etcetera; it's of no interest. But her reply.

I was very touched by your affectionate words. I do not doubt their sincerity! . . . I seemed sad when you last visited me; it's true, I am. You must have noticed that I was somewhat perturbed. I didn't dare tell you that I am at the moment going through a most unpleasant period of crisis which leaves me no peace either by day or night. I have serious commitments to fulfil and I would have to feel relieved from this point of view in order to be myself again and to be at your disposition. I have unfortunately no independent personal means and heavy expenses to keep up; so, even if my heart inclined me towards you, I am too honourable a woman to hide my position from you any longer, being ignorant of yours and not knowing what sacrifices you could make in the immediate future to save me from the overwhelming difficulties in which I find myself. Having read this statement please decide whether you can be the friend on whom I can absolutely rely; otherwise consider this confession as being invalid and forget me for ever.

Léa d'Arsay

My second letter:

10 February 1887

My Dear Friend,

I can assure you I am grateful to you for your frankness . . .

I replied that I could help her, but that I was somewhat apprehensive about these enormous financial difficulties . . .

These first two letters were quite correct and neatly written . . .

Let's continue.

Sunday, 13 February: I go to Rue Stévens; Louise informs me Léa is ill in bed; business about refusing a laxative; until tomorrow then.

Monday, 14 February: Rue Stévens, half-past one; Léa allows me in; pale blue dress; I stay for an hour; I ask her about her money worries, offer to give her ten louis that evening, if she wants me to bring her the money; she agrees, for eleven o'clock, on condition that I leave at once, because of her mother.

Eleven in the evening; she sees me in the dining-room; her mother has invited friends in without telling her beforehand; she can't let me stay; she begs me not to think it's her fault, not to hold it against her; another time, she swears; she's nicer than she's been before; I kiss her for a long time; leave after ten minutes; I give her the ten louis I promised; rendezvous for Wednesday.

Wednesday, 16 February: Two o'clock at Rue Stévens; she was on her way out; she lets me stay half an hour in her room; she puts her hat and coat on; plan to go out next day or the day after for dinner together.

Thursday, 17th: Rue Stévens at one o'clock; I stay for an hour and a half; I have coffee with her; the street singer; we dance; her skirts come undone; she leaves the room to do them up again; bell rings; she comes back; she tells me it's the coalman asking for money; bit of a quarrel; I agree to help her, but I impose the following condition; rendezvous tomorrow evening at nine o'clock; she tells me that if she can't rely on me, nothing doing.

Friday, 18th: Nine o'clock in the evening; Louise is on her own; Léa must have dined in town; she will be back very late; letter for me.

Let's look at that letter.

18th February

I am unfortunately unable to be at home this evening. The situation I am in and which you know about leaves me no freedom; if I had been able to count on what you had promised, I should have remained at home; but I absolutely must get out of this difficult situation immediately. Am I to rely on your good will or not? If you have kept your word, as I believe you have, hand over to Louise what you would have given to me and on Sunday I shall give you my thanks for it.

I miss this incomprehensible girl because she thinks I won't give anything to her, and then wants me to give something to her chambermaid. Let's put these letters back where they belong.

Friday 18th: Nine o'clock. Léa must have dined in town . . . Letter for me.

That's the one.

I refuse to give any money; Louise entreats me; promises; Louise begs me to at least think of her. Her daughter is out to nurse in Auteuil and she needs her wages in order to pay for her board which is in arrears; she tells me Léa is unhappy. I state categorically that Léa cares nothing for me, and that I won't give another penny until she has kept her word. I go, leaving Louise twenty francs.

At this point, my personal minutes break off; what a pity! I've only the beginning of the story. The next Saturday? the next Saturday Léa decided to favour me; in the afternoon, I recall, a beautiful sunny day; I gave her the two hundred francs she needed; that was quite a considerable sum for one kiss; and it's the very devil to break away, once one is caught up in things; and then; to begin the same round again with another woman, for

ever *ad infinitum*; had to get somewhere with that one;
you insist; I've done the right thing. She had been careful
to lock the sitting-room door; I had exactly two hundred
and five francs; in the evening I sent her some roses; it
was then I went to Hanser-Harduin's for the first time;
they've a very pretty sales-girl, with a delightful couldn't-
care-less air about her; I'll go and buy flowers there soon;
amazing girl, that little florist.

Dear Friend,
    You absolutely must come . . .

A rendezvous.

    Unfortunately I cannot be at home tomorrow . . .
    I have to go for an audition . . . Come on Monday
at four . . . a few moments together . . .

Another letter:

    As always because of the situation I am in, I cannot
be free as I would wish . . .
    I've a lot of worries . . .
    I must extricate myself from this impossible situa-
tion . . .

In God's name; my letter giving an ultimatum:

    28th February . . .

    This is it, horrible letter . . . It's this letter which did
all the damage; how could I have written it? my
behaviour for a month before was unfortunately entirely
in accordance with it; why did I write this letter?

Dear Friend,
    I did explain to you that you could only rely on me
to a limited extent. If I had a lot of money at my
disposal, I would ask you to accept what is necessary
for the upkeep of your house. Excuse me, moreover,
for being surprised by your mention of . . . rather
serious financial sacrifice. What I have done is

nothing in comparison to what I should like to do;
but do you deem it to be a laughing matter? For two
months what have you, for your part, done? Your
promises pointed to something more than just an
hour granted one afternoon. I shall not be able to visit
you the day after tomorrow earlier than five o'clock;
please leave me a note if I can come back in the
evening. In which case, count on me. Until then,
yours . . .

Tuesday morning.
   Very moved by your kind words! sorry you cannot
come tomorrow at one; will wait for you until two.
You know I have certain commitments to keep; I
have someone in service I cannot keep on. I would
require one hundred and fifty francs tomorrow evening in order to give her notice; and as soon as I am rid
of the above-mentioned I shall be more free to act.
I'm telling you everything. Try to have this modest
sum sent tomorrow and you will appreciate and judge
for yourself the urgency of doing so. Until tomorrow
then, and you in person or a note extricating me from
my difficulties; with heartfelt greetings . . .

Tuesday, two o'clock
Dear Friend,
   I received your message on my return home. You
weren't very pleased with what I wrote to you
yesterday? I was struck to the very heart when I
wrote it to you. But admit that you have treated me
very badly. Haven't you obliged me to be
unpleasant? I feel, I swear, desperately affected by it.
I had dreamed you would love me a little; I realized it
was a wild dream and I said to myself; too bad, let's
do as others do! . . . Now, please forgive and forget. I
am going to come this very evening; be kind, do not
send me away; I, for my part, will bring you what

you require. Let's leave these unpleasant worries there; you will see that I adore you ...

At nine in the evening she wasn't at home; she had received my letter; she had left me no reply. She could do anything now. Threaten her, be angry with her, and ask her forgiveness! And she might have loved me if I had known how to make myself loved! ...

Tuesday, 1st March, eleven in the evening

It's my plan of what I was going to say; I had been for a very long walk; and back here, alone, I had wanted to decide what I would say to her when she saw me the next day.

Tuesday, 1st March, eleven in the evening.

Once in the bedroom, holding her in my arms, I would say to her: 'Don't you believe I love you? If only what I am going to do could work some good on her poor soul! ...'

The evening I wrote that is the evening when I had met that girl on the boulevard with the wide faraway eyes, in her poor working woman's clothes, walking listlessly under the leafless trees, in the cold of a clear March night; I passed close by her; she feebly cast a lifeless look at me, feebly without a sign, with a faraway look; and I thought of the other girl, so very beautiful, and who I loved; poor, poor soul, sorrowful soul! ... There was a wood fire here; outside a cold sky, bright and dry; not a breath of wind; a deep, distant sky; pale air, with everything rising upwards; in here, the soft warmth of the fire, solitude, and memories.

You don't believe that I love you? – if only what I am going to do could do some good to her poor soul! My friend, I have thought about the things that come between us; I madly desired you; let that be my excuse; I forced you; I implore your pardon. I could stay here

tonight, my friend . . . Goodbye! you are my loved one; I
give you back your body, and leave you, because I love
you.

And I'll take her head in my hands, and kiss her lips.
Goodbye.

Yes, these words, not ill-intentioned entreaties. But
never did I have the opportunity to say these words.

Dear Friend, I absolutely must see you. I shall be
expecting you at ten this evening.
    Yours
    Léa

What else was there that evening? . . . The evening
she was ill? Of course; the night I spent looking after her.
How wounded, hurt, low, breathless she was! I had
waited a long time for her; she had come in in a state of
collapse; she went to bed and I stayed by her bedside; we
put compresses on her forehead; she sent her chambermaid away; I looked after her; I spent the whole night
like that in an armchair; with her mute and motionless,
drowsing; with me in a dream of sadness and pity. In the
morning she awoke; I drew back the curtains; it was
eight o'clock; she smiled at me. The best time of my love,
yes, the most precious. In the afternoon she was better; I
saw her for a quarter of an hour; and next day? It was
next day that she was so disagreeably cheerful, laughing,
singing, shouting.

Léa d'Arsay requests the pleasure of Monsieur
Daniel Prince's company at the Opéra tomorrow.
With kindest regards.

She was pretty that night at the Opéra, in her pink
satin dress and white shoes; Chavainne couldn't help
admitting she was pretty; Chavainne who never wants to
agree with anyone. And that night at the Odéon there
was a tragedy; *Andromaque*; Léa wanted to hear an
actress who was making her debut, I don't know who;

strange whim; we dined at Fayot's; she ordered teal; I was ridiculous not giving a big enough tip; but Léa didn't notice; all the same, I was wrong; from that private room you could see students going by, through the open window facing the Luxembourg Gardens; she had her velvet dress on, her jet hat with the red plume, and the serene dignity she had when in public. Every one of these evenings I used to take her back home, say good night and leave; that was the best thing to do; once or twice, she wanted to leave me on getting out of the carriage; but I always insisted on going up with her for ten minutes; now, it's become a habit and it's really delightful when we are chatting in her room. The letter from Louise, with a baroness's coronet:

> Monsieur Prince, sir, you told me to tell you if mademoiselle was in trouble. I've come to tell you that mademoiselle is in serious trouble at the moment. We need forty francs for the furniture. She's crying all the time because they say if it's not paid by tomorrow evening they'll come and take everything and she says that if it comes to that she doesn't know what she'll do. I mentioned your name but she said you couldn't do anything more for her. I had promised her to go and tell you how she finds herself placed but as I know I can never find you I've decided to write to you without saying anything to mademoiselle, and if we have the good fortune to have you come to our aid I beg of you don't tell mademoiselle who forbade me to because of what you said on Sunday. Forgive me, sir.
>
> Your devoted Louise

Card from Léa:

> Léa d'Arsay thanks Monsieur Prince for his delightful bouquet, and requests him to come and see her next Monday at one in the afternoon.

A letter this time:

> Dear Daniel,
>
> I must again have recourse to your good offices and request you oblige me with the small sum of forty or fifty francs which I urgently need for tomorrow. Would you be so kind as to bring the money yourself? I thank you in advance, with friendliest regards . . .

Again; a card.

> Léa d'Arsay expresses her deepest regret to her friend Daniel Prince; received his letter too late to be able to accept his kind invitation and will fix a day when she can have the pleasure of seeing him, which will be soon.

Another card.

> Léa d'Arsay would be happy to dine with Monsieur Prince this evening; will expect him at seven.

Oh! A whole letter, the one of a week ago, the letter about the jewellery.

> Dear Friend,
>
> You absolutely must let me have two hundred francs in order to save my jewellery, or at least the tickets pledged for this amount at a pawn shop. If you would be good enough to oblige me in this way, you would give great pleasure to your poor little friend Léa, who would be very sorry to see her poor jewellery sold. It's the day after tomorrow, Tuesday, that it will be finally sold off if the money isn't deposited; I have just this very moment received the notification. Be so kind, and I will be nicer and nicer to my only real friend whom I like very much. Marie will call at eleven tomorrow to find out what you decide.

It was a tiresome business, the money due on the jewellery was only one hundred and twenty francs, and there was a fortnight still to go; I paid her one hundred and twenty francs; since then she hasn't asked me for anything; that's already a week ago; she's going to be needing something! she better not ask me for too much though; it's beginning to mount up, all this money.

Dear Friend,
    On returning home, I learned . . .

This is her most recent letter, the day before yesterday.

. . . on returning home I learned you have been to see me; but I didn't have the good fortune to be in. To have more chance of seeing me, come tomorrow (Sunday) at one or half past. I shall be at home. Until tomorrow and with best wishes. Léa

I did indeed go and see her yesterday at one; she was really charming, all smiles, even tender; and what the devil got into me? one moment when she was in my arms, I held her too, too passionately; she looked at me; I murmured 'Léa' with exaggerated tenderness; am I not in sufficient control of myself to behave as I wish to behave? Léa seemed astonished, not annoyed, astonished; slightly mocking, perhaps; why then does she turn all tender like that? it's her fault; she's so pretty, and such a temptress, in the thin, billowing fabrics she wears; otherwise black is what suits her best for a dress, which her impassive breast swells . . . But it's nearly half past nine; it's time to be going. I haven't written down what I was planning to say; totally useless; I'll remember; anyway I've the note of a month ago. Up you get; my hat; in my coat pocket, my gloves. All in order? the letters in the drawer. Before leaving, have to reread this note:

Once in her bedroom. You don't believe I love you? . . . I desired you madly; let that be my excuse . . . Forgive . . . I could stay here tonight . . . I give you back your body . . . Goodbye.

Goodbye, goodbye, let's leave. The gas will be lit on the stairs; I open the door; I snuff out the candles; there; don't let's bump into anything; the door closed; down we go; my gloves; they're clean, yes, perfectly respectable. I'll remember, damn it, I'll easily remember what I have to say to Léa; nothing easier, more natural; she will understand at last why I give up the rights I have over her, and how I love her, and why I do not take her all ... I could stay here tonight, but, my friend, I am leaving ... She will understand; nothing more natural or simpler ... I'll remember ... You don't believe I love you ... I desired you madly ... All right ... I give you back your body ...

vi Up the dark street, the double row of gas-lamps seeming smaller and smaller; no passers-by in the street; the pavement resounding, pale under the pallor of the clear sky and the moon; in the background, the moon in the sky; the pale, elongated crescent of the pale moon; and on each side, the houses ever the same; silent, tall, with high, darkened windows and doors with iron fastenings, the houses; people in these houses? no, silence; silently, I go my solitary way along the houses; I walk on; I go by; to the left, the Rue de Naples; garden walls; the dark leaves on the grey of the walls; over there, way over there, more light, Boulevard Malesherbes, red and yellow lights, carriages, carriages and proud horses; still, through the streets, in a still calm, carriages, between the pavements with their rushing crowds; here, the masonry of a new house, the dull, plaster-coated scaffolding; you can hardly see the newly erected stonework being built; I'd like to climb these masts, up to that far-off roof; from there Paris and its sounds must stretch far into the distance; a man is coming down the street; a working man; here he comes; what loneliness, what pitiful loneliness, far from the agitation of life! and this is the end of the street; Rue Monceau now; more of these tall, majestic houses, and the gas shedding its yellow light; what's in this doorway? ... ah! a man; the concierge from this house; he's smoking his pipe, watching the passers-by; nobody going by; only me; and this fat, old concierge, what's he doing looking at loneliness? here I am in the next street; it suddenly narrows, becomes quite narrow; old houses, whitewashed walls; on the pavement, children, urchins, sitting silently on the ground; and the Rue du Rocher, and so to the boulevard; lights and noise there; movement; rows of gas-lamps, to the right and left; and at an angle, to the left, a carriage under the trees; a group of workmen; the crowded tram sounding its horn, two dogs on the back platform; lighted windows in the houses; that café opposite with its bright white curtains; near me, the din of an omnibus; a young girl with pink cheeks dressed in dark blue; the crowd; the boulevard; I'm going to cross this space and go there; I'm going to be with those people; so I'm going to be over there, the same me, still the same, there and no longer here, and still me; above and in front of the Butte; lights under the clear sky; to the right, along the wall, the reservoir wall; I don't know any of these people; can they see me? who do they think I am? shouts of children playing; massive wheels on the cobble-stones; slow horses; stairways; the sky dimmed by thicker growing trees; my steps monotonously on the asphalt; the song of a barrel-organ, a dance tune, a sort of waltz, the rhythm of a slow waltz ... ♪♪♪ where's the barrel-organ? somewhere in the background, I can hear its soft, piercing voice ... 'love you more than my turkey-cocks' ... a song that goes on and on and begins again ... ♪♪♪ ... the calm of a voice singing out, in a tranquil landscape, in a calm, loving heart, and the restrained desire of a voice beginning to sing; and

another voice answering, the same and yet higher, rising,
calm and thin, rising in desire; and rising again; the
growth of desire; still in the simple setting and in these
simple hearts, the monotonous alternating voices, calmly
rising, of sweet distress; the simple sweet song that swells
and the simple rhythm; between the cool foliage, among
the muted tones of banal sounds swell, in a shrill voice,
the piercing gentle song, the monotonous litany, the
steady rhythm of slow dances; and love rises ... In
unspoiled fields, more than I love them I love you,
friend; here are the pale lovely fields and the wandering,
scattered flocks; I love you more; the flocks are beautiful
when they bleat in the cool foliage, flocks and herds of
dear beasts; I love you more; the fields I dream of are
dear to me; but I love you more, my love, in your clear
eyes; the rows of lights stretch out, and the tree-trunks; I
love you more in your songs; rivers flow with the
shadows, an evening sky, far-off noises; and the lament-
ing voice is further away, the simple voice and its rhythm
fade into the distance; the religious chant fades away; yet
songs, and still songs, and I love you more; cool land-
scapes of night, the trees stretching in rows, and the steps
of the passers-by; movement all round; innumerable
words, tones, mild air, cooler; I shall go into the wood
bordering the mountains; near the meadows, under the
fir-trees; that will be the precious warmth of beloved
nights; we shall all dwell in these lands; oh! what a lovely
time, far from Paris, during those long weeks! but when
will those times come? ... The noises are getting louder;
this is Place Clichy; hurry up; long, dismal walls, without
a break; deeper shadow on the roadway; street girls now,
three street girls talking; they don't notice me; one very
young and frail, with shameless eyes, and what lips! in a
room, bare, indistinct, high-ceilinged, bare and grey, in
the smoky candle light, in the somnolence of the tumult
of the swarming street; yes, a narrow, high-ceilinged
room, and the mean bed, the table, the chair, the grey

walls, and the beast kneeling in the bed, and the lascivious lips, swelling and swelling again while the beast groans and pants for breath ... Here she is, that girl; she is chatting; all three, on the pavement, oblivious to people walking by; I've my lecture tomorrow, boring school, and the exam in three months; I'll pass; so say goodbye to freedom every day, and hello to the responsibility of a job; come on; street girls everywhere now; the café; young people going; a gent who looks like my tailor; what if I met some friend; certainly is better to be on one's own, walking at liberty on a fine evening, with nothing in view, along the streets; the shadow of the foliage ripples on the road, there is a freshness in the air, the pavements gleam white and dry; a group of girls over there, very tall, straight, slim, with seductive ways; over there children; the house fronts glitter; the moon is hidden; there is a rustling, all around; of what? of confused, fragmented, blended sounds, a rustling ... good old April! what a lovely, lovely evening, free like this, thoughtless, on my own like this.

vii But here I am Rue Stévens, in front of Léa's house; this is the hallway all right, the staircase; the winding stairs; the second floor at last; is that it? yes, there of course; let's ring; my button-boots are clean, my tie straight, my moustache properly tweaked up; I have a lot to say to her, a lot I must say to her; she's obviously just come in; she'll be wearing her black cashmere dress; I'm a fool not ringing; if she saw me; I ring; the sound of footsteps inside; the door opens; it's Marie.

'Is Mademoiselle d'Arsay at home?'

'Yes, sir, come in.'

I go in.

'I'll tell mademoiselle you're here.'

She's nice, Marie. This little sitting-room, dear Léa's little sitting-room; let's sit in this chair, near the window; what a pretty flower arrangement! that's the bunch of lilacs I sent her; the mirror; my dress is absolutely in order; I'm quite presentable; not too bad, indeed; Léa likes men with short hair, like mine, provided it's dark . . . Léa . . .

'Hello,' in her exquisite voice.

And her knowingly feminine smile, her kindly mocking eyes, her fairy smile; hello, in her deliciously exquisite voice; and her hair fluttering on her brow, she's here, pretty Léa; no, I mustn't kiss her hand; I'd make myself ridiculous; let's greet her simply:

'How are you, dear?'

'Very well.'

She's wearing her black satin dress. We sit down on the couch, Léa to the left; she has lolled back on the cushions, she's looking at me; she's friendly this evening.

'Well,' she asks me, 'what have you got to say to me?'

I've nothing to say to her, except, yes; why did she write and tell me not to go to the theatre?

'It's a real pity I couldn't fetch you at the theatre.'

'There was no other way; I had to talk to the manager after the play, and sometimes you see him at once, at others you wait for him all evening; he doesn't put himself out, turns up at nine, ten o'clock.'

Don't let's insist; she's certainly making this story up.

'You waited a long time today.'

'Quite a long time; I only got back ten minutes ago; when I came off stage I went to the manager's office; Blanche Fannie was there; she wanted to see the manager before going to get dressed; you know she only appears in the second act; we were so bored in that pokey place! There's only enough room for two chairs; Blanche on her own took up all the room; she's so awfully fat.'

'I can't understand why they still have her playing breeches roles; she's not getting any younger.'

'She's not old; what age do you think she is?'

'. . .'

'She can't be very old; let's see; how old is she? forty?'

Funny girl, Léa, twenty years old and with the childishly serious airs of a coquettish little girl!

'We're going out for a ride, aren't we?' I say to her.

'Oh! I'm tired; I'm worn out; I'm sleepy.'

'What's the matter then?'

'I'm tired.'

'Waiting at the theatre got on your nerves.'

'Oh, it's not that.'

'You were stuck on a chair there, and you can usually never sit still; you can't stay put for two seconds.'

'It's all very well making fun of me, when I haven't moved from this spot for the last quarter of an hour.'

I'm teasing her.

'Whether you move or not, you're always adorable.'

'. . . Charming! . . .'

She never appreciates my witty sallies; there's no way one can joke with women, so what can one say; she stands up; slowly she goes to the window; and her slender, well-rounded body sways; in her neck, the blonde wisps of hair; she draws the curtains aside; she looks out. Indolently one sinks into this couch! and, all around, the pallid light of the white walls and the mirrors. She:

'It's fine tonight; it would perhaps do me good to go out for a while . . .'

'Do you want to then?'

There, now she's agreeing; don't let's look triumphant though; she sits down on the piano; we remain silent. At the restaurant, this evening, the strange man, the lawyer type. One-handed, Léa's thumbing through a pile of scores, with the hand she has on the piano. I'll have to say something; she's going to get bored, she's so frightened of our saying nothing; I absolutely must say something. Here we are face to face; this can't go on; I'd be ridiculous; oh, yes! her problems with that awful mother of hers . . .

'You've come to an arrangement with your mother?'

'Not at all.'

She doesn't seem to want to talk of these things; I was wrong to bring them up; what can I say to her then?

'It is impossible,' she continues, 'to come to an arrangement with her; she would like me to follow her every whim; you can understand that it makes life unbearable.'

'Why do you put up with it?'

'Because I can't do otherwise.'

'What? If your mother bothers you, tell her . . .'

'Oh! yes! she'd make a fine fuss!'

'But you're in your own home.'

'No, I'm not in my own home; that's the trouble; the apartment is rented in her name; the furniture, everything is hers . . . And I'm the one who pays for everything.'

She leans against the piano. I suspected the apartment was her mother's; what's to be done? nothing. Casually she's walking over to this couch; on which she sits; her skirts spread out; on the cushions her sad-looking, pretty head; she raises her arms above her head.

'What a life! What a life! I'm tempted to give everything up.'

'What do you say, my friend?'

'I'd be happier looking after turkeys in Brittany. If my father knew I worked in a theatre!'

'Do you want to go and look after turkeys in Brittany?'

'I wouldn't have to worry myself sick any more; I'd be back with my father's family again; you've no idea what sort of life I lead.'

I go to her; I sit next to her; I take her hand. 'Please my poor dear don't talk like that; what ideas you've got in your head; you know very well I truly love you; why don't you let me take you away somewhere, for us to be together; tell me why not.'

'Come now,' she replies sadly, sweetly, 'come now, you're mad.'

'In what way mad, my friend?'

I look into her eyes; she is leaning back on the cushions; the glow from the candles lights up our faces; sweetly, sadly, she stretches out, pale; I look at her; I'm holding her hands. Smiling she says:

'What extraordinarily long eyelashes you have.'

Still smiling, she looks at me.

'You're a very unhappy little woman.'

She shuts her eyes.

'Oh! how I'd like to be rid of everything! if only there were a way of ending it all, in one go, without suffering, something with instant effect; to go fast asleep, since one is only happy asleep.'

What can I say to her? I can't laugh, nor take her too seriously either; it's embarrassing. She is half stretched out near me, motionless, more or less in a doze.

'Well, go to sleep, mademoiselle.'

I clasp her arms; her eyes are still closed; gently I draw her arms towards me; she does not resist; her delicate head leans back; her naughty, treacherous head, that uses me so insolently; I gently lean back on the cushions; and I draw her breast against me; her breast is against mine; her head is on my shoulder; my arms encircle her waist; she is resting against me; something on my cheek, on my neck, wisps of her hair fluttering; she doesn't move; all along my body, her body; I can feel her; softly I hug her soft, silky hips and her bosom.

'Go to sleep, mademoiselle?'

And, in a very low voice, her eyes closed, in a soft breath, a very low voice, she says:

'Yes.'

The poor, charming, tender little thing lets herself be enlaced by my arms; she rests her dear body against mine; her head rises delicately from her dress as she lies stretched out; and those are her breasts; those her arms, and her tiny hands, this is her neck, and in the whiteness of her neck the fine gold hair escaping; her slim waist, and her ample hips, in the embrace of the black satin; there, the darling tip of her foot; and slowly her bodice swells in long, regular breaths; the buttons on the bodice quiver; the froth of the black lace faintly ripples on her bosom; a brighter light, from the candles, shimmers on her left breast; and womanly life is at work, at work in this incessant movement of the two breasts; quite motionless, her body seems to modulate, imperceptibly; her rounded arms, her breast moving and her neck, her slim waist, her high hips curve in blurred contours, finest grace of delicately softened flesh and fleeting forms, subdued; meanwhile her young face is in repose, and her breath comes from her half-opened lips ... The candles on the mantlepiece burn; their flames shoot up, paling to white, blueish, lighter; all around, the dim shade of the dark greenery, the dim confusion of hand-painted china, and beyond it, the dim light of the mirror and the subdued reflections. The delightful ball I was at this winter, the drawing-room full of flowers and greenery, unobtrusively lit, when the two young girls went by, the pale-skinned English girls! here the warm profusion of things, and my loved one; the warmth little by little from her motionless body; along her body, in my body which she brushes up against, a mounting warmth; only, if she is so unhappy, doesn't she want to change her life? how sweetly soft this warmth, and what perfume emanates from her body! what perfume is it? a blend of subtle, penetrating scents; she herself has mixed their essence; and this scent emanates from all her flesh, from her clothes; it wafts up from her tied-back hair, from her lips too; the poor dear is asleep in my friendly arms; and I am drunk on her scent; this mingled, subtle, intimate scent she has perfumed her body with, is mingled with the very scent of her body, and it is her body's perfume I can sense in the deep essence of the mingling of flowers; yes, her woman's being; and the profound mystery of her sex in love; lecherously, daemonically, when virile mastery of fleshly impulse surrenders to a kiss, thus the terrible, bitter, blanching ecstasy rises ... To possess such joy! ... She moves her head, turns slightly; have I been holding her too tightly? ... She is speaking to me, half-sleeping:

'What is it? I'm tired, what time is it?'

'Not late yet, lie still.'

There, she's quiet again, so delicately pretty, so youthfully flirtatious; what an unhappy life she leads, the one I love needs such love to sweeten her bitterness; poor dear who's going to know bad times at only twenty ... together, rather sleep like this, in oblivion both of us, together, she feels the security of my faith. I am under her spell; and amid the things which are, together, both of us, happily ... so we'll go out together this evening, in the shadows, while music is playing in the distance ... 'you love me' ... 'and you, you love me' ... yes! don't let's say 'I love you' any more, but 'you love me' and 'you love me' and let us kiss ... she sleeps; I feel sleep coming over me; I half close my eyes ... there ... her body; her breast swells and swells; and the sweet scent mingled ... fine April night ... in a while we'll go for a ride ... the cool air ... we're going to leave ... in a while ... the two candles ... there ... along the boulevards ... 'love y' more than m' sheep' ... love y' more ... that girl, slender, with the brazen look, red lips ... the bedroom, the tall mantlepiece ... the room my father ... all three sitting, my father, my mother ... myself ... why is my mother pale? she's looking at me ... we're going to dine, yes, in the grove ... the maid ... bring the table ... Léa

... she is setting the table ... my father ... the concierge ... a letter ... from her? ... thank you ... a
ripple, a rumour, the clouds lifting – and you, eternally
the only one, the original loved one, Antonia ... everything shimmers ... you're mocking ... the gas-lamps
stretching into infinity ... night ... cold and icy night;
... terrible fear!!! what? I'm being pushed; it's – they're
tearing at me, killing me ... Nothing, it's nothing ...
the room ... Léa ... good heavens ... had I fallen
asleep?

'Congratulations, my dear ...' It's Léa ... 'Have
you slept well?' It's Léa on her feet, and laughing: 'Are
you feeling a bit better?'

'And what about you, my dear?'

Laughing, she turns; she walks up and down in the
sitting-room ... She obviously woke up just now, she
saw me dozing off, she suddenly pulled away from me
... Aren't I completely ridiculous? what can I do about
it? What is she thinking? I get up and go and sit on the
piano stool; she's looking in the mirror opposite; speaks
cheerfully:

'So didn't you go to bed yesterday?'

'Indeed I did, mademoiselle, and I slept well too.
Your charm a moment ago hypnotized me ...'

'We'll go out, if you like; it's such lovely weather;
we'll go for an hour's drive to the Champs-Élysées; does
that suit you?'

'It fills me with joy.'

'And I hope you won't fall asleep.'

'No; you'll tell me stories.'

'That's right; I'll keep you happy; you'll tell me the
programme.'

'Don't be unkind.'

God knows that you have to drag the words out of her
some days.

'I'm going to put my hat on.'

She comes towards me; she smiles and I can see her

white teeth; her dewy eyes shine; her lips are all pink, half open; all pink with a little tiny triangle where her white teeth show through; the sweet melancholy of your look, mademoiselle; the white and rosy dimples on your cheeks; your brow bent in graceful melancholy; and there, your wide eyes looking at me.

'My poor dear friend, how I'd like you to be happy!'

I take her arms, her head on my neck, her hair; around my waist her arms; without her noticing I kiss her hair; that's how to be happy; she's sweet, my loved one, she's beautiful and she's tender; she's kind, my love, and it's enchanting to love her! ... She raises her head; astonished, she looks at me, attentively; she raises her hand; signs to me to be quiet; what? she listens; tenderly she asks me:

'What's the matter?'

'What?'

'Are you unwell?'

'No ...'

'Something wrong with your heart?'

She puts her hand to my breast, to the left, she's listening; my heart is indeed beating faster.

'Are you sure?' she asks once again.

'No; it's nothing; I swear to you; it's that you're there; so ...'

And she, softly:

'You're just a child.'

So softly she says it to me, 'You're just a child'; in such a tranquil tone, and so sincerely; her smiling eyes go serious, while she's telling me, 'you're just a child', and with such deep emotion, so feminine and profound, she tells me I'm a child, and retreats, retreats, lovely and gracious.

'Just wait a minute, dear.'

There she is at the door; I reply yes; she goes through the door.

'I'll put my hat on and I'll be back.'

The door has been left ajar slightly; I sit down; I wait; I busy myself waiting, waiting for her.

'I'll just tell Marie to go and fetch a carriage ... Marie!'

'Do you want me to go?'

'No; Marie will go.'

She's speaking to Marie in the bedroom; what's she saying to her? I can't hear; and I can't do anything here; I've nothing to do; tomorrow I'm having lunch with de Rivare; at eleven; in a boulevard café no doubt; when one has been to bed late, it's sometimes somewhat difficult to be at an appointment for eleven or half past ten; the surest means of getting up would be not to go to bed at home; here, for example; because, all in all, why am I here? . . .

'Here I am.'

Léa at the door, wearing her red velvet hat; with gravity, for fun; so, I bow; she curtsies to me in return; outside, the rumbling of a carriage.

'The carriage,' she says; 'let's go down.'

'You're not forgetting anything, Léa?'

'No, my coat's here.'

'Let me have it . . . thank you.'

'Let's go.'

We leave; the soft, warm, furry coat against my arm.

'And your gloves? You've only got one.'

'I was forgetting the other one; it's on the piano; fetch it.'

I was quite certain that she would forget something, I'd told her so.

'Here.'

Marie coming in:

'The carriage is at the door, mademoiselle.'

'I'll be back in an hour, make a bit of fire in the bedroom.'

Must be careful to say goodnight to Marie; Léa goes down, the black satin of her dress bunches up; she goes

down; I follow her; with each step her shoulders are
thrown back; the red feather of the hat on her head sways
to one side; jerks up, sways; holding herself very straight
the young woman goes down; slowly she buttons the long
black glove on her left hand; she goes down each step
with measured tread, still holding herself straight; and
there's the street, a pale reddish glow; and the carriage, a
black mass blocking out the light.

'Aren't you frightened,' I say, 'of catching cold in an
open carriage?'

'No; it's mild out.'

'Are you getting in?'

She gets in. I get in.

'Be careful not to sit on my dress.'

That would mean a lasting grudge against me.

'Shall we go by the Arc-de-l'Étoile?'

'Yes.'

'Cabbie, go along the boulevard to the Arc-de-
l'Etoile.'

I sit down; the carriage moves off; there's Léa grave
and serious like a resident member of the Théâtre-
Français.

viii ••• The carriage going through the streets ...
one in the limitless mass of lives, thus I go
on my way henceforth, for ever one among the others; so
have been created in me the day, the Here and Now, the
time, the individual life; a soul soaring to dreams of
kissing, that is it; the day is a dream of woman; touching
a woman's flesh is my Here and Now; my time is a
woman I draw close to; and here is the course of my life,
this girl this evening ... And they hum with life, the
streets, the boulevards, the muffled noises, the movement of the carriage, its jolting, the wheels over the

cobbles, the bright evening, the two of us sitting in the carriage, the noise and the jolting in the movement, the things streaming past, the delicious night . . .

'Isn't it,' Léa says, 'a really poetic and quite delicious night?'

On leaving, she told, Léa told her chambermaid she would be back in an hour and that she wanted a fire; I'll take her home and we'll go back up together; there's more greenery on this boulevard; I'll go back up with her, I'll stay a quarter of an hour, and I'll leave her, since I must; how pretty, there, half-reclining in the carriage! alternately her face is in the light and shade, alternately in the dim shadow and in the pallor of the lights while the carriage moves along; near the gas-lamps there is indeed bright light, then, after the lamps, a darkening; again; the gaslight to the right is burning more brightly; her lovely white face, mat white, ivory white, white of snow in darkness, in the black that enfolds her, more luminous under the lights, becoming subdued in the shadows, then flaring out again; while over the even wood roadway our carriage goes on its way; gently, between the folds of her dress, I take her hand; she withdraws it ever so slightly; and I say to her:

'Your face in this shadow harmonizes exquisitely with the lights.'

'Really? Do you think so?'

She replies in a mocking tone, in a bored, unkind tone; why is she being like this? gently I go on:

'Yes, I do, Léa; don't you want me to tell you?'

'Yes, I like compliments very much.'

Have to tell her off for using this word.

'Oh? Léa! compliments!'

We fall silent; people are passing by; continually the cabman cracks his long whip which zigzags in the air; I have released Léa's hands; she is often unpleasant when we're out together, she's no doubt frightened of not behaving properly; no way of speaking to her then, except by standing absolutely on ceremony; here's the reservoir wall; just a short while ago I was going by there on my own; now with Léa; she's going to start looking miserable; yet I can't risk saying anything to annoy her. Its black shape pierced by two lights, a tram comes towards us.

Léa: 'Are you going to the Press Fair on Saturday?'

'At the Continental Hotel?'

'Yes.'

'I don't know; maybe; what about you?'

'I've been invited to be a salesgirl.'

'Ah!'

'Lucie Harel's running a boutique, like the novelty shops; there'll be every possible thing for sale.'

'I've heard about it; that'll be lovely; you'll have a stall to yourself?'

'Yes.'

'I'll go then.'

I'll not get away with less than a hundred francs. Am I going to be able to find an excuse for staying at home? Léa would never forgive me; what if the excuse was a good one though? I couldn't say I was ill; I'd have to make out it was something serious; they're such a bother, these receptions; I'll take Chavainne along with me.

'You'll be in costume?'

'Yes, as a soubrette.'

'Bravo.'

'I'm going to have my costume from the pantomine altered. I'll put different pleats on the bodice as they weren't suitable anyway . . .'

Yes, her soubrette's costume, pink satin, with the lace pinafore, short skirt . . .

'I'll fit a belt with the same sort of satin on it and have ribbons put on the sleeves; all that will improve the costume; I'll try to get another pinafore as well, a pinafore that will look really good, you'll see.'

'Another pinafore?'

'I've used the lace from the old one; it wasn't right; don't you think it would be all right with Valenciennes lace?'

'Certainly would.'

She is pleased with her idea; would she, by any chance, be wanting to ask me . . .

'And,' she resumes, 'it isn't very expensive either; you can buy Valencienne at fifteen francs a yard and three yards of insert-lace will easily be enough.'

That's that; I'll pay for her lace; but I won't go to the Fair.

'You've a good idea there, Léa; if all you need is that bit of lace, and if I can help you out, please . . .'

'Thank you; I'd appreciate that.'

Another four or five louis; fifteen francs a yard will become at least twenty or thirty; but I'll be damned if I go anywhere near the place on Saturday; let's talk to her about something else; and not appear to be put out.

'Your pantomine costume was very pretty; it will still be very fetching.'

'It will, won't it?'

'Besides there are always the right sort of people at a Fair.'

'Yes.'

'Do you know if there'll be a lot of people?'

'I've no idea.'

'Ah!'

'How should I know?'

'You might have heard. There won't be any other boutiques apart from Lucie Harel's?'

'That one will be very big, you know.'

'It's an amusing idea setting up a novelty shop; I'm sure it'll be a great success . . .'

She hardly bothers to reply; her look of indifference again; what can I say to her?

'I believe it's not been done before.'

She is silent; she's even half-closed her eyes.

'You'll be really delightful in that costume; only you mustn't sell your goods at exhorbitant prices. Otherwise what on earth would you sell? You mustn't be too friendly either, you know I'll be jealous.'

She gives a faint mocking smile. My jokes create a frosty silence. Aren't we going back soon?

'It's beginning to turn cold,' says Léa.

She's pretending she hasn't heard what I'm saying.

'You're cold, Léa! Do you want us to go back?'

'No; not yet.'

Dark trees, railings, gleams of blue; that's Parc Monceau; behind the railings, under the trees, pathways; it would be pleasant to walk there; would, by any chance, Léa want to?

'Léa, would you like us to get out and walk for a while? if you're cold . . .'

'No; I'm not cold; let's stay in the carriage.'

Too bad; she definitely doesn't want to say or do anything; it's a cool evening; she's going to catch cold.

'Léa, please put your coat on.'

She sits up; she stretches an arm out; I help her into her coat; she seems to resign herself, as if I were doing her violence. Well, isn't that better for her now? so pretty in her furs; her neck is muffled up in the furs; with her black-gloved hands protruding from the furs; she could be so sweet if she wanted to be! she's lovely, sitting still, deep in her furs, her white face seeming to emerge from among the velvets, silks and furs; if only the Desrieux could see her! it would be funny if some friend were to go by; nothing would be better for me in the Desrieux' eyes than to be seen with her; they're really very fashionable, but why have they been so obstinate over square-toed shoes? and de Rivare, if he met me, how amazed he'd be! tomorrow he'd make fun of me over lunch while liberally helping himself to good wine; he'd be so jealous and he'd admire me so much; I'll have to invite him to dinner one evening; we'll go to the 'Cirque'; no, I'll take him to the

Nouveautés; so I'll be able to tell him more about my affair with Léa. Must speak to Léa a bit though; when she doesn't say anything, I don't know what to say to her; the same things that interest her one day bore her the next; she's more temperamental than any woman I know; what shall I talk to her about? about her play? it's a bore; but it's something to talk about.

'Do you know if your rehearsals are beginning soon?'

'I don't think so.'

'Why's that?'

'The play's still bringing in money every evening.'

'You know what the new play is?'

'I've not the slightest idea.'

'You won't be on stage before Act III, you told me?'

'I much prefer to be on stage in only one act.'

'Why's that?'

'I can't understand why one wants to be on stage in every act when one hasn't a leading role. Last year little Manuela was a success with her song in the last act; but look at Darvilly who is much more talented and much prettier than Manuela; her acting this year proves it; it's true that the play's stupid! but Darvilly, who's on stage for half the play, goes unnoticed.'

'It's her own fault, she isn't very good.'

'She's a very good actress, she has a very good voice and she's better than all your walk-ons; those girls finish up by being ridiculous; you're always talking about artists, about singing, about art, and when you see someone who can act, you don't even notice.'

Better stop her with a compliment.

'But it seems to me that the success you have every evening proves the opposite.'

She goes silent; she isn't annoyed; those are the sort of compliments that touch her where it matters and are always well received.

'Just look,' says Léa, pointing, 'that woman in the light-coloured dress on the other side of the boulevard;

what an idea to go out dressed like that at this time of year!'

On the opposite side of the boulevard an elegantly turned out lady in a pale-coloured dress.

'It's strange, admittedly; still, the dress isn't bad.'

'But at this time of year!'

She's looking at me, half-smiling, with an astonished expression.

'It's true that it's not usual.'

'Isn't that so?'

Poor Léa, she can't understand that I'm making fun of her and that she's being ridiculous; she has moments of astonishment and indignation with so little motivation; this afternoon she couldn't get over the story about Jacques.

'There's hardly anyone out this evening,' she says.

'Even so, it's a fine night.'

'Yes, but rather cool.'

'I'm sure you're cold; why won't you go back?'

'No, I'm not cold.'

She's being obstinate; she's cold; she doesn't want to admit it; women are strange creatures! there is certainly more of a chill in the air; a stronger breeze rustles through the foliage; here's the Place des Ternes already; if we go as far as the Champs-Élysées, we won't be back before midnight or one o'clock.

'It's cold,' says Léa; 'let's go back, if you wish.'

At last.

'Cabby, we're going back; Rue Stévens, No 14.'

The cabman stops; the carriage turns; the horse, reined back, stiffens; off we go; at a trot again; the horse's trot and the shaking inside the carriage, at the same time; again the monotonous forward movement; continually the whip cracks; a carriage near us; goes past us; why are we going so slowly? two very old people on the pavement; the sound of the wheels; the slight jolting; the Parc Monceau again, the rotunda; we'll be there in a quarter of an hour; what's Léa going to say to me? I'll go up with her; I must go up with her; I'll go up into her bedroom with her; will she let me? the other day she wanted me to leave at once; yes, but usually I wait until she begins undressing; when the carriage arrives at her door, I'll have to take the precaution of asking to accompany her; she'll alight from the carriage first; since she's on the right, she'll be on the pavement side; she'll at least allow me to take her back into her room; so what's she going to say to me? will she at last let me stay? no, that's not very likely; besides I wouldn't want to; a quarter of an hour in her room while she's taking off her hat and coat; that will be perfect; if she wanted me to stay though! she must think she's going to have to one day or another, at least once; this evening she seems to have arranged to be free; supposing it was this evening! supposing it wasn't quite this evening! she'll have to make her mind up; she can't imagine I want to be a platonic lover for ever; I have never, all things considered, stated any such intention; she mustn't imagine either, that she's reduced me to enduring everything without anything in return; what confusion! We're nearing the long line of lights; more carriages; it's Boulevard Malesherbes; our carriage moves forward; Léa and I; why would she want me today rather than yesterday? she has managed politely to send me on my way for so long now; but I didn't ask for anything, I didn't seem to asking for anything; so how could she have asked me of her own accord? that's what would be wonderful, for her, her to want to, one day! and here she is sitting motionless beside me; how distant is hope! motionless, indifferent and ordinary-looking, here she is; she's staring vaguely in front of her; she's hiding her hands under her coat; her eyes gaze casually ahead; effortlessly we advance in the still night; the high, half-dim houses have windows lit with red; to the left, the trees, the regular trot of the horse on the roadway; the grey-white horse with its regular trot; here, and she, silent and motionless, in a dream, no doubt, she, indifferent, ordinary, motionless and loveless; when will the day come when she will give herself to me, if here she is again loveless, woman's white form! but couldn't there be in the depths of this soul, humble, unbeknown, a tiny scrap of ordinary friendship growing; my constant devotion cannot but have touched her; love filters into the heart that is loved; desire appeals and attracts; it's a force of attraction, loving; why couldn't affection have been born in the deepest part of her being, ready to grow, to become love? If she's without words or eyes for me today, it's because friendship would seem to take root far from lips and looks, but at the bottom of her heart; let's delude ourselves with my most illusory wish; some day she'd love me, the girl sitting there and whose body is by my side, so delicate, the little girl who is unconcernedly sinking back near me, in the cool night, in a dream of not thinking, under the bright, starlit sky. By obscure ways, dim ways, on horizons, in the waving movement of our dream waltz and under the bass harmony's rumble of wheels in the streets, the continuo movement of the happy carriage in which the two of us ride ... Lovingly I speak to my Léa, simply for the words to rise in the evening air, and I speak:

'Léa dear, what are you dreaming of?'

She turns her gaze on me, pale, as if without thought; she is silent; the carriage jolts over the cobbles; once more Léa is looking in front of her, mute, she is not dreaming, not thinking; what are you dreaming of? nothing; what are you dreaming of? I don't know; what are you dreaming of? I can't; what and what are you dreaming of? of nothing, I can't, I don't know, I neither dream nor think; I will not give you the dream, and you will forever be impassive and loveless; she's staring vaguely in front of her; the bright sky, already less bright, still shines; the carriage floats in the mass of trees; and the grey outline of the old, bent-backed cabman rises high above us; and here Léa's voice can be heard:

'I only hope Marie hasn't forgotten the fire?'

'You're cold, Léa.'

'A little.'

'Sit closer to me.'

She squeezes lightly against me and, inclining her head, she smiles.

'That's right,' I say, 'you'll warm up like that.'

'On one side I will.'

'Come closer then.'

'Be quiet, will you!'

She's gently scolding me; we are out of doors; have to behave; yes, people are looking at us; who's this elegant gentleman coming in the opposite direction, with his eyes fixed on us? why is this gentleman looking at us? he still is; all said and done, it's a nuisance; he's going right by the carriage; let's see if he turns round; what did he want with us? did Léa see him? she hasn't been pretending; that was a man who knows Léa; I'm sure he's annoyed; the man's jealous of me; no, it's not everyone who can be out in a carriage at midnight with Léa d'Arsay; is he still to be seen? yes, over there; ah! he's turning round; off with you friend, you can wait under the elm-tree.

'Here we are ... Place Blanche, Léa; we'll soon be back at your house.'

Crack goes the whip in the air; the carriage advances over the cobbles.

'Look there, Léa, they seem to be knocking that house down.'

'What's that house? a café?'

But we're nearly there ... at your house, I said; her house; the decisive moment then? ... it's ridiculous getting all worked up in this way, for no reason; I have the prettiest of young women by my side; I've just been out with her; could I wish for anything better? the gent just now must have been furious; I'm the most fortunate of men ... oh, fatal, fatal anxiety; I'll go mad; aren't I sure of being happy, oughtn't I to be? ... Place Pigalle already; and this cabman speeding along; *passage* Stévens; in a minute, her door; my God, my God, what's she going to say to me? what's she going to do? what am I going to do! the cabman slows down, turns; she's going to send me away again; her house, her room ... the carriage stops; Léa gets up, gets out; it's terrible, this distress; my poor dear, will she finally want to? Léa! she's got out ... what? ...

'Aren't you going to pay the cabman then?'

I'm not paying the cabman, it's true; sorry; two francs fifty; there ... Léa rings the door bell ... I'm done for; oh! I beg you ...

'May I accompany you?'

'If you wish.'

That's a bit of luck ... the carriage is going ... damn it, let's go up ... what time is it? it's not midnight, we've time; when I come home late, my concierge keeps me waiting for a quarter of an hour on end at the door; it's intolerable.

ix Léa precedes me up the stairs; we go up; on the pale walls, our shadows; how much money do I have on me? I had fifty francs in my card-case; in my pocket four louis; that comes to, fifty and eighty, one hundred and thirty francs; I've more money at home; no matter, the end of the month will be difficult; Léa's got to be reasonable; for the moment, let's go up; we're there; the open door; Marie.

'Good evening, Marie.'

'Good evening, sir ...'

Léa: 'You haven't forgotten the fire, Marie?'

'No, mademoiselle, if mademoiselle would like to go to her room ...'

At the end of the passage, the dressing-room door;

beyond that, the bedroom; casually Léa moves forward, with her sweetly casualness, should I follow her? wait till she tells me to? she would forget; but what if she sends me away? too bad, it would be too stupid to stay in the passage; I go in; she can scold me if she wants; and I go through the dressing-room, the bedroom door; in the bedroom the wood fire is glowing; a glow from the night-light from the ceiling too; and, on the little table, two candles; Léa is sitting, by the fire; the white alabaster glow of the dimmed light, and the bright red of the fire running, quivering incessantly over the logs; near it in an armchair, the young woman; she catches the warmth, still wearing her hat and gloves, motionless, in shadow; and the same shooting flame shines from the two candles; the fire reflects, golden, dark on her dress; the lovely, soft warmth.

'You were cold, weren't you, Léa?'

She didn't want to come back in, the stubborn girl.

'You ought to take your hat and coat off.'

She remains in front of the fire, in the armchair; is she insisting on being too warm now? but she gets up, swiftly and sharply up; and her voice comes quickly:

'Yes, it's too hot in here.'

She takes off her hat, throws it on the bed; she pushes her hair back into place; she pulls off her gloves, casts them on the bed; I lean against the mantlepiece; she is unbuttoning her coat; I go and help her.

'No thank you, Marie will do it.'

Marie helps her; I go back to the fireplace; Marie takes the coat; the fire is warming my calves; Léa turns round, she smiles.

'Well then, what are you doing with your hat in your hand and your coat buttoned up?'

What does she want? does she want me to take my coat off? why? to stay? could it be possible? I've replied in a few words . . . there she is still smiling . . .

'If you allow me . . .' I was saying.

And slowly she turns, slowly, her hips swaying, towards the wardrobe with the mirror, opposite the fire-place; near the window, on a chair, I put my hat, my coat; my hat on my coat. Léa in front of the wardrobe mirror, rearranges the ruffles of her bodice on her breast, and the black ribbon round her neck; I am standing against the wall, next to the curtain drawn over the window; in the mirror I see her sweet face and pretty looks, this body alternately shown off and hidden by the clothes; fashion is wonderful nowadays, able alternately to hide and display a woman's form. Moving with feline grace, tossing her hair from the matt skin of her brow, she comes towards me; was I thinking of it? would she like to this evening? she has told me to put down my coat; what then? I take one step towards her; then we stand still; real tenderness in her look! I've won then! is it to be the day at last? caressingly, she murmurs:

'Be a good boy and go into the sitting-room just for five minutes.'

'Yes, very well, as you wish.'

She takes a candle-stick from the mantelpiece, lights the candles. So she agrees; she wants me to wait for her.

'You're going to wait here; five minutes, and whatever you do, don't play the piano.'

And closing the door: 'See you in a moment.'

Here I am in the sitting-room again; what a dif-ference from an hour ago! Léa obviously wants me to stay, obviously; otherwise she wouldn't have me wait until she finishes undressing; and she's so friendly this evening! I can be in no doubt, she wants me to stay; but why tonight rather than another night? and why *not* tonight? no doubt about it, she's letting me stay; the very idea makes me quiver! to think that in a minute she'll call me, that I'll go into her bedroom; that I'll hold her in my arms, that I'll loosen her long, silky, perfumed clothes; and that in her bed in just a little while! ... let's not get carried away; let's see, better be careful about what I am

going to do; it would first be a good idea for me to take all
the necessary precautions, while I'm on my own; it's
been nearly six hours since the urinal in the Boulevard
Sébastopol ... the closet is to the left in the entrance
hall; have to feel at ease for love talk; but have to be
careful getting out of the room! without making any
noise, without being heard; there's probably a light in the
hall; besides I have some matches; let's open the door;
careful! quietly does it; on tiptoe ... I'm in luck! there's
a light on; that's it, the door's ajar; here we go ... and be
careful not to wet myself ... Relief at last! not a needless
precaution; I leave the door ajar, just as it was; the sitting-room door; gently does it; there; that's fine! nobody
will have heard me; and now let's sit down comfortably
in this armchair. Léa is getting undressed; she is going to
wrap a dressing-gown round her; it's extraordinary that
she has never wanted to take off or put on as much as a
bootee in my presence; what's the time? ... quarter to
twelve; Léa isn't usually long dressing; she'll call me in a
minute. I'm being absolutely ridiculous; not two hours
ago I prepared what I wanted to do, things I decided
upon a month ago, and I'm not even thinking about that;
it's simple though; Léa wants me to stay with her
tonight; well, I must refuse, I shall give her the best
proof of my love, by respecting my love; by not accepting
her giving her body in the way she deems herself obliged
to do, by not doing like the others who are merely con-
sumed by vain passion, but by loving her profoundly and
wanting to be loved; that's it; instead of accepting her
sacrifice, I will offer her my own; and what if she were
offended? no; I shall tell her why I am going, and she will
be moved. I'm cowardly and stupid; now I'm wavering;
no, I'm not; devil take it, it's not that difficult; have to
choose, to have this girl for a night like the others, or to
love and make a friend of her; no need to prepare fine
phrases or rack my brains; in a few minutes now I will
simply say goodnight ... and she'll think I'm shy and

foolish, or, better still, that I'm suffering from an attack
of syphilis brought on by my platonism. God, how slow
she is getting ready! what's the time? ... ten to twelve;
will she never be finished? ... several times already she's
kept me waiting here only to turn me out after a quarter
of an hour of her kittenish ways; it's exasperating to wait
and not know what to expect; Léa's just making a fool of
me; does she think I'm enjoying myself, sitting in this
room, hoping for her to deign to open the door? and I am
going to play at being generous and magnanimous, stake
everything on pure love, rather than make the most of
the opportunity of a night's pleasure; it's nothing but a
pretence and a joke; Léa is sending me away because I
can't force her to let me stay; I let her play her little game
with me and I invent this sublime pretext of wanting to
win her through respect; I've less strength of will than a
stupid child; have to put an end to this; so, this evening,
too bad, I'm going to bed with her; it would be too
idiotic: an affair begun so long ago, at such continual
expense, and which would lead to nothing; all that
money and trouble for the pleasure of looking at a girl's
pretty face; a young mademoiselle playing breeches roles
at the Nouveautés; what an idiotic thing! it's worth two
hundred francs and no more; banking on feelings in that
world! a girl who makes proposals every night on stage
and frequents houses of ill-repute when she's hard up;
yes, I wouldn't be the least bit surprised if she went
there; and the chambermaid there to console the
gentlemen to whom fate has been unkind; I'd certainly
be able to put my money to better use than by paying for
the lace for her costumes; it'll be a pretty sight at the
Continental on Saturday; I'll cut a fine figure in the middle of all those people she'll be flirting with and who'll
leave her their cards next day; and there's the heat and
the crowd like at the Arts Ball where my hat got crushed;
and those boutiques you leave without having enough on
you for a cab home ... What a time she is this evening!

it's enough to make me lose patience. I'm going to knock on the door. No, I can't do that. What patience one needs! I think I can hear her. From here you can't hear anything in the bedroom. Yes; she's opening the door; at last!

'Now, dear, what *are* you doing there? Are you getting very bored?'

In a long, flowing peignoir, cream white, slightly gathered in at the waist, she is all white in the creamy white, flowing folds.

'May I come in?'

'Come in.'

By the fire, she goes and stretches out in the low armchair; on a chair, her white skirts; the black dress hanging up nearby; the fire in the hearth is nearly out; a soft, uniform heat; by the window there's my hat and coat; I take a low chair, and I go and sit by Léa; she is stretched out in the chair, her hands held out; in the blue armchair with the wide embroidered edging, she is white, but rosy-cheeked: against the wardrobe is a little plush-topped table and on it a score of tiny objects, caskets, ivory trinkets, scissors, things that remain ill-defined in the very white light of the bedroom. We are sitting in the soft   and   silent   tranquillity   of   the   bedroom . . .

'You haven't told me what you did this afternoon, after you'd left me.'

She's speaking to me; I reply.

'Oh! nothing special.'

How pretty she is this evening!

'At least you dined and went home?'

'You want to know exactly what I did?'

'Yes, tell me about it.'

'Well, after leaving here I went to see a young gentleman, a friend, in whose company I had a quarter of an hour's walk.'

She smiles.

'And you told this friend about me.'

'Naturally.'

'And your friend was very jealous of you. So where have you been?'

Where? 'Where have I been?' ... This evening ... the busy crowd rushing through Paris, six in the evening; the crowded streets; the carriages hurrying and slowing. Palais-Royal ...

'I was at the Palais-Royal.'

The blonde woman I met in front of the windows of the Magasin du Louvre, so provocative and slim, tall, proud, unfortunately lost in the crowd of passers-by.

'My friend had to go and see *Ruy Blas* at the Théâtre-Français today; I refused to go with him.'

'For my sake; that's heroic.'

It would have been interesting to see *Ruy Blas* again; but I refused, then I had dinner.

'Then I had dinner, where? in a restaurant along the Avenue de l'Opéra; you can't know very ordinary places like that. Do you want to know what I had to eat?'

'You'll tell me the next time we have dinner together. And did you see any of your friends there as well?'

'Not a single one.'

But the very pretty woman sitting opposite me, with the very bald man, a bailiff or consul; the very pretty woman I'd have liked to see again and who was laughing.

'Near me, that's all, there was a very beautiful woman escorted by an old gentleman who was no doubt a consul or a solicitor.'

'Congratulations.'

In the restaurant vivid with brilliant colouring and luminosity, the comfort of the leisurely dinner, observing strangers. Wine, gambling, women ... And suddenly, very bright in the night street, and against the shadows, the façade of the Eden Theatre, Excelsior as seen of old, lines of dancing-girls; and my friend, the one who's going to get married, the worthily happy one, the beloved of his loved one.

'I went home, without anything untoward happening, having simply seen a man loved by the woman he loves, if you'll allow me to mention such a thing.'

'Certainly a rare thing, a man who loves.'

'You really think so?'

'There are so few women that a man can love; a woman several men declare their love to is loved by nobody.'

Ill-chosen, Léa's words; what shall I say to her that doesn't offend her? Why aren't they loved, all – all women, unless they don't want to be.

'If a woman isn't loved,' I say, 'it's often because she doesn't want to be.'

For, guilty or worthy, every woman is an accomplice in the non-love of the one who's seen her. Léa smiles, slightly mocking; she stares into the dying fire; she is more or less as she is in her photograph.

'Did they give you my card immediately at your house?' she asks.

Yes; but if I hadn't been back home? . . .

'You were going there.'

'I had an hour to waste before coming here; I stayed at home.'

'Doing what?'

'Nothing much; I wrote a bit.'

And then, the night, beautiful, at the window overlooking the garden and the trees, the tall trees in front of my window, the garden which is always empty, without flowers, majestic, and that night perfume from the open windows; and then, through the empty streets and the noisy boulevards, the same night, with the barrel-organ and the familiar refrains, so sweet in the shadows . . . shall I tell Léa?

'On the way here tonight, I was pursued by a barrel-organ and its wailing noises.'

'But you usually like music.'

'More than ever, but less than you.'

And her letters ... 'Léa d'Arsay requests the company of Monsieur Daniel Prince ...' Why should Léa know that I have been rereading her letters? she'd only laugh; and what could I tell her about her sad letters? and my plans, once more, to sacrifice my love for her! perhaps she is right, and that it's rare for a man to love, and that she has never been loved; could it be that I don't love her either then? I'm sorry I love her so little, so little, when I try so hard to love!

'You've had,' she continues, 'a very nice day.'

'And an even better evening, in spite of the horrid impropriety of falling asleep.'

She laughs.

'And, to finish with, a lovely carriage ride, with a very charming, but very naughty young woman.'

Wasn't she really naughty? and the gentleman who followed us along the boulevard; the hill of Montmartre visible in the mist; the line of houses with their bright windows and the dark trees in the night; so graceful with her show of dignity, at once serious and funny, now unpretendingly charming; she has raised her head, pale and blonde, from amid the blonde pallor of the flowing fabrics; and the slender body of a child-woman, slight, slim, rounded; an inviting smile, promising caresses, a softness ready to sink into someone's arms; for at this time when day has flown and is no more, after the death of the dreary day, it is night, the time of love.

... Oh, my friend, your lips do lie, and on the winds they fly ...

And her hands; and, from her hands, through my hands and my arms and my heart, a flush, a thrill, a warmth, a poignancy, rises to my very eyes; am I going to waver? Goodbye to respect – long-drawn-out expressions of respect – for undemanding love, the noble schemes, late-flowering loves, so lengthily prepared, departures, renunciations, goodbye to the renunciations, I want her! and I gaze at her in her carnal pallor that announces joy, the woman I would not renounce for a dream. But she is withdrawing her hands from mine; I step back two paces; she comes towards me; she puts her hands on my shoulders; and, as I grow intoxicated and carried away with her, she speaks to me:

'You will come to the Fair at the Continental on Saturday; you'll see how pretty I'll be . . .'

'Yes, of course.'

'I'd be very sorry not to see you; and then, I'll be a credit to you . . .'

'Yes, indeed . . .'

'You'll bring me, won't you, that pinafore for my costume?'

Her costume? . . . yes, that pinafore, that money I promised her . . . I'd forgotten all about it. She wants the money at once; I promised it her; besides, it's the very least; let's get it over with at once . . .

'If you could tell me what you need, Léa, and excuse me for leaving you to . . .'

'I don't know . . . it would come to . . . at the very most . . . about a hundred francs.'

'Allow me to make you a gift of the money.'

I've a fifty-franc note in my card-case, a few louis in my purse; only twenty-franc coins; that will add up to one hundred and ten francs; that's it; three louis and fifty francs, there, on the mantelpiece.

'Kind of you,' says Léa.

She comes back towards me; I've pleased her; it's been rather expensive again; but she'll be pleased with me and nice to me; and then that way I haven't so many scruples about staying tonight, and more right to do so; and can I not then prove my love without refusing it? so tenderly, so gently, so simply shall I love her tonight that it will be worth all speeches and renunciations; undoubtedly, if I know how to behave, I will be more successful by staying with her, in proving that my love is real; that's what has to be done; and, my lips in her hair, I say:

'So, you're letting me stay?'

Her wide eyes, her wide eyes astonished, as if pitying . . . what do they mean?

'Oh! not tonight; I beg of you; I can't . . .'

What? not tonight? She doesn't want to?

'Next time, I promise . . . tonight I can't.'

Once again, again, she doesn't want to? . . . I can't force her . . . she really doesn't want to.

'Léa, you don't want to?'

'I swear . . . , I . . .'

But why insist?

'Good night then.'

Why did I ask her? Why didn't I keep to my resolution, and leave as I was going to, honour intact?

'Good night.'

I kiss her brow; delight in partings and impossibilities, fatal and desperate delight!

'Come on Wednesday at three o'clock,' she says.

'Many thanks, I will.'

Why did I again want to possess her? she who I'm again not going to possess. I must go; here's my coat, my hat.

'Goodbye,' she says. 'Wednesday, at three.'

She is taking the candlestick and is opening the sitting-room door; Marie is there; we cross the hall.

'Wednesday, at three,' I say.

No, I won't see her any more; I mustn't see her any more; why should I see her again? gone for ever, the possibilities of love between us . . . Pale and unforgettably beautiful, my friend stretches out her hand to me.

'Goodbye.'

'Goodbye.'

She gives a friendly smile; on her breast the lights glimmer, blonde and nocturnal.

Notes to The Bays are Sere

p.7   *Ruy Blas* verse drama by Victor Hugo, first published in 1838.

p.15   *Robert le Diable* opera by Giacomo Meyerbeer, libretto by Eugène Scribe (with G. Delavigne), first performed in 1831.
    Le Chalet comic opera in one act by Adolphe Adam, libretto by Scribe and Melésville, first performed in 1845.

p.15   The reference is to a 'social' problem of pronunciation. The still very provincial Daniel Prince is showing how over-sensitive he is about 'correct' pronunciation. He does not want to reveal his social origins. The reference to 'Mendès' may be an anti-semitic and/or anti-Southern jibe.

p.16   *Tortoni's* one of the great Paris cafés, on the corner of the Boulevard des Italiens and the Rue Taitbout. Famous for its cuisine and frequented by men of letters and politicians. Tortoni's closed in 1894.

p. 16   *La Dame Blanche* opera by Adrien Boïeldieu, libretto by Scribe (after Walter Scott), first performed in 1825.

p. 16   *Bignon's* a restaurant on the Boulevard des Capucines, the meeting and dining-out place for many leading artists, journalists and men of letters during the Second Empire.

p.19   *Fortunio* a novel by Théophile Gautier, published in 1840.

p.23   *Madame de Ségur* French-language author of Russian descent (*née* Sophie Rostopchine) whose stories are still popular with French children.

Interior Monologue

Its first appearance
and origins, and its place
in the work of
James Joyce

The different parts of this essay formed the basis of public lectures given in May 1930 in Marburg, Berlin and Leipzig

Until the publication in 1919 and 1920 of the first extracts from James Joyce's *Ulysses*, hardly anything was known about monologue except what comes more or less under the dictionary definition: words spoken in a play by a character alone on stage.

Like the famous monologue[1]* from *Hamlet*: 'To be or not to be ...': Hamlet is on stage alone; he is expressing his thoughts; he could content himself with thinking, and not talk; but theatre requires him to think aloud.

In theory, therefore, the speaking character must be alone. However, there is a monologue when, while not alone, he speaks as if he were, although in the theatre this is more often called an 'aside'. But whether there are other characters on stage or not, the essential condition is that the one speaking is not heard and does not want to be heard. Conversely, speaking to someone who does not reply, like Turelure in the last act of *L'Otage*,[2] is called in ordinary parlance 'monologuing' (*monologuer*), but in fact is not monologue any more.

It is easy to see how monologue, originating in the theatre, could without difficulty be introduced in a book, into the novel, for example. The author, instead of relating that his character is thinking this or that, has him say to himself what he is thinking, in the same way as on stage. In a passage from *Le Père Goriot* we shall come back to, Balzac could have written: 'Rastignac thought everyone was making fun of him ...' He uses monologue and writes: ' "Everyone is making fun of me," Rastignac said to himself ...'

In the novel it is even less necessary than in drama for the character to be alone; to produce monologue, it is

* [See p. 146 for notes added by the translator. Footnotes are Dujardin's, with modernized references in square brackets.]

enough for the character to express his thoughts without intending them to be heard. And monologue can consist as much of a long piece as of a few sentences inserted into a narrative or a dialogue.

Whatever refinements have been added, this traditional monologue is as old as literature itself.

With what is nowadays termed interior monologue, for example Mrs Bloom's in the final chapter of *Ulysses*, there is nobody who hasn't had the feeling, on a first reading and preliminary to any analysis, that a great innovation has been made in literature.

Our interest will be to investigate what constitutes this innovation, how it can be defined and what its origins are; but it will first be advisable to recall how it came into being.

How it started

It is not my purpose here to give the biography or to analyse the work of James Joyce,* and I shall remain within the limits of our subject. The great writer evidently carried within him the need for that new method whereby his genius was to express itself, and we shall shortly see that it was in fact from the age of about twenty, between 1901 and 1903, that he became aware of this. The idea germinated for several years without any outward manifestations, and there is no trace of it in his first two books, *Chamber Music*, published in 1907, and *Dubliners*, completed in the same year but not published until 1914.‡

* I refer readers to Valery Larbaud's preface to the French translation of *Dubliners* cited below.

† Translated into French by Y. Fernandez, H. du Pasquier and J.-P. Reynaud as *Gens de Dublin*, 1924, preface by Valery Larbaud.

At the same period he was finishing his first novel, begun in 1904, *A Portrait of the Artist as a Young Man*, which came out in New York in 1916 and established his reputation.*

Attempts have been made to find interior monologue in *A Portrait of the Artist as a Young Man*; in actual fact there are only a few lines of it – this on the confession of the author himself, who told me he had written them more or less unconsciously – which merely serves the better to confirm what was at work within him.

Another sign of this process is to be found in the draft of *Ulysses* begun at the same time as he was writing *Dubliners*; far from having the huge proportions of the final version of *Ulysses*, this *proto-Ulysses* would only have been a short story, but it was already conceived as the picture of one day in the life of the main character. After having put it aside in order to write *A Portrait of the Artist as a Young Man*, James Joyce came back to it once *A Portrait* was finished and worked on it for seven years, from 1914 to 1921, in Trieste, Zurich and Paris.

In 1919 and 1920 extracts from it appeared in a New York magazine, *The Little Review*, which was prosecuted and taken to court because of the supposedly immoral passages in the work.

Immediately, even before it reached the bookshops, the stir created was enormous. As Philippe Soupault has said, 'the prevailing literary climate in Great Britain and the United States was completely transformed by it';† but it wasn't only the literary climate of English-speaking countries: the whole world of letters was affected.

As far as France was concerned the stir created came to a head with a public lecture given by Valery Larbaud at the Maison des Amis du Livre on 7 December 1921, subsequently published in the *Nouvelle Revue Française*

* Translated into French by Ludmila Savitzky as *Dedalus*, 1924.
† *Europe*, June 1929.

in April 1922, and later reprinted as the preface to
Dubliners.

Ulysses was to come out in book form in February
1922, from Shakespeare and Co. in Paris, because it was
banned in England and the USA.*

> How [writes Jean Cassou] can one tell the story of
> this day in Dublin which is longer than all the cen-
> turies of history, how describe the stellar movements
> which separate Stephen Dedalus and Leopold Bloom
> and then bring them together again? How can one
> map out the routes by which one cuts through the
> undergrowth of all languages, slang, vocabulary from
> the Middle Ages, from journalism, conversational
> style, academicisms, dialogue, unrestrained pure
> poetry, finally to reach Mrs Bloom's interior mono-
> logue? . . .†

To give an idea of the impression *Ulysses* produced
on young writers, I shall quote these lines by Pierre
d'Exideuil:

> Everything that goes through the mind of an extra-
> ordinarily ordinary individual – ideas, memories,
> boastings, and with the minute detail and evocative
> incoherence which can reign there, everything a
> man's thought at every moment perceives as the
> occurrence of vaguely ridiculous impulses – all this is
> conveyed with the pomposity of collective and
> individual pride and stupidity in which we all share.
> All those seething thoughts stirs in us like a doomed
> flock; a flock in mad course. Wildly incoherent
> dreams, hilarious corruptions of meanings, fiendish
> visions, scatological feats, gusts of poetry – such is
> the swift and silent orgy which takes shape within us,

---

* The French translation by Auguste Morel and Stuart Gilbert,
revised by Valery Larbaud, came out in 1929.
† *Nouvelles littéraires*, 9 March 1929.

just as in the depths of Plato's Cavern, shadows, no less disturbing, found form.*

The formula of interior monologue, in accordance with which part of the book was written, had achieved the height of fame, and was immediately employed in France by Valery Larbaud in *Amants, heureux amants* and in America by William Carlos Williams.[3] Soon (1924), in his delightful novel *Juliette au pays des hommes*, Jean Giraudoux could write that 'what intrigued Paris at that time, was certainly not death, but interior monologue'. And immediately the question arose: what were the origins of this sensational innovation?

The celebrity of James Joyce is in no way affected if one looks for what the erudite world would call its 'sources', just as Victor Bérard has researched the sources of the *Odyssey* itself, just as theologians research those of the Sermon on the Mount. But who knows when the question would have been elucidated, if James Joyce, with a generosity unparalleled in the history of letters, had not revealed that thirty-five years before the publication of *Ulysses*, interior monologue had in fact been used in my novel, *Les Lauriers sont coupés*.

It was in fact in 1887 that *Les Lauriers sont coupés* appeared in the *Revue indépendante*, and in the following year in book form. What was its theme? Edmond Jaloux has summed it up in the following manner:

> In *Les Lauriers sont coupés*, almost nothing happens: a young man is in love with a pretty girl, gives her some money, goes out with her and finally obtains nothing. He leaves, stating that he will not see her again, but it is not absolutely certain that he will keep his word.†

* *Revue Nouvelle*, July–August 1929.
† *Nouvelles littéraires*, 17 January 1925.

The specific originality of the work was that interior monologue was employed there for the first time, not fortuitously, but systematically and continually, from beginning to end. In the words of Joyce quoted by Valery Larbaud, 'the reader was, in *Les Lauriers sont coupés*, placed inside the thought processes of the main character, and it is the uninterrupted unfolding of this thought process which, completely replacing conventional narrative form, informed the reader of what this character is doing and what happens to him.'*

The book had achieved little in terms of public success. Like all volumes published by the *Revue indépendante* bookshop, 420 numbered copies had been printed, including twenty on untrimmed paper; a certain number were distributed as review copies, and a very small number were actually sold; when the review ceased publication the remaining stock was sold off to the Vanier and Deman bookshops at a ridiculously low price, apart from a few untrimmed volumes which I myself preferred to destroy.

The book's reception by those who received complimentary copies was hardly any better – with a few exceptions; it is true that the exceptions made up in quality for their number.

First a letter from Mallarmé, 8 April 1888:

You know I particularly appreciated this novel on my first reading it in the *Revue indépendante*; leafing through it today, I can see you have set down a cursory method of notation that turns upon itself, whose sole aim, independent of large-scale literary structures, poetry or decoratively convoluted phraseology, is to express, without misapplication of the sublime means involved, everyday experience which is so difficult to grasp. So there is here less a happy result of

---

* Preface to the definitive edition, 1924 [see note 14 below].

chance than one of those discoveries we are all tending towards in our different ways.*

I shall always regret that Mallarmé *said* to me but never *wrote* to me what he had thought of the book on its serial publication; while excluding it from the heady definition he gave of literature, he had been the only one (apart from Huysmans perhaps) to feel what Joyce was to discover later on: the enormous possibilities of interior monologue. I recall his phrase 'the moment gripped by the throat . . .'

Huysmans, as I said, also seemed to have an intuitive grasp of it . . . 'It's strange . . . it's strange . . .' he repeated without being more precise. From him, I have a note in which he merely recalls the sense of novelty he had experienced.

J. H. Rosny who, from the first, showed an unflagging interest in the book, must be set alongside Mallarmé and Huysmans.

From Emile Hennequin, then considered an important critic, I received a letter recognizing the book as 'a novel of character analysis reduced to a single enumeration of a series of impulses of the soul'.

From Loti I received a somewhat embarrassed note.

In 1890 a letter of several pages, couched in unfriendly terms, from Charles Le Goffic, which I shall come back to.

A little later, a note from Ajalbert, as part of the questionnaire by Jules Huret, in which he classes the book with interesting examples of Symbolism.

A letter from Courteline, who declares himself to be a 'great admirer of *Les Lauriers sont coupés*'.

A few brief mentions, here and there, in different journals. Add to this some friendly words from Paul

---

* I possess a second letter from Mallarmé about *Les Lauriers sont coupés*, expressed in terms no less precious to me.

Adam; congratulations from Edmond de Goncourt who honoured the book with a special binding. Later a letter (9 August 1897) from Rémy de Gourmont telling me he had followed this little book with delight in the *Revue indépendante* in 1887; and later on still, several pages in the *IIe Livre des masques*.

George Moore, whom I have been corresponding with since 1886, had written to me from London on 17 May 1887, while the novel was being serialized:

> Your story is very good, uncommonly good: the daily life of the soul unveiled for the first time; a kind of symphony in full stops and commas. All I am afraid of is monotony. We shall see; in any case it is new.[4]

I also received a few words from him in the following December; then ten years later, 22 July 1897, a letter in which he told me I had found the most original literary form of our time, but that the psychology was somewhat Naturalistic ... 'That seems to you a contradiction in terms;' he added, 'but it is not, it is sound criticism'.[5]

I cannot recall anything else.

In 1897 Mercure de France, who were bringing out the main Symbolist works again, published a new edition of the book. Finally, *Gil Blas Illustrated* reprinted it, but that, it has to be remarked, was for personal reasons.

The publication of a new edition did not save the book from sinking into oblivion, and one of my biographers,[6] in a booklet he devoted to me in 1923, did not even mention it as figuring amongst my works! Another sign: when the untrimmed copy I had given Goncourt, which he had had bound and had inscribed in his own hand, was offered to the bookseller Camille Bloch several years after the sale of Goncourt's library, it was laughingly refused by this usually erudite and sensible man.

In his preface to the definitive edition, Larbaud has explained the causes of this neglect too well for me to

want to go over them again. More and more occupied
with my study of the history of religions and my dramatic
writing, I myself had finally nearly forgotten this book
from my youth, when James Joyce pronounced the
words 'Lazarus, Come forth'.

The circumstances of this literary resurrection will
perhaps be of interest – because of the side-issues
involved – to people curious about the history of interior
monologue. They are like a film consisting of many different episodes.

The first episode dates back to 1901–03; it could be
called 'Christopher Columbus's Egg' or 'Denis Papin's
Pot'.[7] This is how the scene goes: a young writer, twenty
years old (none other than James Joyce), reads *Les
Lauriers sont coupés* while on a trip to Paris.

And there we have to stop for a moment. Why did
Joyce adopt the interior monologue formula? Obviously,
as stated above, because he had it within him; the occasion which opened his eyes to it merely made him conscious of himself. This occasion was when he read the
little French novel where precisely that method had been
created. But this is the insight of a man of genius;
whereas nobody (apart from Mallarmé, and perhaps
Huysmans and Rosny) had seen the enormous possibilities of the method roughed out in this book, *Joyce*
noticed them, not immediately no doubt, but taking
into consideration their whole range which went
infinitely further than I had first managed to sketch out.

. . . Back to our film.

The second episode takes place in 1917. James Joyce
is in Zurich; he is in the process of writing *Ulysses* (1914–
21); he sees in a Swiss newspaper that I am having a play
performed in Geneva; he writes to me to ask whether I
really am the author of *Les Lauriers sont coupés*; he doesn't
know where I live; but he thinks the French Consulate

must have the address of a Frenchman who is having a play performed in Geneva. Needless to say, I never received the letter.

Third episode. Late in 1921. *Ulysses* is finished; extracts from it have been published; the book itself is at the printer's. James Joyce is chatting to a group of authors, one of whom is Valery Larbaud. They express their admiration for what they think is the great author's invention. Joyce interrupts them and states that interior monologue was not invented by him, but some thirty-five years before, by a French writer, and he gives my name and the title of my book.

This statement, however, goes more or less unnoticed. Valery Larbaud has even told me that he had attached so little significance to it that day that he forgot the title of my book and only remembered the fact that Joyce had talked to him about me. Indeed, in his lecture of 7 December 1921, he not only fails to talk about the 'sources' of *Ulysses*, but seems to attribute the invention of interior monologue to Joyce himself, without however being categorical about this.

Not one of the writers who concern themselves more and more with the new method instituted by Joyce knows or remembers *Les Lauriers sont coupés*. In February–March 1922, André Gide gives six public lectures on Dostoyevsky* in which, while considering interior monologue, he refuses to credit James Joyce with its invention and sees it as dating back to Edgar Allan Poe, Robert Browning and Dostoyevsky himself, without making any mention of *Les Lauriers sont coupés*.†

At the same time as André Gide was giving his lec-

---

* Published as *Dostoievsky*, 1923 [English translation, *Dostoevsky*, Dent, 1925].

† André Gide whom I asked recently whether he had read my book when it came out (even though he was still at school) replied in a letter of 4 July 1930, whose amusing opening I will quote for everyone's benefit: 'On the other hand [that is

tures on Dostoyevsky, René Lalou was completing his *Histoire de la littérature contemporaine* which was to come out in the autumn of the following year, 1922. René Lalou had read *Les Lauriers sont coupés*, but he had mainly been struck by shortcomings that I defend so little that I shall shortly come back to them; and now that justice has been done as far as the work's qualities are concerned, I can understand why he let himself be put off by the annoyance these failings caused him.* In any case he too is seen attributing interior monologue to Dostoyevsky, to Browning and, going further than Gide, to Proust and even to Paul Morand.

Larbaud himself, in a review of Lalou's book he published in the February 1923 *Nouvelle Revue Française*, and which he had probably written in December 1922, failed to point out this omission along with the others he listed ... But can I reproach anyone with this slip since I myself, in the article of protest against Lalou's book which I published in the *Cahiers Idéalistes* of February 1923, mentioned *Les Lauriers sont coupés* without one word about its technique?

The fourth 'episode' takes place at a time that can be dated as being between the end of December 1922 and the end of February 1923. James Joyce is again with Valery Larbaud; he talks about *Les Lauriers sont coupés* again; he insists; and the 'film' picks up these words [in English]:

'Read it; you shall see what it is.'

---

how the letter begins] I remember the performance of *Antonia* very well ...' And concerning interior monologue: 'The dates are in any case there,' he added, 'to certify that you were the precursor.'

* Since then he has given a very fair explanation of this in a note to be appended to the next edition of his *Histoire de la littérature contemporaine*. As for predecessors of interior monologue, the information set out further below will be included in the same edition.

Fifth episode. A writers' meeting. Valery Larbaud hasn't yet read *Les Lauriers sont coupés* but has been deeply affected by what James Joyce has revealed to him; he gives an account of the conversation; he says how much he has been affected: he asks if they know my book; he says he is impatient to read it . . .

General embarrassment . . .

I am not going to give any names; the affair is past history; besides, most of the 'opponents' of that time have changed their minds.

It is a known fact that a writer's popularity varies. Édouard Dujardin's popularity, which had fallen to quite a low level in the pre-war years, had suddenly risen at the end of the war and in the years just after, but, for reasons which had nothing to do with literature, there had been a reaction, within – it is true – a fairly narrow circle, but precisely the one which the writers taking part in our fifth episode belonged to.

Not one of these really holds a grudge against the man; but they hold his social and political tendencies against him, and from there, it is only a short step to denigrating his literary work; Symbolism, which they refuse to hear spoken of in the group, is pretext enough. Those who have read *Les Lauriers sont coupés* are only capable of remembering the failings which had already been a stumbling-block for René Lalou; dated style; unreadable book . . . Finally, they want to promote *Ulysses*, and some of them wonder if it is the right moment to draw critical attention to a work the innovatory nature of which could be set against it . . . Joyce himself, the great writer, has not been affected by this apprehension; but a great writer's admirers do not always share his mentality, and what disciples observe the least willingly in a mentor are his moral qualities . . . The person who is to bring out the French translation[8] is precisely the one to show the most generosity; she protests that such fears are ridiculous and that they would grieve Joyce if he knew about them; she is ignored, and these are the essentially French, even essentially Parisian words recorded by the film:

'Only Joyce would need to dredge this book up!'

Valery Larbaud, however, does not take this view; he refuses to follow the advice of those who try to persuade him against reading the book: he decides to go in person and ask for it at the Mercure de France office, reads it, and here I can only quote the account he himself gives of his impressions:

> I have been prepared to find failings in every line, period corruptions, dated words and expressions, Symbolist gibberish, etc. On the contrary, I was confronted with a fine work of French literature, unspoiled and pure, where traces of a time and a trend were so few as to be insignificant (besides, these have been deleted from the definitive edition), and which, on the whole, stood up to comparison with the best works of imaginative prose in our language.

And in the preface to the definitive (1924) edition:

> I noted that *Les Lauriers sont coupés*, although totally different in style and spirit from James Joyce's work, had in fact to be considered as one of the sources for the form of *Ulysses*. But I was above all astounded to think that such a book, of such obvious literary worth, and which contained a completely new and attractive literary technique, full of all sorts of possibilities, capable of renewing the novel form or of replacing it entirely, had gone unnoticed for so many years.

In 1921 Larbaud had dedicated his novella, *Amants, heureux amants*, to the great Irish author he considered to be the inventor of this form. When he read *Les Lauriers sont coupés* for the first time, he had just finished *Mon plus secret conseil*, in the summer of 1923, and felt obliged to dedicate it to me in the following terms: 'To Édouard Dujardin, author of *Les Lauriers sont coupés* (1887), "a quo"'. It can be said that this somewhat sibylline dedication marks the time, after thirty-five years of indifference, of the renewal of interest in my book by the literary public.

A year later Larbaud followed this up by writing the preface for the definitive edition of *Les Lauriers sont coupés,** which was to cause the commotion that is now common knowledge.

James Joyce had brought *Les Lauriers sont coupés* out of the tomb; Valery Larbaud welcomed the author returned to life, took him by the hand, and guided him to the world of the living. This frame will form, if you like, the sixth and final episode.

The article which Edmond Jaloux devoted to it in *Les Nouvelles littéraires* of 17 January 1925, thus associating himself with the work accomplished by Valery Larbaud, was the book's consecration.

It is not very frequent [he said] that a book which has gone more or less unnoticed on publication is retrieved after long years from neglect, and is suddenly found to have the status of an important work. However, it does happen. We are doubtless under the illusion that such a mistake is no longer possible, and yet in fifty years' time it is likely that out of the mass of books that appear every day, three or four will stand out, which will probably be those to which was attached the least importance at the time of their publication, while all the new books we are successively wild about will have in their turn reverted to being old 'new books', that is to say outdated ones

---

* Published by Albert Messein, [Paris] 1924. An English translation by Stuart Gilbert, one of the translators of *Ulysses*, is to come out under the title *We'll to the Woods No More*.

... This is what has just happened in the case of *Les Lauriers sont coupés* ...

Apart from in *Les Lauriers sont coupés*, had interior monologue been employed before *Ulysses?*

Arthur Schnitzler, who is about my age, published in 1901 his *Leutnant Gustl*, which is supposed to be written according to this technique. There would be grounds for investigating whether, because it happens to be written in the first person, the book really consists of the profoundly essential characteristics of interior monologue. One cannot deny, in any case, that it is near to it, and it is interesting to note that it was written in the very same year as Joyce was reading *Les Lauriers sont coupés* for the first time. Did Arthur Schnitzler know the book?

A few years ago, Valery Larbaud and Mademoiselle Edith Weyel, a student from the University of Frankfurt, who was writing a thesis on interior monologue, requested Ernst Robert Curtius to ask Schnitzler this question. In a letter to Mademoiselle Weyel, dated Adelboden, 5 August 1926, which I myself have read, Arthur Schnitzler replied that he did not know the book, adding that, shortly after the publication of *Leutnant Gustl*, Georg Brandes had written to him to tell him about it.

Without going so far as to put Georg Brandes's gesture on the same level as that of James Joyce, it is strange to note that, while *Les Lauriers sont coupés* was forgotten by my compatriots, it remained fresh in the memory of an Irishman and a Dane who were – something that I find particularly affecting – on the one hand a critic of standing, and on the other the greatest writer of our time.

As to who had employed interior monologue before *Ulysses*, in addition to the problem of Schnitzler, there is the problem of Dostoyevsky, Browning and others, who are said to have used it even before *Les Lauriers sont coupés*. We shall examine these examples when we have defined interior monologue as such. We shall show that, in the alleged passages, it is a question of something quite different. However, if one wished to identify some of the characteristics of interior monologue in these works, it could only be with reference to aspirations or tendencies in that direction, and the problem could only ever clearly be seen by studying the previous history of the technique. Only one thing remains in fact undisputed: the first deliberate, continuous and systematic use of interior monologue dates from *Les Lauriers sont coupés* in 1887, and its being established in all its glory dates from *Ulysses*, extracts from which first appeared in 1919.

Valery Larbaud has brought to my notice, for its curiosity value, the sudden and brief appearance of interior monologue (three words) in a novel by Armando Palacio Valdés, *El Cuarto Poder*, published in Spain in about 1890.[9] One can read this (I am quoting from memory): 'He had behaved in a stupid manner. He had cut a sorry figure. I've cut a sorry figure. He should have ...' After which the third person narrative continues as usual.

Obviously this is an example of interior monologue – unless, as Yves Gandon has suggested to me, this sudden appearance of the first person is merely a printer's error! Whatever the truth of the matter, half a line, lost in the middle of a book, will never, as Larbaud has pertinently remarked, be anything but a curiosity.

Where does the expression 'interior monologue' come from?

Valery Larbaud attributes its origin to Paul Bourget,* who used it in his novel *Cosmopolis*, published

---

* Autograph manuscript, March–April 1930.

in 1893, where one can read, following a monologue by the main character straight out of Stendhal (in no way 'interior monologue') these lines:

> This interior monologue was not very different from what would have been said in comparable circumstances by any young man interested in a young girl whose mother behaves badly (Vol. I, p. 40).

Paul Bourget knew *Les Lauriers sont coupés*; he showed his sympathy for the *Revue indépendante* to which he had contributed an article, but it is all too obvious that in this text from *Cosmopolis* he was far from having the new technique in view.

The invention of the expression, with its present meaning, seems to be due to Valery Larbaud himself.

Attempting a Definition

The writer of a novel puts himself in the situation of an observer who is supposed to witness all the doings and gestures of the character he presents and possesses the faculty of entering his innermost thoughts, either limiting himself to narrating them to his readers, or attempting to explain the way they unfold, just as a well-informed witness is supposed to reveal in court what he has seen and heard (you swear to tell the truth, the whole truth and nothing but the truth), with or without giving a psychological portrait of the accused.

Certain conventional narrative novels are an unqualified success. Taking psychological novels (for example, from among the most recent, those of Bernanos), some could be considered as three-hundred-page analyses writ-

ten by a critic about stories which would normally be
only one hundred and fifty pages long. Novels which set
out to narrate without passing judgement do not abstain
any more than the others from giving explanations. As
for those in which the main character says 'I', the latter is
mainly being substituted for the author as a means of
expressing the workings of his psychology. And many are
the readers, I imagine, who are wearied to the point of
exasperation with this continual intervention of an author
who does not allow his character to lift a finger or say one
word without explaining the reason . . . the reason . . .

Drama at least has the advantage of sparing us from
all this troublesome business (except in the case when it
reappears in the form of a confidant, or of exaggerating
the amount of self-knowledge attributed to the main
character). If so many poets have been attracted by the
theatre, it is not because this gives them the somewhat
vulgar (and generally dearly paid for) pleasure of realiz-
ing their conceptions in the flesh in a paint and paste-
board atmosphere, but precisely because it allows them
to have the innermost voices they hear in their hearts
speak out loud. Such, finally, is the interest, in the
theatre, not merely of the monologues one occasionally
comes across there, which are fairly few and far between,
but of the passages of dialogue in which the character
speaks as if he were speaking to himself, either in lines he
seems to be addressing to an interlocutor when in fact he
isn't, or in a sentence inserted into the speech, or merely
in a clause where the cry of the subconscious gushes up,
all being nothing more or less than scraps of concealed
monologue.* In this way, genuine theatrical dialogue is
continually a combination of disguised monologues
through which the spirit of the character speaks, and of
dialogues proper – with the happy absence of any author
to interrupt with his comments. The beauty of the dra-

* Obvious examples among hundreds of others: Phèdre's entry
and her declaration to Hippolyte in Racine's tragedy.

matic genre does not, as certain realists have felt, consist in faithfully reproducing the conversation that two people might really have had; it consists in bringing to the surface the things that are locked in their subconscious and which in reality would never have been on their lips. Wagner did all this through his orchestra; the psychological novelist analyses them from his professorial chair; Racine expresses them, not only in the lines of dialogue, but also in the monologues (genuine monologues or disguised monologues) which he continually mixes in with them.

And this is primarily what is facilitated by interior monologue in the novel.

The primary object of interior monologue is, while remaining within the conditions of the framework imposed by the novel, to suppress authorial intervention (or at least apparent authorial intervention) and to allow the character to express himself directly, as traditional monologue does in drama.

Interior monologue is therefore, before anything else, a monologue ... I mean that it has the same basis as traditional monologue in drama, that is to say it is first of all speech through which the character himself, in front of us, directly sets out his thoughts.

Secondly, interior monologue is speech without listeners; and in that it still follows the rules governing traditional monologue.

In addition, it is unspoken speech; so English critics call it 'unspoken' or 'silent monologue'. Is it in this way different from traditional monologue? Not any more so than other forms; for we know that, if in the theatre the monologue is recited aloud, it is by virtue of a convention which absolutely requires it to be so; but as soon as the play is read instead of being listened to, nothing obliges one to imagine the character speaking out loud. Moreover, in the novel, traditional monologue is never supposed to be spoken aloud, except in exceptional cases;

in general, this sort of monologue aims at expressing
thoughts and not at reporting words spoken.

When Valery Larbaud, in a letter to René Lalou of 29
February 1924, wrote that it was the 'voiceless monologue of consciousness', he merely emphasized a characteristic it has in common with traditional monologue;
when he said it was 'undeclaimable', adding that one can
only read it out loud 'in a tone as near as possible to
words spoken in a dream' I am sure he was only asking
from the reader of Mrs Bloom's monologue, what I, if I
were a theatre director, would ask of the actor reciting
the 'To be or not to be' soliloquy . . .

Does it follow from there that interior monologue
must necessarily, like traditional monologue, use the first
person? In the theatre, it is still a monologue when,
talking to himself, the character speaks to himself as
'You', as is current usage in certain regions, or when he
speaks in the third person like Negroes in travel stories,
and as Robert Browning, we shall see, has Caliban speak;
the second and third person are in fact in these cases only
a disguised first person. If we leave drama aside and
concentrate on the novel, there is also monologue when a
writer, narrating in the third person, transcribes the
thoughts of his character in the same way as the
historians of antiquity gave the words of their heroes in
'indirect speech', or in the same way as Flaubert and the
Naturalists make use of their narratives in the imperfect
tense, on condition however that the novelist excludes all
personal intervention. An example from *Ulysses* is the
passage which begins with the explanation of Gerty's
thoughts and becomes her interior monologue while
remaining in the third person;* this is what we would
call, by analogy with 'indirect speech', 'indirect interior
monologue'. Here again, the 'He' (or 'She') covers the
same 'I' as in conventional monologue.

* Page 397 in the French translation. [The Gerty MacDowall
passage is in Chapter 13 of *Ulysses*.]

Let us therefore bear in mind that interior monologue, by its very nature as monologue is, above all, in
the first place speech by the character being presented to
us; second, speech without an audience; third, unspoken
speech. And let us look elsewhere for its characteristics.
By reviewing certain of the definitions which have been
given since the publication of *Ulysses* brought it under
scrutiny, we shall at the same time be able to see what
view of it was taken, and assemble the elements of the
definition we shall put forward ourselves, adding to them
and correcting them as the need arises. We beg to be
excused for having brought together texts relating on the
one hand to interior monologue as modestly sketched out
in *Les Lauriers sont coupés*, and on the other to its brilliant
creation in *Ulysses*; this chapter is centred on looking for
the characteristics of a technique and not on a critical
appreciation of its application.

Interior monologue, said Valery Larbaud as early as
1924, in the preface quoted above, is the expression 'of
the most intimate, most spontaneous thoughts, those
which appear to form unconsciously, prior to organized
speech'. Thus it allows one 'to penetrate so deeply the
upsurge of thought in the Self and to grasp it so near to
its point of conception . . .'

We have seen the same writer, with reference to
James Joyce, characterize interior monologue in *Les
Lauriers sont coupés* as 'the uninterrupted development of
a character's thought'.

'Its essential characteristic,' says Edmond Jaloux,
repeating the terms employed by Valery Larbaud, 'is to
represent not only interior speech, but intimate thoughts
in formation.'

These first three texts provide a fine summary of
what is generally thought about interior monologue and
substantially set out its different basic characteristic elements. We shall find them at the bottom of most of the
articles we are going to quote. If, however, we try to

differentiate between these various elements, we can see that it is the subject matter of interior monologue, that is to say the subject matter of the thing described in it, which has attracted the closest attention on the part of the critics who, in order to communicate their message, have accumulated the most varied images.

Edmond Jaloux, in the same article, explains that the novelty of the technique of *Les Lauriers sont coupés* 'resides in that extraordinary refinement involved in grasping all the nuances of the mind, in fusing the external and the internal world, in short, vivid, simple sentences, the perpetual workings of volition, of thought, and of the unconscious mind, which spins and unravels almost imperceptible webs in the depths of our soul'.

This has the result, he further states, of evoking 'that state of complete confusion in which things outside and inside clash, are fused and telescope into each other to arrive at that impression of life which makes up the essential part of our consciousness . . .'.

In this way is expressed, he adds, that indiscernible, unstable, swarming element, which is almost frightening in its protean plasticity and which has its ephemeral existence in the depths of our minds and 'gives to reality the intensity of a hallucination . . .'.

As early as 1924, Jean Giraudoux, with the amused perspicacity for which he is famous, had listed several of the characteristics of interior monologue in the novel to which he added interior monologue's consecration as *the* event of the time. 'Interior monologue,' he had explained, 'was a movement of frankness such that the coverings which had been forced on the soul from the time of Aristotle till that of the Symbolists had been shaken off. It was this soulquake which had been shaking Parisian literati for two months . . .' And already he was speaking about 'monsters unleashed by confession' and 'the suction pad effect of interior monologue'.*

* *Juliette au pays des hommes*, pp. 149, 156, 159.

A few years later, Pierre d'Exideuil compared interior monologue to 'a diving-bell which suddenly plunges us into marine depths. Amidst a magic or unreal vegetation suspended in the mass of water, grows a profuse fauna, fauna composed of strange animals and fish with their bodies made transparent by the conical glare of the spotlights. We can see them in movement at the same time as we can study the contractions of their bodies, their comings and goings, their habits, their reflexes. If they catch something to eat, we can then follow the food through their insides right to the cloaca.'*

For Eugène Montfort, interior monologue (in its raw state) ought to catch 'everything audible that is strange and confused when one is looking for a station to hear a programme by moving the pointer on the wave-band of a wireless set. It is a mixture of incomprehensible sounds, in no order, of fragmented words, bursts of odd voices, of diabolical whistling, which one feels freed from when one has at last found the beam, the wavelength one was looking for'.†

Eugène Montfort adds that it is impossible to render things as they are; and it is to this point that we shall return later.

The *Revue des Deux Mondes* has even published Louis Gillet's study of James Joyce, which, although somewhat critical, shows none the less a rare degree of understanding.

> Mr Joyce is attempting against impossible odds, without omissions or suppressions, to note down everything that remains unformulated, this reservoir of vague perceptions, of obtuse sensations, of tortuous associations, these rough drafts, these beginnings, these approximations of ideas, this fluid, floating, elusive material, this powder, this chaos of

* *Revue Nouvelle*, article quoted above.
† *Les Marges*, February 1929.

feelings, of reminiscences, of images or of fragments of images which make up 'thought' in its natural state, thought being formed rather than perfected thought.*

It is [continues Louis Gillet] the substance of the soul that one is trying to grasp, thought being born, the searching X-ray photograph of fleeting life in its perpetual becoming.

All this implies, of course, that things are only rendered in interior monologue as far as they are thought by the character, and as they are thought by him, without attention being paid to what they may be from an objective point of view. This is what James Joyce expresses so well when he says that in *Les Lauriers sont coupés* 'the reader is placed, from the very first lines, within the thought processes of the character ...' (for the rest of the quotation, see above, p. 88). The character in *Les Lauriers sont coupés* reveals not what is happening around him, but what he sees happening; not the movement he makes, but those he is conscious of making; not the words spoken to him, but the ones he hears; all that, as he incorporates it in his own and only reality. In other words, as Edmond Jaloux writes, everything there is a state of consciousness.

While mainly drawing attention to the extraordinary richness of the states of mind described by interior monologue and to its subjective character, the critics who have studied it have in the main emphasized the spirit in which this description has been conceived.

We have just heard Valery Larbaud speak of 'non-organized speech' and of 'intimate thoughts being formed'. Pierre d'Exideuil explains in the article quoted above: 'thought not yet filtered and settled ... thought in its raw state ...'

* *Revue des Deux Mondes*, 1 August 1925, reprinted in *Esquisses anglaises*, 1930.

This is what attracted the attention of the critic from the *Revue des Deux Mondes*:

> Normally [writes Louis Gillet], our words conform to a structure, at least to a grammatical construction, to the requirements of reasoning. Now frameworks are to be broken, the sentence unhinged from logic, words liberated from syntactic forms are to be ordered according to spontaneous associations or even not associated together at all.

Interior monologue has been compared to a film being projected: as André Berge specifies, 'a film shot "live" and in particularly difficult circumstances and which would then be shown in slow motion on the screen of a quiet public cinema'.*

Marc Chadourne compares interior monologue (a term he dislikes) to a film (i.e. film image) of consciousness unrolled by the writer.†

'All ideas and images, psychological and emotional feelings,' he says, 'which one after the other or simultaneously develop in a brain, Joyce endeavours to photograph raw ...' (It would be better to say as if they were raw ...) 'These films,' he continues, 'criss-cross and overlap in a puzzle which, indecipherable at first, reveals to the attentive reader endowed with memory a marvellously unified panoramic view. And this,' he adds, 'is Joyce's greatest innovation ... This film of consciousness and of the subconscious at intervals brings forth associations, clusters of feelings experienced, of images and ideas, varying in each case ...'

Taking up this idea of the 'film (film image) of consciousness', Marcel Thiébault outlines how Joyce, in interior monologue, reproduces 'all the thoughts which run through the brain of the character under consideration – in the order or apparent disorder in which they

---

* *Cahier du Mois*, January 1925.
† *Revue Européenne*, May 1929.

come, nothing being neglected, even concerning the sad necessities of our human machines.'* And he rightly opposes this to traditional monologue in which 'writers took away from their characters' thoughts the elements which appeared essential to them and organized them according to the rules of logic'.

Stuart Gilbert, one of the translators of, and author of a perceptive commentary on *Ulysses*, defines interior monologue as 'an exact, almost photographic reproduction of thoughts according to the way in which they take shape in the consciousness of the person thinking, "nuclei" which by a sort of capillary action attract other associations, which give an initial impression of incoherence . . .'†

I shall continue this series of remarks by quoting the translation I have been given of an article in Japanese which a Tokyo review devoted to *Les Lauriers sont coupés*, in which the author, M. D. Horiguchi, gives an excellent explanation of how interior monologue 'bestows on literature the possibility of expressing the thoughts that well up in the deepest recesses of our hearts, the fleeting thoughts that spring forth and then vanish without rising to the level of our conscious thoughts'.[10]

Yves Gandon adds to this outline of interior monologue a fresh comment, writing that 'no doubt only a poet has any chance of succeeding in this audacious enterprise'.‡

Almost at the same time, Louis Gillet, in the article quoted above, related the word poetry to interior monologue. 'More and more,' he said, 'poetry and even the theatre are endeavouring at the expense of what is rational to extend the twilight area of the blurred and inarticulate.'

These exceptions apart, critics do not seem to have

* *Revue de Paris*, 15 June 1929.
† *Nouvelle Revue Française*, April 1929.
‡ *Vient de paraître*, December 1925.

realized that the conception of interior monologue they were setting out was about the same as we have of poetry today. In fact the interpretations we have just collected almost amount to a sort of definition. It has in any case become impossible for us to attribute a poetic quality to a work in which reasoning plays a part and which does not spring directly from the depths of the subconscious. I personally acclaim in interior monologue one of the manifestations of this dazzling introduction of poetry into the novel, which characterizes the epoch.

This 'poetic' dimension of interior monologue, this presentation of thought being born without any concern with logic, could only be expressed through sentences devoid of concern with reasoning. We have seen Edmond Jaloux noticing how these series of little touches one after the other necessitated the series of 'short little phrases' one finds in *Les Lauriers sont coupés*. The form seems to have been dictated by the content. But it isn't so much of 'short little phrases' one must speak as of very simple, very direct sentences, constructed as little as possible (I mean as un-Ciceronian as possible), of sentences reduced to a *grammatical minimum*. In fact, the cases of interior monologue critics have wanted to find in the long sentences with parenthetical clauses by Marcel Proust, for example, do not come into this category at all. By the simple fact of being 'constructed', a parenthetical sentence totally loses any cinematic character in its representation of thought. The subject is not even worthy of discussion.

We can go even further. At the same time as being a return to the basic forms of poetry, interior monologue is a return (obviously in modernized form) to primitive forms of language; and this is an illustration of the very doctrine of the musical origin of poetry. Pierre Exideuil has noted that 'interior language does not obey the physiological rules of audible expression' propounded by Father Jousse. Jules de Gaultier in fact established that poetry consisted in a sort of return to primitive language, which itself was only 'the continuation and exteriorization in the aural world of the vibration of nerves associated with the actual reality of physiological emotion', man then transmitting to man 'in an entirely adequate fashion' his 'state of feelings'.* Thus, poetry would seem to be 'a biological attempt with a view to reconstructing, with the new methods appropriate to the circumstances imposed by the new language, the ancient power of speech'. Jules de Gaultier is less fortunate in the choice of examples he gives to back up his theory.†

The 'poetic' character of interior monologue has necessarily led us to its 'musical' character, which could hardly have been less noticed by the critics, with the exception however of Marcel Brion who has insisted on the musical aspect of Joyce's work, and has gone to the lengths of writing that 'the only effective means of approach to the first reading of *Ulysses*, the "spadework" reading, would be to sight-read it as one does a sonata or fugue'.‡

Most critics have compared interior monologue to all sorts of things – film, wireless, X-ray, diving-bell; they have not, at least as far as I know, pointed to the analogy, the relationship, say, that these short sentences in succession have with musical motifs as, for example, employed by Richard Wagner. But we must make clear what is to be understood by 'musical motif', especially by Wagnerian motif.

The 'motif' in music, in accepted usage, is understood to be a very short phrase, so short that it can be as little as two notes, or sometimes a single chord – in contrast with the (more or less) long phrase in melodies,

---

* See in particular *Mercure de France*, 1 March 1924.
† I have already pointed to the curious case of this philosopher, so perceptive in the realm of abstract ideas, whose eyes cloud over as soon as he descends to the world of appearances.
‡ *Revue hebdomadaire*, 20 April 1929.

popular songs, or operatic arias. However, Wagnerian motif is to be distinguished from traditional motif in that the latter is a theme subject to development (and consequently ought to be called 'theme' rather than 'motif'), whereas Wagnerian motif, while sometimes employed by Wagner as a theme as in classical symphonies, is most often employed by him without development, especially in the *Ring* and in *Parsifal.* In its pure state, the Wagnerian motif is an isolated phrase which always carries an emotional significance, but which is not logically linked with those that precede and those that follow; and that is how interior monologue derives from it. Just as a page of a Wagner score is most often a succession of undeveloped motifs each of which expresses an impulse of the soul, interior monologue is a succession of short sentences each of which also expresses an impulse of the soul, being alike in that they are not linked together according to a rational order but according to a purely emotional order, irrespective of all intellectual arrangement.

Often there is in Wagner, it will be argued, more rational arrangement than I conceive of. I have already recognized the fact that he often employs thematic development in the manner of classical symphonies; I willingly acknowledge that the appearance of motifs is not always as spontaneous as might be; there are sometimes some very un-Wagnerian things in Wagner; but it is all too evident that the influence of an innovator works through what new things he brings and not from what he keeps from the past.

But that is not all. In music one must distinguish – in theory at least – between 'motif' and 'leitmotif'.

In Wagner, motifs are mainly known as leitmotifs, that is to say motifs which reappear in the drama every time the same emotion appears. A music-drama could easily be made up of non-recurring motifs, that is to say motifs which would not be *leit*motifs. In the same way, interior monologue could be made up of ordinary motifs, all different; in actual fact and in the very nature of things, leitmotif was to play a considerable part in it.

Marcel Thiébault and Stuart Gilbert, in the studies quoted above, have remarked on these recurring motifs. I beg to be excused for comparing once again the more modest attempt which was *Les Lauriers sont coupés* and the brilliant realization of *Ulysses*; if however one looks closely at *Les Lauriers sont coupés*, one will see the book is full of leitmotifs ... One will find a very obvious example of this at the beginning of the eighth chapter, with the recapitulation of motifs from the prelude or, in the middle of the last chapter, in the brief account the hero gives Léa of the way he has spent his day; this account is systematically constructed from motifs from the novel, some repeated in their initial state, the others deliberately deformed.*

Gabriel Marcel allows me the opportunity of confirming the poetic and musical origin of interior monologue, in a rather unfortunate article in which he reproaches *Les Lauriers sont coupés* precisely with transposing procedures from poetry and music.†

Alas, dear Sir, that was my very project!

Fortunately I can find another confirmation of my point of view in the comprehensive and penetrating article Valery Larbaud has devoted to James Joyce. This is what we can read on page XXXIII of this study (preface to *Dubliners*):

> Over this framework, or rather the compartments prepared in this way, Joyce has little by little organized his text. It is in actual fact the construction of a mosaic. I have seen his rough drafts. They are entirely made up of sentences in abridged form cros-

---

* The same procedure is found in *Antonia*, in *Les Epoux de Heur-le-Port* and in *Le Mystère du dieu mort et ressuscité*.
† *Nouvelle Revue Française*, February 1925.

sed through with strokes of different coloured pencils. These are notes aimed at reminding him of the complete sentences, and the pencil strokes indicate, according to their colour, that the sentence crossed out has been put in such and such an episode. It reminds one of the boxes of little coloured cubes used by mosaicists.

For someone with a musical background like myself, it reminds one of Wagnerian leitmotifs.

From this series of observations we can conclude that interior monologue, like all monologue, is a speech by a character, the object of which is to introduce us directly into the interior life of that character, without the author intervening with explanations or commentaries, and which, like any monologue, is unheard and unspoken.

However, it is to be distinguished from conventional monologue in that, in its subject matter, it is the expression of the most intimate thought, closest to the unconscious; in conception, it is speech before any logical organization, reproducing this thought as it comes into being and in its apparently raw state; in its form, it is realized through sentences in direct speech reduced to a syntactic minimum. Thus it corresponds essentially to the conception we have today of poetry.

From which I draw up this attempt at a definition:

Interior monologue is, like poetry, unheard, unspoken speech, through which a character expresses his most intimate thoughts, closest to the unconscious, prior to all logical organization, that is to say as it comes into being, by means of sentences in direct speech reduced to their syntactic minimum, in order to give the impression of raw experience.

Is the interior monologue technique, as we have
attempted to define it, viable? The example of *Ulysses*
would be reply enough, if this admirable success by a
writer of genius had not, like all great works, given rise to
objections, sometimes rather unexpected ones. I shall
give one example of these.

> Interior monologue [writes André Billy], besides
> being the dullest and most facile of procedures, has
> the inconvenience of being the most wearisome.*

One could counter André Billy's argument by saying
that the most difficult things are sometimes those which
appear the most facile, and that facility as well as dull
platitudes are more readily recognizable in certain judgements about which one can say that they are at best
simplistic. Does what the editor of *L'Oeuvre* writes about
James Joyce's novel itself go any deeper? I am sure André
Billy never talks about books he has not read. This is no
doubt why the same man, who analyses certain novels
with such perception and originality, can only appreciate
the dimensions of *Ulysses*. One would have thought, in
any case, that noting down the pagination is no more
sufficient to appreciate the work of a master like Joyce
than, to appreciate the work of a new writer, it would be
sufficient to cast a glance at the 'Recent Books' notes
compiled by the publisher.

The objections that Auguste Bailly brings to bear† on
interior monologue are, in contrast, by a critic who has
made a close study of the work he is talking about. For
him, the 'slice of interior life' represented by the new
technique is no less arbitrary or false than analysis in the
traditional psychological novel, and it is for this reason,
he says, that 'the author is obliged to present it as a sort
of unbroken line', whereas 'we do not think on one level,
but simultaneously on several levels'.‡

---

* *L'Oeuvre*, 25 June 1929.   † *Candide*, 23 May 1929.
‡ On Jean-Richard Bloch's attempt, see page 143 below.

The question cannot be discussed in a few lines; a psychologist would say, I believe, not that we think simultaneously on several levels, but that our thought moves from one level to another with a rapidity which seems to be, but is not, simultaneity; and it is precisely this disconnected flow of which interior monologue gives an impression; Joyce's 'unbroken line' is in fact a broken one.

The critics have also been concerned with what we have called the 'raw experience' of interior monologue. Without faulting Joyce's book, Eugène Montfort contended, in the article quoted above, that 'the formless magma' which was at the basis of interior monologue could never be reproduced as such, and that a selection from it had to be made.

In the *Revue des Deux Mondes* article devoted to the great Irish writer, Louis Gillet reproaches him with saying everything; but at the same time he accuses him of employing every kind of artifice, 'all the wiles, all the tricks, St John's wort in all its forms', and of substituting for the thoughts of the unfortunate Bloom 'the whims of his own wit, the embellishments, fireworks, and flourishes of his dizzying and burlesque imagination'.

In a later article devoted to Virginia Woolf,* the same critic raises the subject again; after having, with characteristic penetrating, eloquent wit, reminded the reader of what *Ulysses* sets out to do, he concludes:

> An illusory project, because no language exists which can translate what is beyond language. The author himself is not to blame in going beyond the limits of his project and developing immense lyrico-epic, satirical, dramatic fugues, which have nothing more to do with the original outline. The book begun by a realist ends up as phantasmagoria.

* *Revue des Deux Mondes*, 1 September 1929, also reprinted in *Esquisses anglaises*.

According to Marcel Thiébault, 'it would be unjust to reproach Joyce with saying *everything* and with serving up a formless mish-mash of thought ... Making these films of consciousness is not the result of laziness,' he adds, 'because in reality it is not re-production (which is technically impossible) but re-creation.

Though appearing to be in contradiction, these views coincide. Total reproduction, real 'reproduction of the film of consciousness' is something almost impossible to imagine. And that is why we have several times made clear that interior monologue must not render thought 'raw', but give the impression of it. And in this way it proves itself to be a work of art much more than the logical analysis of the psychological novel.

It could even be said that it hardly seems possible that it can be achieved continuously and absolutely strictly. In the article already quoted, Gabriel Marcel criticizes *Les Lauriers sont coupés* for its 'discursive passages' ... If *Les Lauriers sont coupés* had contained no departure from its own guidelines, it would have achieved what no work of art has ever achieved ... One could find the same 'mistakes' even in the interior monologues of *Ulysses*; Wagner is not without his un-Wagnerian passages; there is sometimes a bit of Lefranc de Pompignan in Hugo.[11] It is rather mean to limit oneself to looking for weaknesses in a work, instead of studying what it was striving towards, especially when this produced something innovatory.

On what is perhaps psychological,
dramatic or intimate monologue, but is not
interior monologue

Now that the elements of a definition of interior monologue have been assembled, it will be easy – without
making the definition we have proposed an article of faith
– for us to distinguish between what has been taken for
interior monologue and what it really is.

We have observed that interior monologue and conventional monologue are both unheard speech (with the
exception of the theatrical convention which demands
they be recited out loud) and unspoken speech. So one
sees Hamlet in Shakespeare's play or Rastignac in *Le
Père Goriot* 'monologuing', and nobody professes to find
interior monologue in their soliloquies. But if no confusion is possible in the case of monologues in
Shakespeare or Balzac, it more easily comes about in the
case of half-way techniques, such as those which have
been termed psychological monologue or 'dramatic
monologue' and which are to be found, respectively, in
Dostoyevsky and Browning.

We have already related how, in one of his 1922
lectures, André Gide had stated that Dostoyevsky, Edgar
Allan Poe and Robert Browning had employed this literary technique, even adding that they 'had brought it to
the most diversified and subtle perfection it could attain'.

In a conversation they had shortly afterwards, Valery
Larbaud thought he had convinced him of his mistake;
but the retreat effected by André Gide was only of short
duration; the letter he wrote to me on 4 July 1930 shows
him to have gone back to his original position.

> Certain stories by Poe [he said], among others,
> 'The Tell-Tale Heart' and admirable poems by
> Browning (in particular *Sludge*) remain no less, in my

view, perfect, unsurpassable realizations of interior monologue. Also Dostoyevsky's unforgettable 'The Gentle Creature'.

This does not tally too well with the sentence I have quoted from the same letter in which he writes: 'the dates are ... there to prove you [i.e. me] as precursor.' But let us leave this detail aside ... We have found an analogous opinion from René Lalou; we shall find a similar one in Charles Du Bos, and it would not be difficult to make a more extensive list.

One would only have to reproach these views with giving too wide a definition of the term 'interior monologue', and it would only be a question of words, if the views under consideration did not contain a serious misapprehension as to what fundamentally new element interior monologue has contributed to literature.

Most of the critics we have quoted have written that interior monologue had the specific aim of guiding us in the unconscious of the character, that is to say, to express everything unformulated ... viz diving-bell, wireless, x-ray, etc ... and this is, in fact, the supreme realization of interior monologue, especially when handled by a James Joyce. But the fact that Joyce's interior monologue expresses a greater number of feelings and sensations, and that it penetrates more deeply into the lower depths of the soul of the character, I can see only as a difference in tendency or realization, not its essentially characteristic innovation.

The essential innovation introduced by interior monologue consists in the fact that its aim is to evoke the uninterrupted flow of thoughts going through the character's being, as they are born and in the order they are born, without any explanation of logical sequence and giving the impression of 'raw' experience. We were saying earlier that a concrete choice is necessary; what is peculiar to interior monologue is not absence of choice, but that choice is not made according to rational logic. The difference does not consist in the fact that conventional monologue expresses *less* intimate thoughts than interior monologue, but in that it coordinates them, demonstrates their logical sequence, that is to say explains them, and most often is content to summarize them.

Dostoyevsky has described with genius those illogical, inconsistent, self-contradictory characters at the mercy of their unconscious impulses; however, a writer can show that a character is illogical, and remain perfectly logical in his description. Dostoyevsky may have expressed this seething mass of embryonic thought, of thought in formation; but instead of expressing it as such, as Joyce has done, as it is born in the mind, he has explained it, analysed it, which is a traditional procedure.

If we go to the bottom of things, we can see that this dark, teeming unconscious has been expressed by the great classical writers as well, in the rationalized discourse of their time; but they tended to make no more intellectual use of it than Dostoyevsky. In *Phèdre* and *Andromaque* there are certainly no abnormal, degenerate or alcoholic characters; you are not confronted with those ridiculous confessions to be found at every turn, nor any of that brothel-house Satanism now commonplace in Russian literature; however, Racine has not penetrated any less far into the human soul. If he has depicted Western and not Russian characters, who will regret it? In any case, one ought to guard against confusing the profound and the morbid.

Half a century ago, Zola and the Naturalists imagined they could produce something more truthful than classical writers because they gave free expression to ruffians. Our contemporaries are under the same illusion when they imply that it is more profound to describe the mental state of a degenerate than that of a man in good health – as if it sufficed to put on stage somebody totally paralysed in order to go one better than Racine and Molière!

Joyce had no need to attend the Russian school of novel writing in order to study the depths of humanity. In fact, interior monologue did not invent the probing of human profundities; it made of it a new means of expression, which is not to be found in the monologues of Raskolnikov or Stavrogin any more than in those of Phèdre or Hermione.

Far from having employed what we term interior monologue, Dostoyevsky in a sense gave it its death sentence, in that after having seen the possibility of it, he stated that he refused to use it. Here, in effect, is the strange extract I have taken from one of his stories, entitled 'A Nasty Story':

> Everybody knows that whole trains of thought can sometimes pass through our heads in the twinkling of an eye, like so many sensations, without being translated into any kind of human, much less literary, language. But we shall try to translate our hero's sensations of that kind and present to our readers at any rate the substance of them, what were, so to speak, their most essential and plausible aspects.*

Dostoyevsky, we can see, after having apologized for this lack of logic, announces that he is going to 'try to translate', which is, in exact terms, *the contrary of interior monologue*. He has reached exactly the same position as Balzac who, after the monologue by Rastignac I have quoted, writes the following lines: 'These words are the brief formulation for the thousand and one thoughts between which he wavered.'

The error of someone who, like André Gide, is a

* French translation, *Une fâcheuse histoire*, Nelson, Paris, 1926, p. 28 [English translation, 'A Nasty Story', in *The Gambler and Other Stories*, translated by Jessie Coulson, Penguin Books, Harmondsworth, 1966, p. 195].

masterly critic as well as a great writer, springs from the fact that, in his conception of interior monologue, he has not taken sufficiently into account the elements which constitute the profound innovation of the technique achieved by James Joyce. And the proof lies in the fact that the same André Gide who can recognize interior monologue in the works of Dostoyevsky, is not far from recognizing it in his own works:

> I also believe [he wrote on 4th July last] I have several times employed the form so dear to you, particularly in certain chapters of *Les Caves du Vatican*, in which the murder of Fleurissoire by Lafcadio is revealed, explained, only through the latter's monologue. My *Bethsabé* is merely a long monologue by David; but, when it takes shape on the stage, Larbaud would object, can one still say it remains 'interior'?

Les Caves du Vatican is a masterpiece; Lafcadio's monologue is one of the most admirable passages in our literature, just as certain novels by Dostoyevsky are among the most powerful that have ever been written ... As for André Gide's monologues, we have only to repeat what we have said about Dostoyevsky's.

Is it necessary to add that it is not impossible to find in these writers, especially in Dostoyevsky and Browning, words, whole sentences exhibiting the characteristics of interior monologue? When a movement is about to come into existence, premonitory signs of it can frequently be seen to appear; but we repeat that what counts, to register the birth of a technique, is its deliberate, systematic and continuous use, as it was sketched out in *Les Lauriers sont coupés* and realized in *Ulysses*.

Mention was also made of the name of Marcel Proust in 1922. A few years later in an article devoted to *Les*

Lauriers sont coupés Robert Kemp put forward the same argument.

> The work of Marcel Proust [he wrote] is teeming with interior monologues. When Marcel awakes, listens to the noises in the street, guesses what the weather is like from the colour of his curtains, sifts through the impressions he has felt in the company of Albertine and discusses within himself the sincerity and the virtue of his friend, is that not interior monologue?*

No, Robert Kemp, it is not interior monologue. For, first of all, even if Proust had wanted this, the very construction of his sentences loaded with parentheses is *a priori* irreconcilable with the expression of thought coming into being and, secondly, his aim, on the contrary, is to explain the inferences of this thoughts, and, far from setting them out in an illogical sequence, to demonstrate how they connect together.

I shall take an example that I believe to be convincing. It is the passage from *Albertine disparue* (pp. 113–14) beginning with the words: 'And because, behind its multi-coloured marble balusters, Mamma was sitting reading while she waited for me . . .'†

From the very first words, we can see Proust announcing his formal intention of demonstrating how his thoughts are deduced from each other. The 'because' alone is at the opposite pole to interior monologue.

I have heard quoted as evidence the passages relative to Vinteuil's sonata (*Du côté de chez Swann*), to Albertine asleep (*La Prisonnière*) to the death of Bergotte (ibid):

---

* *Liberté*, 22 January 1925, and returning to the attack in an article of 22 April 1929 devoted to *Ulysses*.

† [*À la recherche du temps perdu*, vol. IV, Gallimard, 1989, p. 204; *Remembrance of Things Past*, vol. III (*The Fugitive*), translated by C.K. Scott Moncrieff and Terence Kilmartin, Penguin Books, 1983, p. 639.]

there as elsewhere, Proust's primary aim is to explain. And where there is explanation, there is no interior monologue.

I shall reply in like manner to Charles du Bos who, referring to *Anna Karenina*, wrote in 1924 and, not a little foolhardily, repeated in 1930 the following:

> At the decisive turning-point in her destiny, Anna Karenina reaches the station and we hear the most incredible interior monologue, that interior monologue about the recent invention of which genre everybody has just been wanting to tell us.*

It is perfectly obvious that literature was not born in the years directly preceding 1924, any more than it was born with Mallarmé, or with the Romantics, or with Racine, or with the Pléiade. It is simply a question of knowing whether, in the years immediately preceding 1924, a particular innovation, unknown in previous times, did not come to light.

As far as Edgar Allan Poe's stories are concerned, 'The Tell-Tale Heart' may well be a first-person narrative, yet it is never anything but a narrative, however great its pathos.

The name of Stendhal, too, has been put forward. Now, at the time when I was putting the finishing touches to this essay, I was reading an article by Henri Martineau, the title of which is sufficient indication of its subject matter, 'Stendhal précurseur de James Joyce',† together with the following lines from the (so-far unpublished) notebooks by the young Stendhal:

> One thinks much faster than one speaks. Let us suppose a man could speak as fast as he thinks and

* *Entretiens sur Tolstoi*, 1924; *Approximations*, 1930.
† *Figaro*, 27 September 1930. The passage from Stendhal quoted forms part of the *Pensées/Filosofia nova* published by Henri Martineau a few months later in Divan Editions, vol. II, pp. 123–4; see also pp. 179 et seq.

feels, that this man, for a whole day, said, so as to be heard only by one man, everything he thought and felt, that there was that same day, always by his side, an invisible stenographer who was able to write as fast as the former could think and speak. Let us suppose that the stenographer, after having noted down all the thoughts and feelings of our man, translated them to us the next day into ordinary script, we should have a character depicted for one day as life-like as possible.

Henri Martineau, in this article, does not mention the words interior monologue; but no text is better suited to showing how far Stendhal is from it. In the project he outlines there is not the slightest trace, in fact, of an inference concerning the pre-logical characteristics inherent in this technique, and there is, on the contrary, a preoccupation with the expression of absolutely 'raw' thought that James Joyce, as we have seen, never envisaged. Even more than Dostoyevsky, than Proust, than Poe and than Tolstoy, Stendhal is at the opposite pole to interior monologue. Much closer to it was that delightful and outstanding man, George Moore, when in 1906 he wrote the two lines, as delectable as they are characteristic, and which I am obliged to quote in the original:

> My nonsense thoughts amuse me; I follow my thoughts as a child follows butterflies.*

The French translation is: 'Mes pensées vagabondes [roaming] m'amusent: je les suis comme un enfant suit des papillons.' If George Moore had said that his thoughts were 'roaming', he would only have said what anybody else might have said; with the word 'nonsense' which signifies devoid of meaning, the intuition of the great writer has expressed everything that was irrational

---

* *Memoirs of My Dead Life*, 1906, Chapter I; French translation, *Mémoire de ma vie morte*, 1922; complete edition, 1928.

in the sequence of thoughts unfurled in what was later to be termed [in English] 'unspoken monologue'. This is what George Moore himself recently confirmed to me in a letter dated 8 November 1930:

> The word 'vagabond' [he wrote] does not fully express my thought; 'irrational' which you suggest expresses it better; but 'irrational' is a word I detest. This is my interpretation of interior monologue: when reason ceases to step into the wings to crank things up, we begin to hear an exquisite music. The cage is open and the birds (our thoughts) sing in free verse.

There would be a case, as well, for studying Max Jacob, who, in a series of works which tend more and more towards interior monologue, succeeded in producing, in 1922, that masterpiece, *Le Cabinet noir*, which displays so many of its characteristics.

Louis Gillet thinks he has found something similar in Charles Péguy's attempt to reproduce the internal movement of thought, an attempt which 'came to him', writes Louis Gillet, 'from Bergson and from a superstitious attitude about the spontaneous, about the unformed, about consciousness coming into being; he had misgivings about corrections; about being directive; he gave in his copy with crossings-out, incorporating them in his sentences ...', without being aware that this is the very thing 'which gives his work such great monotony and made it look exactly like what he most hated; written according to formulas'.

On the contrary, it seems that reproducing all of thought's 'crossings-out', when thought is moving according to a rational order, is a quite different thing from expressing its pre-logical antecedents, and that the principal characteristic of interior monologue will always be to evolve according to the irrational.

We have seen René Lalou in 1922, in his *Histoire de la
littérature contemporaine* referring to Paul Morand, Marcel
Proust, Dostoyevsky and Browning as the earliest mas-
ters of the genre. In a review of Larbaud's *Amants,
heureux amants* published two years later,* he dropped
the first three. Recently queried by me on this subject, he
wrote, on 8 August 1930, that he had intentionally 'no
longer retained the names of Morand and Proust' and
that the use of monologue seemed 'less clear-cut in
Dostoyevsky, where it represents only a brief incursion
in his work (except perhaps in *Notes from the Under-
ground?*), than in Browning where whole, self-contained
and independent poems are monologues'.

Let us then consider the case of Browning who, we
have seen, is also proposed by André Gide. This is what
René Lalou writes in his 1924 article:

> Robert Browning had seen all the possibilities of
> interior monologue, witness the solitary meditation
> of the Pope and the logically disorganized chatter by
> Hyacinthus in *The Ring and the Book*, or again the
> extraordinary *Caliban upon Setebos*, in which Caliban
> is so afraid of being heard that he does not dare to
> speak in his own name, expressing his thoughts in the
> grammatical guise of an anonymous third person.

I must admit that however much I have thought
about it, scratched my head over it, I find it impossible to
understand how the fact of speaking about oneself in the
third person and anonymously indicates that 'one is
afraid of being heard ...'. If, not content with speaking
of himself in the third person, our good old Negro,
instead of saying 'Nice Negro like jam', speaks of himself
anonymously and says 'Li likes jam ...', does it mean he
does not want to be heard?

The important thing is to ascertain whether Brown-

* *Vient de paraître*, March 1924.

ing's monologues are really unheard speech and unspoken speech; it is also important to know if they proceed from a logical order or from an irrational order. Having myself only an imperfect knowledge of Browning's work, I have preferred to have recourse to Valery Larbaud's competence in the matter, as specialized as René Lalou's on English literature, and I received the following reply:

> The examples put forward [writes Larbaud], when the invention of interior monologue was being attributed to Robert Browning, were ill-chosen. *My Last Duchess* and *Mr Sludge the Medium* both presume the presence of a real and visible interlocutor and change the monologue into a dialogue.
>
> The same objection applies to the monologue by Robert Browning in which the person speaking addresses himself to someone who is absent or to an imaginary audience. We have there in fact merely the extreme extension of a technique common in seventeenth-century novelists (for example the declaration to a portrait).
>
> However, there is in the work of Robert Browning a class of long monologues (1,500 to 2,000 lines) in which nothing allows us to suppose that the character speaking is addressing himself to an interlocutor, either real or imaginary; and, at first sight, nothing seems to distinguish them from what today goes under the name of interior monologue. (This is the case of 'Dominus Hyacinthus de Archangelis' referred to by René Lalou.) But, if we examine these monologues more closely, we find specifically *dramatic* characteristics in them, different from – and up to a point the opposite of – those of interior monologue.
>
> First of all, we can always suppose they are spoken, according to the convention which allows

monologues in the theatre, and because a man who is
deeply moved 'talks to himself'. Next, and most
important, these monologues belong to drama
because of their material and their limitations: everything in them contributes to the portrait of a given
character in a given set of circumstances. (So the
external present, the fortuitous, which play such a
significant role in interior monologue, only play a
limited role.) One can therefore say that each of these
monologues is in itself a comedy or a drama out of
which we only hear the hero, through whom we learn
everything; and one could imagine *Tartuffe* or *Le
Misanthrope* reworked in the following way: the
characters and events presented through the solitary
chatter of the hero meditating and reminiscing, and,
at the same time, involuntarily giving his self-
portrait.

Robert Browning's monologue has therefore been
appositely named by applying the term *dramatic* to it,
and it was necessary to invent a new expression to
designate the *non-dramatic* monologue practised in
Les Lauriers sont coupés.

Valery Larbaud's conclusion seems to be the right
one. The critics' mistake consisted in confusing things
which must be kept separate. Already in his *Histoire de la
littérature contemporaine*, René Lalou seemed to have
realized the difference between interior monologue and
the various forms of traditional monologue, by designat-
ing 'interior' monologue, which he attributes to Joyce
and to Larbaud, and 'intimate' monologue which he
attributes to Dostoyevsky and to Browning. As I asked
him if he considered the two expressions to be
synonymous, he replied in the letter quoted above:

I have tried to distinguish a nuance by speaking
first of 'interior monologue' then of 'intimate mono-

logue'. I have understood by the term 'intimate monologue' a more direct psychological means of expression employed by Browning and Dostoyevsky, with the art form of the former remaining that of the dramatic poem and of the latter, the novel. If one adopted this nuance of vocabulary, one could without ambiguity reserve the name 'interior monologue' for a work whose genre would be the *form* itself. In other words, interior monologue would have become, with you, Joyce and Larbaud, a separate genre.

We do not feel that the term 'intimate monologue' will have much success; there is only an imperceptible difference between 'intimate' and 'interior', and the terms 'psychological' monologue and 'dramatic' mono-logue give a better definition of the traditional monologue which existed before 1887. The important thing in any case, and this is more than a question of words, is to recognize that interior monologue, born in 1887 and brought to a peak of achievement by a genius thirty years later, has contributed something innovatory to literature from the formal point of view.

The Origins of Interior Monologue

The fact that interior monologue was created in 1887 and not thirty years later leaves the question of its origins unanswered.

Indeed, the word 'origins' can be taken to have two meanings. The origins of interior monologue (which we could in this case call the literary origins) can be under-stood by taking into account the series of literary forms which, for several centuries, have established a tradition according to which the creation of this technique has been possible thanks to a given set of circumstances.

Otherwise, one can understand by origins of interior monologue (and in this case it would be rather its historical origins) the actual circumstances, the historical facts which made this creation possible.

I shall only make a brief mention of the 'literary' origins; Valery Larbaud has wanted to study them and perseveres in wanting to, and I only need to sum up the conclusions he has reached. For him, the study of the origins of interior monologue consists in finding the series of literary forms characterized, he specifies, by the use of the first person singular,* the apparently immediate and spontaneous expression of intimate thoughts, and the stylization of talking to oneself, which have established the tradition according to which (thanks to a given set of circumstances, as we said just now) its creation was made possible. In his opinion, this tradition, in France, is a direct line through Montaigne, Madame de Lafayette, Stendhal, the 'gratuitous' long soliloquy and the asides in Romantic drama; but he himself recognizes that there must be many other links in this chain of monologues which, without themselves having anything in common with interior monologue, prepared for its invention.†

My studies in sociological history have progressively led me to be more interested in the circumstances, in other words in the historical facts, and further still in the development which made the creation of a new technique not only possible but necessary. As far as I am personally concerned, a distance of nearly half a century will allow me, I hope, to speak about this with objectivity. But the personal aspect of the question is of secondary interest: in addition, the personal element can only be considered from a sociological point of view as the reduction to the individual level of a general phenomenon.

* For my reservations on this, see pages 98–9 above.
† I would say, for example, the 'disguised' monologues of Racine; see above, page 101.

Some critics seem to believe that interior monologue could just as well have been created one hundred or two hundred years earlier. Others, reserving for me the glory of its invention (for which I thank them) write that, by a sort of prophetic intuition (they do me too much honour), I was thirty years ahead of my time ... One would be at a loss to understand such a complete absence of method in self-respecting writers, if one did not remember the extent to which the historical disciplines are alien to some of the most intelligent, the shrewdest, and the most sensitive of our critics. In fact, the critics who express such opinions have remained at the stage of certain 'lycée'-teachers in my youth who imagined the great universal writers, from Homer to Hugo, in the guise of schoolboys side by side on the benches of the same class, each one doing his 'home-work' to the best of his ability.

A new technique has its origins in the necessities of the period from which it emerges, not from those whose preoccupations are outdated, nor from those of a future time; this is a law of literary evolution that it is surprising to see unrecognized. Interior monologue could not have been born in a period of literary evolution uncongenial to it; if it was born in 1887, however modest that birth was, it is because the literary evolution of that period demanded it.

Obviously, like any new technique, it possibly had antecedents, and one is justified in investigating how it could possibly be prefigured; but it could only be prefigured to the extent to which the development from which it sprang was also to be prefigured; if the psychological monologues of a Dostoyevsky or the dramatic monologues of a Browning display certain of its characteristics, this is as premonitory signs of the movement which was to be inaugurated even before the two writers had died.

Taking an opposite point of view, one cannot auto-

matically deny that interior monologue must have started
somewhere – we are not saying prior to the development
which was to produce it, but at a moment in that
development before it ought naturally to have appeared;
and this is what we shall shortly have to come back to.
What matters in any case, is to determine which literary
movement it is connected with and from which one,
sooner or later, it was going to have to spring.

As to ascertaining who was the 'inventor' of interior
monologue, the question is of the sort that the least sociological notion of literary history indicates should not be
asked, and I can only repeat here what I said, a few years
ago, in my essay on *Les Premiers poètes du vers libre.**

Just as in the social and religious domains, 'invention' in art and literature, far from being the personal
work of the writer who first embodied it, is the product
of the aspirations of a generation realized by one man of
that generation, who himself will have hardly understood
the import of his contribution.

The truth is that interior monologue was to be, and
essentially was, a manifestation of what was most profound in the great movement first expressed in the poems
of Mallarmé and of Rimbaud, which started in about
1885 with the entry into literature of the Symbolist generation, and which, in actual fact, renewed French
literature throughout its whole range.

What did the young writers of 1885 mean by poetry?
This question has dominated the history of French
literature for half a century. To them poetry meant the
expression of an interior life. There was a total reaction
against Romanticism and the Parnassian movement; the
external world no longer exists for the young writers of
1885 except as conceived of by the mind. Everything in
the literature of this period concerns the soul; the
external world is only scenery put up and dismantled on
the orders of the poet. But we sought this essential

* Mercure de France, 1922, pp. 25–7.

reality, this interior life which the classical writers had looked for in what they called reason, in the area till then despised (today we would say repressed) of the unconscious. The very aim we attributed to poetry led us to exclude from it everything to do with reasoning, with narrative, with logical demonstration. We were the ones who unshackled poetry from rationalism.

Lastly, the Symbolist generation operated the introduction of poetry into every literary field. Up till then, there had been verse and prose; thereafter there was poetry and non-poetry.

I will not undertake to study this immense movement here; its history is, moreover, well known; I shall limit myself to drawing attention to the aspect of it which is most familiar to me and which, in my opinion, was the most important: the influence of music.

By establishing the fundamental opposition between the world of 'Representation' and the world of 'Life Force' Schopenhauer taught us that, if the first was connected with the conceptual arts, the second was completely beyond him.[12] Symbolism established as a guiding principle the differentiation of the two fields.

So, which was the art form, free of anything conceptual, to which Schopenhauer had accorded the power of expressing the world of the Life Force? Music. This is why Wagner had such a considerable influence in 1885; Wagner was, first of all, the medium through which most of us came to Schopenhauer and, later, his magnificent example, going beyond all that the old philosopher of Frankfurt could have imagined, demonstrated how music could be the Life Force. We deliberately placed poetry on the Schopenhauer level of music. And that is what is meant by saying that Symbolism, liberating poetry from the servitude of intellectualism, restored to it its musical value.

The limited scope of this study does not allow us to examine the connections between Bergsonian philosophy and the movement of 1885. Let us simply recall that Henri Bergson, although our senior by only a few years (he was born in 1859), only began to outline the tenets of his philosophy at the end of the nineteenth century, and that the work which really set them forth, *L'Evolution créatrice*, dates from 1907. If Bergson gave expression to certain of the tenets of Symbolism, it cannot at all be said that he inspired them; he seems rather to be one of those who inherited their legacy. Whatever the exact truth of the matter, the huge success he obtained at the beginning of the century is proof, one among others, of the extent to which the movement of 1885 was a profound and lasting renewal.

Like Bergsonism, Freudianism was hardly known before the beginning of this century; it comes out of the same movement, through the importance it has given to the deepest levels of the unconscious in the formation of thought.

To limit ourselves more to what particularly concerns our object of study, we shall only keep to the main characteristics of the movement of 1885; that is to say, the life consciousness taken over as the subject of poetry, the musical conception – namely the de-intellectualization of poetry – and finally, the shattering entry of this conception of poetry into prose and especially into the novel are precisely the fundamental principles of interior monologue.

It remains to be seen whether it was to be one of the first creations of the movement or one of its last.

I must apologise for moving from an important general question to a very personal one about which I have incidentally often been asked: how did the man writing these lines come to conceive of interior monologue? The interest of this, I repeat, is to see a general phenomenon in a specific individual case.

It is all too obvious that, in 1885, I was subject to the same influences as the group I was in; but there is one influence I came under more than the others: that of German music, and I can say that I contributed to propagating this around me. Just now I pointed to the analogy, generally not recognized, between musical motifs and the short phrases in direct speech of interior monologue. I am going to divulge a secret: *Les Lauriers sont coupés* was undertaken with the wild ambition of transposing into the literary field Wagnerian procedures which I defined for myself as follows: the life of the soul expressed through the incessant eruption of musical motifs, coming up to speak, one after the other, undefined and in succession, the 'states' of thought, feeling, impressions, brought into existence, or tentatively brought into existence, in an undefined succession of short phrases, each rendering one of these states of thought, in no logical order, in the form of bursts of thought rising from the depths of the self, from what we today would call the unconscious or the subconscious . . .

The critics hardly seem to have considered the fact that interior monologue came out of the movement of 1885. One writer who, intending to attack Symbolism, has been able to recognize how it manifested itself, was more clear-sighted. I am referring to Charles Le Goffic who, in his book *Les Romanciers d'aujourd'hui*, published in 1890, grouped *Les Lauriers sont coupés*, to which he devoted several pages from which I take the following lines, with other Symbolist works.

Suppose a novelist sets himself the following project: in the disorder of mental life, with the perpetual confusion of feelings, ideas and impressions, in the tumult external circumstances creates for the logical development of thought, and the sudden switches within this thought itself, to commit to memory and try to describe in minute detail all the feelings, ideas, impressions, which can go through a human mind from seven to ten in the evening. If with a project like that you don't manage to put together a monologue for Coquelin Cadet, I tell you, you won't have been faithful to your project . . .'[13]

Except for the allusion to the monologues of Coquelin Cadet, very much in vogue in 1890, the analysis of interior monologue is sufficiently discerning to prove that Charles Le Goffic knew what he was talking about when he made it a product of the Symbolist movement.

Thirty-five years later, with the insight borne out by his whole article, Louis Gillet too, in the *Revue des Deux Mondes*, was to point to the real origins of interior monologue.

It is strange [he said of *Ulysses*] that this sort of total novel, the most sustained effort that has been made to exhaust the sum of all of reality, came both from Naturalism and from the Pandora's Box of Symbolism. And yet that is understandable, because the whole of reality consists in the clear or confused consciousness we have of it. 'The soul,' Mr Joyce states, 'the soul, in a sense, is all that exists.'

'Our soul alone lives,' I wrote at the beginning of my first book.

One guesses why Louis Gillet links Naturalism and Symbolism here; but what he says about reality, about the consciousness we have of it and of the soul, only really applies to the latter.

A complete study of the movement that began in 1885 would conclude with Surrealism which pushed it to its extreme logical consequences by trying to express, directly and without any rational clarification, the prod-ucts of the unconscious. When they published *Les*

Champs magnétiques in 1921, André Breton and Philippe Soupault had not read *Les Lauriers sont coupés* and were not familiar with the extracts from *Ulysses* which had just come out in New York; the characteristics of interior monologue were nonetheless present in their work, as well as in the poems which followed and in the attempts at automatic writing. What is automatic writing, after all, if not the raw material (uncorrected raw material) of the thoughts which come out of the unconscious independently of all intellectualizing elaboration?

We can conclude from the foregoing that, if interior monologue cannot be considered the final product of the movement of 1885, it is even more difficult to see in it one of its first manifestations. The very fact that it intended to go to the well-springs of the unconscious and, without diminishing it altogether, reduce to a minimum and conceal rational elaboration, makes it necessary to situate it at a very advanced stage of the movement's development. If things had taken their normal course, interior monologue would have been the last manifestation of Symbolism. It is in this way that we could say that *Les Lauriers sont coupés* was the offspring of the movement of 1885,[14] albeit the premature offspring.

And that is what explains, at least partially, not merely why the book had no success in 1887 or 1888, but why it had no reverberation and remained an isolated experiment. And it is in this manner that one can reply to a possible objection: if interior monologue in *Les Lauriers sont coupés* was the expression of the tendencies of the time, why didn't this book have on its appearance the success which, it seems, a work which fulfils the expectations of its contemporaries must always obtain?

Just now I protested, with all the confidence that the feeling one is master of a method can give, against the critics who, without having any method themselves, have sought for the historical origins of interior monologue other than in the circumstances which gave rise to it, or who presented it as anticipating a later development. Yet the fact that the Symbolist movement began in around 1885 does not at all mean that it was sufficiently ripe in 1887 or 1888 for it to have been from that very moment the time for interior monologue. One therefore has no right to state that *Les Lauriers sont coupés* came before its time, if one understands by that that it anticipated a movement that was to come into being thirty years later; one has that right, if one means that, although stemming from the Symbolist movement, it came before its time.

However, a work's lack of success can also be explained, at least at a secondary level, by its qualities or rather by the failings proper to it, and by the circumstances of its publication.

Will it be said of *Les Lauriers sont coupés* that it was the imperfect realization of a happy idea?

I shall not, at a distance of half a century, make a play of modesty. The testimony of Joyce, of Larbaud and Jaloux alone would prevent me from thinking it was an entirely failed work. Perhaps in the first enthusiasm of discovery Larbaud was encouraged to exaggerate somewhat, when he stated that *Les Lauriers sont coupés* was 'a perfect masterpiece to put next to the greatest novels of French literature ...'. It is for me praise enough that Edmond Jaloux was able to write in his *Nouvelles littéraires* article that 'there are passages in *Les Lauriers sont coupés* that are really wonderfully successful ...'. Many statements, in any case, have largely outweighed a few unfavourable opinions. However, if the book is not a failure, neither is it, and especially was it, when it came out in the *Revue indépendante* in 1887, a completely successful book.

I can see one of the causes of the lack of success of *Les Lauriers sont coupés* in 1887 in the excesses of 'Symbolist' language, which I made even more complicated with supposed grammatical reforms! Without defending failings which I have for long deplored, I shall however ask writers, who still continue today to bring harsh judgements on the language of their forebears, if they are perfectly sure that the language they themselves use (see any anthology of 'modern poetry', for example) will be more appreciated in forty years' time.

Little by little, moreover, my friends and I rid ourselves of these errors. The first edition of *Les Lauriers sont coupés* published in book form in the following year was already somewhat toned down, though only slightly so.[15] More wide-ranging were the corrections introduced by the 1897 Mercure de France edition. In the latest edition, in 1924, I tried to clarify things without losing any of the original atmosphere ... What would the fate of *Les Lauriers sont coupés* have been if the text published in 1887 had been 'readable'? ...

Another reason can, to a certain extent, explain the book's lack of success. If I had wanted to make a profession of faith of the dedication I inscribed on its first page, I could have dedicated my book to Richard Wagner. Would it have been understood? ... Wagner's name would in any case have been evocative ... I dedicated my novel to Racine, 'supreme novelist of souls'.

Such a dedication was not merely a reaction against the injustices perpetuated by the Romantics; it was not simply the affirmation of my profound admiration for classical beauty; it indicated my intention to link, against all odds, my experiment with tradition; most of all it carried the ambition, astonishingly pure in a twenty-five-year-old writer, of continuing, by other means and on a different level, the Racinian triumph of poetry. This is what was completely misunderstood. There was too great a distance between the rule of reason according to which the seventeenth century had developed and the irrational order I was trying to penetrate. Most of my friends asked me why I had dedicated my book to Racine. Instead of guiding my readers, my dedication spread disarray amongst them.

Larbaud obligingly explained in his preface, what
other causes, through the years that followed, contributed to the fact that my book was forgotten until
Joyce revived it.[16] I shall not go over these again. Today
we can see that the sort of lack of consideration which
Symbolism went through before the War is being diss-
ipated, at least among writers who do not wallow in their
own ignorance. We are beginning to understand that
Symbolism is memorable for more than the tawdry
finery, so obviously out of date, with which it covered
itself forty years ago. The basic characteristic of the great
literary movements is precisely to bring about an agitation where the worst mixes with the best. We can smile
at the attitudes the young writers of 1885 took pleasure
in, as we can smile at the attitudes of the young writers of
1830, as we shall smile at the young writers of 1931; but
let us consider rather the work achieved. All the good
work which is being done at present was born from 1885;
from 1885 dates the liberation of poetry, the new meaning given to poetry, and this triumphal entry of poetry
into the novel which is the basic characteristic of contemporary literature.

Symbolism, in reality, was only the beginning of the
great antirationalist movement which was to transform
literature and which not only continues today, but is just
reaching its full strength. 'We are at present living in the
Symbolist era,' one of the most refined and perceptive
minds of the times wrote recently.*

Romanticism, like seventeenth-century French Classi-
cism, was lucky enough to produce the great men in which
it was incarnated. The movement of 1885 had its men-
tors, Mallarmé and Rimbaud, who belonged however to the previous generation; in the generation born
to literary life in 1885, no great name was found to give it
expression. Will it find one in the generation that followed? Nothing can be more probable, because it is only

* Bernard Fay, *Revue Européenne*, August–September 1930.

through this generation that the movement has found its full realization. I should not be surprised if, for posterity, the writer of genius who will represent the movement of 1885 will not be the Irish author who began writing in the first years of the twentieth century.

Interior Monologue in Contemporary Writers

I should have liked to study, among contemporary French writers, those who employ interior monologue and the way in which they employ it. I shall content myself with a few brief indications and, without professing to give a complete list, I shall limit myself to referring to those whose books I have read.

We can recall that the first one in France was Valery Larbaud, whose realization of it is that of a great writer. Let us indicate the precise dates: *Amants, heureux amants*, written in 1921, published in November of the same year; *Mon plus secret conseil*, written in 1921–2, published in September 1923; both now in book form (and prefaced by *Beauté, mon seul souci*) under the general title, *Amants, heureux amants* published end of 1923.

From among works written entirely in interior monologue technique, one must mention at least one of the fine stories by Jean Schlumberger published under the general title, *Les Yeux de dix-huit ans*; Dominique Braga's novel '*5ooo*', a sporting tale; another sporting novel, *Quinze rounds* by Henri Decoin, the story of a boxing-match; several short pieces at least one of which is completely successful, *La Servante en colère* by Adrienne Monnier, either under her own name or under the pen-name Sollier; and a very stylish novella by Emmanuel Berl, *Saturne*.

The present tendency, followed, it is true, by *Ulysses* itself, seems rather to insert passages of interior monologue along with passages in narrative, dramatic, or dialogue form. This is to be found in *Jean Darien* by Léon Bopp. I shall also make mention of the novel of a writer who is particularly dear to me, something which does not prevent me from judging it objectively, *La Guérison immorale* by Marie Dujardin, and the previously published stories, a collection of which is to be entitled *Divertissements dans les places*, and in which are to be found examples of an astonishing mastery of what I called 'indirect interior monologue', that is to say in the third person.

In the work of other writers, interior monologue is employed in a still more fragmentary fashion, in a few pages or even a few sentences which are interpolated in a narrative or in an analysis. This is the method employed by Pierre-Jean Jouve in the three admirable novels he has published: *Paulina 1880, Le Monde désert* and *Hécate*. The same too as Marie-Anne Comnène, in *Rosa Colonna*. Also Albert Cohen in his moving *Solal*; let us note in particular, pages 235–239, the large-scale interior monologue by Aude, with its deformations of vocabulary and significant disruptions of meaning.

If the number of writers employing genuine interior monologue is not great, the number of those inspired by it is. First among these to merit mention is the great poet Léon-Paul Fargue in certain of the pieces collected in the volumes entitled *Espaces* and *La Lampe à huile*.

Among novelists, François Berge from his first novel, *La Fille Aztèque*, Ribemont-Dessaigues and his terrifying *Frontières humaines*, George Pillement, whose *La Valencia*, without ever being interior monologue, is impregnated with an exquisite atmosphere of personal confidences ... As for André Berge, he recognizes that his novels are only fairly loosely connected with the new technique; 'I am convinced, however,' he adds, 'that many passages in these books would be different from what they are, if I hadn't known interior monologue; I at least owe to it a greater facility of transition between narrative and my characters' meditations.' This is what many young writers could agree with him in saying.

It is perhaps the atmosphere of interior monologue which has given one of the best of these, Jean Cassou, although he has never formally employed it, the possibility of renewing Romantic inspiration (always on a rather surface level) by bringing to it the feelings of penetrating confession which run through the following captivating and profound works: *Les Harmonies viennoises, Le Pays qui n'est à personne, La Clé des songes.*

The immense poetic novel where vision is always a state of mind, Jean-Richard Bloch's *La Nuit Kurde,* only contains a very few passages written in accordance with the new technique, but is suffused with its spirit. Moreover, it is to him we owe the experiment which I mentioned above, and which excited the enthusiasm of the American critics when the book was translated into English. It is in Chapter VI of Part 3 where we have 'Saad and Mirzo each occupied with a subject that interests the very marrow of his life, ... saying one thing with his lips, while thinking another with his mind, and dreaming a third without knowing it ...', where the narrator resorts to a musical technique and sets out the six texts one above the other, so that the reader's eyes can take them in at once.[17]

Let us take as a further proof of the almost daily increase in the influence of interior monologue, a writer, Jacques Lacretelle, whose works seem to be at some distance from this technique, and who has written about solitude and the nature of reverie that solitude allows,* pages which we might have appended to the definitions of interior monologue we collected, if the term itself had

* *À la recontre de France,* 1930, previously published in the July *Nouvelle Revue Française* of the same year.

been used there, and which in any case convey a most accurate and fine sense of it – all that in opposition to the man who was anti interior monologue in person, Anatole France!

But perhaps the most decisive factor is that interior monologue has finally broken into the work of the one novelist of ours who more than any other has remained attached to the old procedure of professorial analysis. See, among other examples, page 71 of *L'Imposture*.

One can wonder whether, after having taken up such a place in the novel, interior monologue is not destined to go into the theatre, in order to renew it, so to speak. We can well imagine, in the course of a dialogue, a series of 'disguised' monologues which would differ from the 'disguised' monologues of Racine in that, instead of being the translation into rational terms of the character's thoughts, the latter would be expressed anterior to their logical organization, that is to say as they come into being and in an apparently 'raw' state – in other words, in which the character would let the intertwined voices of his heart speak directly during the dialogue . . .

Whatever the possibilities of introducing interior monologue into drama, its introduction into the novel is nowadays an established fact, and Valery Larbaud remains convinced, as he already stated in 1924, that it is the technique of the future.

> Many authors [he wrote to me recently] are afraid of disconcerting the public by using this new technique, still considered to be 'extremely avant-garde', its dangerous facility making it unusable by mediocre craftsmen. It will certainly be popularized in the end, however; but before then, fine works will have been written in interior monologue, or in a form of prose that the influence of this form will have touched

upon. These works, like those of the Symbolist period, will enjoy real success, through the passage of time, away from the general public. The elite, among which figure neither pedants nor those who in France go under the name of snobs, an elite which comes together secretly and silently, behind the mass in thrall to publicity and fashion, will acclaim these works. From there they will spread their light. Then the popularizers can come. In ten or twenty years perhaps.

One fact, in any case, can confirm Valery Larbaud's prediction: masterpieces of the stature of *Ulysses* have always opened the way to a new form of literature.

As this was going to press, I rediscovered a delightful little work by Ernest Gaubert, *Flore d'Eveil,* published in Montpellier in 1899, in which the main character is seen reading *Les Lauriers sont coupés* 'for the twentieth time', and of which several passages show its influence and so can be cited as one of the oldest attempts at interior monologue.

Translator's notes
to Interior Monologue

1 Dujardin's general term has been retained here rather than the usual English 'soliloquy'.

2 By Paul Claudel.

3 In *The Great American Novel*, published in Paris, like *Amants, heureux amants*, in 1927.

4 *Letters from George Moore to Édouard Dujardin, 1886–1922*, translated from the French by John Eglinton, Crosby Gaige, New York, 1929, p. 20.

5 ibid., p. 40.

6 Presumably Joseph Rivière (see Bibliography), although he was hardly a 'biographer'.

7 Metaphors for ingenious inventions.

8 Adrienne Monnier; the French translation of *Ulysses* was published in August 1927.

9 *El Cuarto Poder* was published in Madrid in 1888 (English translation, *The Fourth Estate*, translated by Rachel Challice, Grant Richards, 1901).

10 The reference is to an article by Horiguchi Daigaku entitled 'Interior Monologue as a New Fictional Form', in the journal *Shinchō* (Tokyo), no. 14, August 1925. Horiguchi (1892–1981) was a poet and translator of French poetry. I am indebted to Dr Peter Kornicki of the Japan Research Centre of the University of Cambridge (England) for identifying and translating this passage, which does not correspond exactly to the rough French translation quoted by Dujardin.

11 Jean-Jacques le Franc, Marquis de Pompignan (1709–84), a writer who attacked the *encyclopédistes* and was savagely criticized by Voltaire.

12 See Bryan Magee's demonstration of the use of these terms in his *Schopenhauer*, Oxford University Press, 1983.

13 Coquelin Cadet was a well-known theatrical humorist towards the end of the nineteenth century.

14 The formulation originates with Teodor de Wyzewa.

15 In successive editions of *Les Lauriers*, Dujardin increasingly cut out the (outmoded) 'modish' Symbolist vocabulary, with its insistence, for example, on nouns ending in '-ance'. For details of the textual changes, see the edition edited by Carmen Licari (see Bibliography), pp. 29ff.

16 As reasons for the neglect of *Les Lauriers*, Larbaud instances the largely subterranean existence of the Symbolists, so that, for instance, Mallarmé himself was little known; and the fact that Dujardin had produced so much other work which had the effect of concealing his early books (see the preface to *Les Lauriers sont coupés*, Messein, 1924, pp. 12–13).

17 See Jean-Richard Bloch, *A Night in Kurdistan*, translated by Stephen Haden Guest, Victor Gollancz, 1930, pp. 189ff. In this English edition the texts are set out alongside each other, three columns per page, for eight successive pages.

Select Bibliography

WORKS BY ÉDOUARD DUJARDIN
(published in Paris unless stated otherwise)

Les Lauriers sont coupés, published in *La Revue Indépendante* (May–August 1887); in book form by the Librairie de la *Revue Independante*, 1888; reprinted in a collection with *Les Hantises* ('poèmes de jeunesse'), Mercure de France, 1897; 'Édition Définitive', with preface by Valery Larbaud, Messein, 1924; 10/18 paperback edition, with preface by Olivier de Magny, Union générale des éditeurs, 1968; reprint of 1924 edition, Le Chemin Vert, 1981; English translation by Stuart Gilbert, *We'll to the Woods No More*, introduction by James Laughlin, New Directions, New York, 1938; reprinted with an introduction by Leon Edel, New Directions, New York, 1957.

Le Monologue intérieur, Albert Messein, 1931.

Les Lauriers sont coupés suivi de Le Monologue intérieur, edited and with an introduction by Carmen Licari, Bulzoni (Rome), 1977.

L'Initiation au péché et à l'amour (novel), Mercure de France, 1899.

Poésies, Mercure de France, 1913.

Trois poèmes en prose mêlée de vers, preface by the author, Messein, 1936.

Antonia, légende dramatique en trois parties (*Théâtre*, Vol. I), Mercure de France, 1944.

Les Argonautes (including *Marthe et Marie, Les époux d'Heur-le-Port, Les enfants prodigues*) (*Théâtre*, Vol. II), Mercure de France, 1924.

Le Mystère du dieu mort et ressuscité, Messein, 1924.

Le Retour éternel, Moly-Sabata (distributed by Messein), no date.

Mallarmé par un des siens, Messein, 1936.

La Source du fleuve chrétien, I: Le Judaïsme, Mercure de France, 1906.

Histoire ancienne du Dieu Jésus: Grandeur et Décadence de la Critique. Sa Rénovation. Le cas de l'abbé Turmel, Messein, 1931.

Histoire ancienne du Dieu Jésus. La première génération chrétienne. Son destin révolutionnaire, Messein, 1935.

Rencontres avec Houston Stewart Chamberlain, Grasset, 1943.

'La Tetralogie à Londres', *Renaissance musicale*, vol. 2, 14 May 1882, p. 155.

'Les Représentations de Bayreuth', *Mercure de France*, XIX, August 1896, pp. 198–206.

'La Revue Wagnérienne', *La Revue musicale*, 1 October, 1923, double pagination: 141–60, 237–56.

'Die französische Literatur der Gegenwart', *Deutsche Rundschau*, November 1924, pp. 218–22.

'La vivante continuité du symbolisme', *Mercure de France*, 1, vii, 1924, pp. 55–73.

'Ferréus' (pseud.), *Annuaire du duel, 1880–1891*, Perrin et Cie, Paris, 1891

BACKGROUND MATERIAL & SECONDARY SOURCES

Ajalbert, Jean, *Mémoires en vrac, Au temps du symbolisme, 1880–1890*, Albin Michel, Paris, 1938.

Alajouanine, Th., *Valery Larbaud sous divers visages*, Gallimard, Paris, 1973.

Banta, Melissa and Silvermann, Oscar A. (eds), *James Joyce. Letters to Sylvia Beach, 1921–1940*, Indiana University Press, Bloomington, 1987.

Bowling, Lawrence Edward: 'What is the Stream of Consciousness Technique?', *Proceedings of the Modern Languages Association*, 65 (1950), p. 333–45.

Blake, Nancy, 'Le Nouveau roman de 1890: Barrès, Dujardin, Gide et Gourmont', in *Agencer un univers nouveau: le temps de la genèse, 1870–1914*, edited by Louis Forestier, Lettres Modernes, Minard, Paris 1977, pp. 45–62.

Blanche, Jacques-Emile, *Portraits of a Life-time*, translated by Walter Clément from *Mes Modèles* (Stock, 1928), Dent, London, 1937.

Blisset, William, 'George Moore and Literary Wagnerism', in *George Moore's Mind and Art*, edited by Graham Owens, Oliver and Boyd, Edinburgh, 1968, pp. 53–76.

Budgen, Frank, *James Joyce and the Making of 'Ulysses' and other writings*, with an introduction by Clive Hart, Oxford University Press, 1972.

Cassou, Jean, 'Édouard Dujardin et l'évolution du Symbolisme', *Revue Européenne*, 1 March, 1924, pp. 16–24.

Coeuroy, André, *Wagner et l'esprit romantique*, Collection 'Idées', Gallimard, 1965.

Cunard, Nancy M., *Memoirs of George Moore*, Rupert Hart-Davis, London, 1956.

Dahl, Lüsa, *Linguistic Features of the Stream of Consciousness Techniques of James Joyce, Virginia Woolf and Eugene O'Neill*, Annales Universitatis Turkuensis, Turku, 1970.

'A Comment on Similarities between Dujardin's "Monologue intérieur" and James Joyce's Interior Monologue', *Neuphilologische Mitteilungen*, Helsinki, LXXIII, 1972, pp. 45–54.

D'Annunzio, Gabriele, *Il Piacere*, Rome, 1889; translated by G. Harding as *The Child of Pleasure*, London, 1898; *L'innocente*, Naples, 1892; translated by A. Hornblow, New York, 1898.

Decaudin, Michel, 'Le Symbolisme en 1885–1886 d'après la correspondance inédite d'Édouard Dujardin', in *Autour du Symbolisme*, edited by P. G. Castex, Paris, 1955, pp. 272–3.

La Crise des valeurs symbolistes, Librairie Privat, Toulouse, 1960.

De Gourmont, Rémy, *Le Livre des masques* (illustrated by F. Valloton), Mercure de France, Paris, 1963.

Delovoy, Robert L., *Le Symbolisme*, Skira, 1982.

Dinar, André, *La Croisade symboliste*, Paris, 1943.

Dujardin, Marie, *La Belle que voici*, Les Editions universelles, Paris, 1949.

'Souvenir d'Édouard Dujardin', *Synthèses (Revue Internationale*, Brussel), Year 14, May 1959, No. 15, pp. 90–98.

Edel, Leon, *The Modern Psychological Novel*, Universal Library edition, Grosset and Dunlap, New York, 1964 (originally published as *The Psychological Novel, 1900–1950*, Rupert Hart-Davis, London, 1955).

Ellmann, Richard, *James Joyce*, New and revised edition, Oxford University Press, Oxford, 1983.

Friedman, Melvin, *Stream of Consciousness: A Study in Literary Method*, Yale University Press, New Haven, Connecticut, 1955.

Furness, Raymond, *Wagner and Literature*, Manchester University Press, Manchester 1982.

Fletcher, Ian (ed.), *Romantic Mythologies*, Routledge, London, 1967.

Gilbert, Stuart, *James Joyce's 'Ulysses'*, revised edition, Penguin, 1963.

Goléa, Antoine, 'Le Langage poétique de Richard Wagner', *Obliques*, Wagner special number, Paris, 1979, p. 125–38.

Handler, Philip, 'The Case for Édouard Dujardin', *Romantic Review*, 56 (1965), pp. 195–202.

Heppenstall, Rayner, 'The Bays are Sere', *London Magazine*, August 1960, pp. 47–51.

Höhnisch, Erika, *Das gefangene Ich*, Carl Winter Universitätsverlag, Heidelberg, 1967.

Houston, John Porter, *Fictional Technique in France, 1802–1927. An Introduction*, Louisiana State University Press, Baton Rouge, 1972.

Humphrey, Robert, *Stream of Consciousness in the Modern Novel*, 'Perspectives in Criticism' No. 3, University of California Press, Berkeley, 1954.

Joyce, James, *Letters*, 3 vols, Faber and Faber, London, and Viking Press, New York, 1966.

Kearns, Edward J., 'L'Image dans la poésie symboliste française', unpublished Ph.D. thesis, University of Reading, 1958.

King, C. D., 'Édouard Dujardin, Inner Monologue and the Stream of Consciousness', *French Studies*, VII, 1953, pp. 116–28.

'Édouard Dujardin and the Genesis of the Inner Monologue', *French Studies*, IX, 1955, p. 101–15.

Larbaud, Valery, *Amants, heureux amants*, Gallimard, Paris, 1943.

Technique, Gallimard, Paris, 1932.

Lehmann, A. G., *The Symbolist Aesthetic in France, 1885–1895*, second edn, Blackwell, Oxford, 1968.

Licari, Carmen, 'Une Hantise d'Édouard Dujardin' in *Critica testuale ed esegesi de testo: studi in onore di Marco Boni*, Bologna, 1983, pp. 343–7.

Lucie-Smith, Edward, *Symbolist Art*, Thames and Hudson, 1972.

Mabire, Jean, 'Un Héraut wagnérien: Édouard Dujardin, 1861–1949', *Nouvelle École*, no. 31–2, Richard Wagner 2, Spring 1979, p. 94–117.

McKilligan, Kathleen M., *Dujardin 'Les Lauriers sont coupés' and the interior monologue*, Occasional Papers in Modern Languages, No. 13, University of Hull, 1977.

'The Trials and Tribulations of a Symbolist Editor. Dujardin and the *Revue Indépendante*', *Nottingham French Studies*, vol. XX, no. 2, 1981, pp. 37–50.

'Theory and Practice in French Wagnerian Drama: Dujardin and *La Légende d'Antonia*', *Comparative Drama*, XIII, 1979–80, pp. 283–99.

Magee, Bryan, *Aspects of Wagner*, Alan Ross, 1968.

Mallarme, Stéphane, *Œuvres complètes*, Bibliothèque de la Pléiade, Gallimard, 1945.

Marie, Aristide, *La Forêt symboliste*, Firmin-Didot, Paris, 1936 (reprinted by Slatkine, 1970).

Martin, Stoddard, *Wagner to 'The Waste Land'. A Study of the Relationship of Wagner to English Literature*, Macmillan, 1982.

Mercier, Vivian, 'Justice for Edouard Dujardin', *James Joyce Quarterly*, 4 (1966–67), pp. 209–13.

Moore, George, *Confessions of a Young Man*, Tauchnitz edition, vol. 3812, Leipzig, 1905.

Hail and Farewell, Leipzig, 1912–14: vol. 1, *Ave*, Tauchnitz, vol. 4314, 1912; vol. 2, *Salve*, 1912 (not consulted); vol. 3, *Vale*, Tauchnitz, vol. 4490, 1914.

Letters from George Moore to Édouard Dujardin, 1886–1922, Crosby Gaige, New York, 1929.

Conversations in Ebury Street, Heinemann, London, 1930.

Letters to Nancy Cunard, 1985–1933, edited by Rupert Hart-Davis, Rupert Hart-Davis, London, 1957.

La Revue Indépendante, reprint of the Paris edition, 1884–92, Slatkine Reprints, Geneva, 1971.

La Revue Wagnérienne, February 1885–July 1888, Slatkine Reprints, 1968.

La Revue Musicale, special number: Richard Wagner and France, 1 October 1923.

Rey, Pierre-Louis, 'Les Lauriers sont coupés', *Nouvelle revue française*, 346, 1 November 1981, p. 124–6.

Riviere, Joseph, *1893–1923. Notes à propos des représentations du 'Mystère du dieu mort' et ressuscité d'Édouard Dujardin*, Editions de Soi-Même, Picard, Paris, 1923.

Rothenstein, William, *Men and Memories, Vol. I: 1872–1900*, Faber and Faber, London, 1931.

Scarfe, Francis, *The Art of Paul Valéry. A Study in Dramatic Monologue*, Glasgow University Publications, No. 97, Heinemann, London, 1954.

Schnitzler, Arthur, *Leutnant Gustl*, first published in *Die Neue Freie Presse*, 25 December 1900, pp. 35–41: translated by Kenneth Burke in *The Dial*, 79, II, August 1925, pp. 89–117.

Schwarz, W. L., 'The Interior Monologue in 1845', *Modern Language Notes*, June 1948, p. 409.

Surowska, Barbara, 'Schnitzlers innerer monolog im Verhältnis zu Dujardin und Dostojewski', in *Theatrum Europaeum*, Festschrift for Elida Maria Szarota, edited by Richard Brinkmann, Fink, Munich, 1982, pp. 549–58.

Swift, Bernard, 'The Hypothesis of the French Symbolist Novel', *Modern Language Review*, 68, 1973, pp. 776–87.

Uitti, Karl D., *The Concept of Self in the Symbolist Novel*, Mouton, The Hague, 1961.

Wagner, Richard, *Parsifal*, translated by Judith Gautier, Colin, Paris, 1893.

Wagner, review of the London Wagner Society, edited by Stuart Spencer.

Weissmann, Frida, *Du monologue intérieur à la sous-conversation: Dujardin et Valery Larbaud*, Nizet, Paris, 1978.

'Édouard Dujardin, le monologue intérieur et Racine', *Revue d'Histoire littéraire de la France*, 74, 1974, pp. 489–94.

'Autour du monologue intérieur. La correspondance de Dujardin et Valery Larbaud', *Cahiers des Amis de Valery Larbaud*, 14, March 1976, pp. 1–45.

Wilson, A. N., *Jesus: The Evidence*, Weidenfeld and Nicolson, London, 1986.

Wyzewska, Isabelle, *La Revue Wagnérienne, essai sur l'interprétation esthétique de Wagner en France*, Librairie académique Perrin, Paris, 1934.

Wyzewa, Teodor de, 'Édouard Dujardin', *Les Hommes d'aujourd'hui*, vol. 1, no. 388. no date (1891?), unnumbered pages.

'Les Livres', *Revue libre*, May 1888, pp. 75–6; August–September 1988, pp. 190–1.

Name index

This is an augmented version of Édouard Dujardin's own index to *Interior Monologue*, from which some names were omitted.

28/10/95